George Gissing in 1895
Reprinted from *The Album*
by permission of The British Library

WILL WARBURTON

A Romance of Real Life

George Gissing

New Introduction by John Halperin

THE HOGARTH PRESS
LONDON

Published in 1985 by
The Hogarth Press
Chatto and Windus Ltd
40 William IV Street, London WC2N 4DF

First published in Great Britain by Archibald Constable & Co Ltd 1905
Hogarth edition offset from the original British edition

British Library Cataloguing in Publication Data

Gissing, George
Will Warburton: a romance of real life.
I. Title
823'.8[F] PR4716.W5
ISBN 0 7012 0718 3

Printed in Finland by
Werner Söderström Oy

INTRODUCTION

Writers' lives are rarely as interesting as their books. The life of George Gissing is an exception.

Born in 1857, the son of a Yorkshire pharmacist, he was expelled from college at the age of eighteen for stealing money in order to support his mistress, a girl of his own age who, if not a confirmed prostitute, accepted money from men in order to finance her drinking habits. He went in disgrace to America, where he almost starved to death in 1877; then he returned to England, and led a life as fascinating in its tragic grandeur as any of his novels. He married twice and subsequently entered into a common-law union with a Frenchwoman (his second wife was still alive). He died in France at the age of forty-six.

Gissing came from Wakefield, although the family did not originate in the north and were, to some extent, outsiders in that setting. His father imbued him with an interest in literature (especially the classics), botany and politics. His mother held narrow evangelical views, which George Gissing found repellent – at any rate, by the time he was in his teens. He lost his father when he was thirteen and, leaving his four younger brothers and sisters behind, was sent to a nearby boarding school. While there he earned a scholarship to Owens College, now the University of Manchester. His academic performance at Owens was brilliant, and in 1876 he won a full scholarship to the University of London, where he intended to read classics.

In this same year, however, his academic career came abruptly to an end. He had become entangled with the promiscuous, working-class Helen ('Nell') Harrison; from her he contracted a venereal disease, though it has never been clear if this was serious or long-lasting. In an attempt to rehabilitate her by transforming her into a sempstress, he stole money from coat-pockets in his college: he planned to buy her a sewing machine. He was caught, prosecuted, sentenced to one month's hard labour, and expelled from Owens – an extraordinarily harsh punishment by modern standards. His school prizes were rescinded, and his scholarship to London cancelled.

Like many another nineteenth-century black sheep, Gissing was packed off to America, where it was hoped he would make his fortune. One cold day in Chicago, when the only alternative seemed to be starvation, Gissing sat down in the common room of an hotel and wrote the first of what was destined to be a long line of fictional productions (twenty-three novels, at least 111 short stories). A melodramatic tale of English life, it was bought by the editor of the *Chicago Tribune*, and subsequently Gissing supported himself for several months by selling stories to local journals. At last he could sell no more, and decided to return to England. He came back to London towards the end of 1877 and, not long afterwards, Nell Harrison joined him there. He supported himself, and presumably her, by giving lessons, and presently started his first novel, *Workers in the Dawn* (published 1880), one of whose themes is the disastrous nature of a marriage between two such people. Nevertheless, he did marry Nell, in October 1879. It was not to be the last time that Gissing in his fiction dealt graphically with the appalling results of actions which he himself was to take in his private life.

Workers in the Dawn, being autobiographical and set amongst the poor, indicated the path Gissing was to follow as a novelist for the next few years. *The Unclassed* was published in 1884. *Demos*, his first popular success, appeared in 1886, as did *Isabel Clarendon*. *Thyrza* (1887), *A Life's Morning* (1888) and *The Nether World* (1889), one of his most powerful novels, rounded out the initial period of Gissing's productivity, during which he wrote a great deal and earned almost nothing.

In 1888 Nell, from whom he had been separated for the last four years, died, and Gissing, freed from having to support her, made the first of his trips to the Continent. The change of scene, the unusual presence of some money in his pockets, and a feeling that he had by now said much of what he wished to say about the pulverising effects of poverty upon human beings, led him to more middle-class subject matter and characters. The result was a series of great books which represent Gissing at his finest as a novelist: *The Emancipated* (1890), *New Grub Street* (1891), *Denzil Quarrier* and *Born in Exile* (both 1892), *The Odd Women* (1893), *In the Year of Jubilee* (1894), *Eve's Ransom* and *Sleeping Fires* (both 1895), *The Paying Guest* (1896) and *The Whirlpool* (1897). During the 1890s Gissing's name was often linked with Meredith's and Hardy's when the leading novelists of the day were mentioned. He was acquainted with both of them, and particularly admired Meredith. During this middle period of his career Gissing was also in demand as a writer of stories and commanded relatively high prices for his short fiction.

Late in 1890 he met Edith Underwood, another uneducated working-class girl; he probably made her acquaintance at a music hall. He married her in 1891, even as he was reading proofs of *New Grub Street* – a novel which documents, among other things, the catastrophes which can overtake men of letters when they marry beneath themselves. This marriage produced two sons, and another explosive separation several years later.

Gissing's last years as a writer were marginally more prosperous and happy than his earlier ones, except for his declining health. In 1899 he embarked upon an informal but intense union with Gabrielle Fleury; a woman of consciously intellectual and refined tastes, she aspired to translate *New Grub Street* into French. He lived with her and her family in Paris, on and off, before moving to the south of France in a vain attempt to nurse his weak lungs. During the final five years of his life he published *Charles Dickens: A Critical Study* (1898), the first monograph on Dickens; *By the Ionian Sea* (1900), a moving account of his travels in Italy; and a final group of novels, including *The Town Traveller* (1898), *The Crown of Life* (1899), *Our Friend the Charlatan* (1901), and *The Private Papers of Henry Ryecroft* (1902), a pseudo-memoir that enjoyed instant popular success. *Veranilda* (1904), an unfinished historical novel, and *Will Warburton* (1905) appeared posthumously. He continued to write short stories up to the time of his death, and these have been published between 1897 and 1970 in several collections.

Gissing died near St Jean de Luz, in the Basque country, in December 1903, of pleuritis and pneumonia, which proved too much for lungs already weakened by chronic emphysema. Over his death bed Gabrielle Fleury and his friend H.G.Wells debated the respective merits of French and English nursing methods. Wells described Gissing's last moments when he came to write the death scene of George Ponderevo in *Tono-Bungay* (1908).

Gissing's novels, in the new century, soon disappeared from public view – an unjust fate for such good fiction. They remained neglected until the 1960s, when interest in them revived. Since then, much has been written about him, but it is only recently that his work has, once more, begun to be appreciated by the wider audience it deserves.

Gissing gives us a unique view of Victorian society, but his are the concerns of almost every generation. Perhaps the most class-conscious of the English novelists – a class-obsessed breed – in his books Gissing examines again and again the complicated connections between money, marriage, and social status. More sensitively than any other English novelist and more consistently than any other, he skilfully shows the effects on individuals of poverty and class prejudice, and how these things affect and even shape the relation of the sexes. Many of his novels focus on the question of what happens when a man or woman marries exogamously – that is, beyond the confines of his or her natural class – just as he had done himself. Like Dickens, and for something of the same reasons, Gissing saw himself as an outsider from what should have been his proper social milieu – as a man in exile.

Will Warburton, the last of Gissing's twenty-three novels, was written while he was dying (1902-3) and published posthumously in 1905. Despite the fact that he referred to it disparagingly during his last months, it is one of his greatest books, another in the long line of neglected masterpieces he gave to a largely indifferent posterity. A brilliant examination of the psychological impact of class barriers and pressures on a sensitive nature, *Will Warburton* describes, from the inside, the pathology of class fear and the ways in which it can govern human intercourse.

Will's attitudes toward class are recognizably and consistently Gissing's, articulated in various ways in all of his novels. 'Social grades were an inseparable part of his view of life; he recognized the existence of his superiors – though resolved to have as little to do with them as possible, and took it as a matter of course that multitudes of men should stand below his level.' Gissing goes on to define in Will the brand of middle-class paranoia to which he himself was subject throughout his adult life: 'No man was less pretentious; but his liberality of thought and behaviour consisted with a personal pride which was very much at the mercy of circumstance. Even as he could not endure subjection, so did he shrink from the thought of losing dignity in the eyes of his social inferiors.' That last clause says much: it refers to the continuously percolating guilt about his past and the fear of revelation which haunted Gissing throughout his life – and explains as well a good deal of his social conservatism.

The very short chapters, some of them only two or three pages, betray the novelist's failing strength. 'The struggle was telling upon his health; it showed in his face, in his bearing,' Gissing writes of Warburton. He enumerates some of his sick hero's anxieties:

> What if some accident . . . threw him among the weaklings? He saw . . . himself, a helpless burden upon [others]. Nay, was there not rat poison to be purchased? How – he cried within himself – how, in the name of sense and mercy, is mankind content to live on in such a world as this? By what devil are they haunted, that . . . they neglect the means of solace suggested to every humane and rational mind . . .

Overwhelmed by the hateful unreason of it all, he felt as though his brain reeled on the verge of madness . . . life weighed upon him with a burden such as he had never imagined. Never had he understood before what was meant by the sickening weariness of routine.

This gives us a fearsome glimpse into the mind of the dying novelist, detesting his invalidism (he was suffering from emphysema) and the bleak prospects he faced if he managed to go on living. He had always worried about being incapacitated, unable to work, dependent on others. Suicide was a 'means of solace' he had considered, and rejected, often before. Feeling more strongly than ever 'the humiliating circumstances of human life', as he wrote in his Commonplace Book, Gissing in *Will Warburton* returned to the despairing tone of his early slumlife novels – *Workers in the Dawn* (1880), *The Unclassed* (1884), *Isabel Clarendon* (1886), *Thyrza* (1887), *The Nether World* (1889). 'A horror of life seized him,' Gissing writes of Will. 'He understood, with fearful sympathy, the impulse of those who, rather than be any longer hustled in this howling mob, dash themselves to destruction.'

Another theme – the commercialization of art – links *Will Warburton* to some of Gissing's novels of the Nineties. *New Grub Street* (1891), *In the Year of Jubilee* (1894), *The Whirlpool* (1897), and *The Crown of Life* (1899) contain devastating commentary on English philistinism – on the fear and loathing of artists Gissing saw as a peculiarly English trait. He was well before Galsworthy, Forster and Lawrence in noting the vulgarity of advertising, the mind-numbing noise of urban machinery, and the spoliation by commercial interests of quiet suburbs and rural landscapes. But in so far as it focuses on the status of art itself and of artists in society – many of them painters and many of them starving – *Will Warburton* is also a return to an earlier vintage. Norbert Franks, the hungry painter who succeeds by prostituting his art, could have stepped out of the pages of any of Gissing's first ten novels. Again we are told that the artist must starve to succeed and that often he is ruined by marriage. Franks, who is to *Will Warburton* what Jasper Milvain is to *New Grub Street*, discovers these things for himself; ultimately his goal in life is to make enough money to induce Rosamund Elvan to marry him. To make money as an artist, *Will Warburton* argues, one must discard standards and ideals. Success comes with selling out, with artistic vulgarity. This is a very bitter book – written by an impecunious artist who had not sold out.

'Fate has a grudge against the foolishly secure,' the novel says, and this might be its epigraph. Here is the Gissing of his own hungry twenties and thirties reborn at the end of his life as a result of the terrible struggles of his last years.

Gissing's life and Will's are to intersect in the south of France – 'in exile', to use a favourite phrase of the novelist's when discussing himself. Gissing had always expected to end his days out of England, as several of his earlier novels show, and what the author thought and wrote about had an unerring tendency to happen to him. In *Will Warburton*, he gives full vent to the autobiographical impulse which runs through his books: among other things it is a poignant spiritual account of what might have been, and what was – a fascinating testament from the last months of his life.

John Halperin, London 1985

CHAPTER I

THE sea-wind in his hair, his eyes agleam with the fresh memory of Alpine snows, Will Warburton sprang out of the cab, paid the driver a double fare, flung on to his shoulder a heavy bag and ran up, two steps at a stride, to a flat on the fourth floor of the many-tenanted building hard by Chelsea Bridge. His rat-tat-tat brought to the door a thin yellow face, cautious in espial, through the narrow opening.

"Is it you, sir?"

"All right, Mrs. Hopper! How are you?—how are you?"

He threw his bag into the passage, and cordially grasped the woman's hands.

"Dinner ready? Savagely hungry. Give me three minutes, and serve."

For about that length of time there sounded in the bedroom a splashing and a blowing; then Warburton came forth with red cheeks. He seized upon a little pile of letters and packets which lay on his writing-table, broke envelopes, rent wrappers, and read with now an ejaculation of pleasure, now a grunt of disgust, and again a mirthful half roar. Then, dinner—the feeding of a famished man of robust appetite and digestion, a man three or four years on the green side of thirty. It was a speedy business, in not much more than a quarter of an hour there disappeared a noble steak and its appurtenances, a golden-crusted apple tart, a substantial slice of ripe Cheddar, two bottles of creamy Bass.

"Now I can talk!" cried Will to his servant, as he threw himself into a deep chair, and began lighting his pipe. "What's the news? I seem to have been away three months rather than three weeks."

"Mr. Franks called yesterday, sir, late in the afternoon, when I was here cleaning. He was very glad to hear you'd be back to-day, and said he might look in to-night."

"Good! What else?"

"My brother-in-law wishes to see you, sir. He's in trouble again—lost his place at Boxon's a few days ago. I don't exac'ly know how it happened, but he'll explain everything. He's very unfortunate, sir, is Allchin."

"Tell him to come before nine to-morrow morning, if he can."

"Yes, sir. I'm sure it's very kind of you, sir."

"What else?"

"Nothing as I can think of just now, sir."

Warburton knew from the woman's way of speaking that she had something still in her mind; but his pipe being well lit, and a pleasant lassitude creeping over him, he merely nodded. Mrs. Hopper cleared the table, and withdrew.

The window looked across the gardens of Chelsea Hospital (old-time Ranelagh) to the westward reach of the river, beyond which lay Battersea Park, with its lawns and foliage. A beam of the July sunset struck suddenly through the room. Warburton was aware of it with half-closed eyes; he wished to stir himself, and look forth, but languor held his limbs, and wreathing tobacco-smoke kept his thoughts among the mountains. He might have quite dozed off had not a sudden noise from within aroused him—the unmistakable crash of falling crockery. It made him laugh, a laugh of humorous expostulation. A minute or two passed, then came a timid tap at his door, and Mrs. Hopper showed her face.

"Another accident, sir, I'm sorry to say," were her faltering words.

"Extensive?"

"A dish and two plates, I'm sorry to say, sir."

"Oh, that's nothing."

"Of course I shall make them good, sir."

"Pooh! Aren't there plates enough?"

"Oh, quite enough—just yet, sir."

Warburton subdued a chuckle, and looked with friendly smile at his domestic, who stood squeezing herself between the edge of the door and the jamb—her habit when embarrassed. Mrs. Hopper had served him for three years; he knew all her weaknesses, but thought more of her virtues, chief of which were honest intention and a moderate aptitude for plain cooking. A glance about this room would have proved to any visitor that Mrs. Hopper's ideas of cleanliness were by no means rigid, her master had made himself to a certain extent responsible for this defect; he paid little attention to dust, provided that things were in their wonted order. Mrs. Hopper was not a resident domestic; she came at stated hours. Obviously a widow, she had a poor, loose-hung, trailing little body, which no nourishment could plump or fortify. Her visage was habitually doleful, but contracted itself at moments into a grin of quaint drollery, which betrayed her for something of a humorist.

"My fingers is all gone silly to-day, sir," she

pursued. "I daresay it's because I haven't had much sleep these last few nights."

"How's that?"

"It's my poor sister, sir—my sister Liza, I mean—she's had one of her worst headaches—the extra special, we call 'em. This time it's lasted more than three days, and not one minute of rest has the poor thing got."

Warburton was all sympathy; he inquired about the case as though it were that of an intimate friend. Change of air and repose were obvious remedies; no less obviously, these things were out of the question for a working woman who lived on a few shillings a week.

"Do you know of any place she could go to?" asked Warburton, adding carelessly, "if the means were provided."

Mrs. Hopper squeezed herself more tightly than ever between door and jamb. Her head was bent in an abashed way, and when she spoke it was in a thick, gurgling tone, only just intelligible.

"There's a little lodging 'ouse at Southend, sir, where we used to go when my 'usband could afford it."

"Well, look here. Get a doctor's opinion whether Southend would do; if not, which place would. And just send her away. Don't worry about the money."

Experience enabled Mrs. Hopper to interpret this advice. She stammered gratitude.

"How's your other sister—Mrs. Allchin?" Warburton inquired kindly.

"Why, sir, she's doing pretty well in her 'ealth, sir, but her baby died yesterday week. I hope you'll excuse me, sir, for all this bad news just when you come back from your holiday, and when it's natural as you don't feel in very good spirits."

Will had much ado not to laugh. On his return from a holiday, Mrs. Hopper always presumed him to be despondent in view of the resumption of daily work. He was beginning to talk of Mrs. Allchin's troubles, when at the outer door sounded a long nervous knock.

"Ha! That's Mr. Franks."

Mrs. Hopper ran to admit the visitor.

CHAPTER II

"WARBURTON!" cried a high-pitched voice from the passage. "Have you seen *The Art World*?"

And there rushed into the room a tall, auburn-headed young man of five-and-twenty, his comely face glowing in excitement. With one hand he grasped his friend's, in the other he held out a magazine.

"You haven't seen it! Look here! What d'you think of that, confound you!"

He had opened the magazine so as to display an illustration, entitled "Sanctuary," and stated to be after a painting by Norbert Franks.

"Isn't it good? Doesn't it come out well? —deuce take you, why don't you speak?"

"Not bad—for a photogravure," said Warburton, who had the air of a grave elder in the presence of this ebullient youth.

"Be hanged! We know all about that. The thing is that it's *there*. Don't you feel any surprise? Haven't you got anything to say? Don't you see what this means, you old ragamuffin?"

"Shouldn't wonder if it meant coin of the realm—for your shrewd dealer."

"For me too, my boy, for me too! Not out of this thing, of course. But I've arrived, I'm *lancé*, the way is clear! Why, you don't seem to know what it means getting into *The Art World*."

"I seem to remember," said Warburton, smiling,

"that a month or two ago, you hadn't language contemptuous enough for this magazine and all connected with it."

"Don't be an ass!" shrilled the other, who was all this time circling about the little room with much gesticulation. "Of course one talks like that when one hasn't enough to eat and can't sell a picture. I don't pretend to have altered my opinion about photogravures, and all that. But come now, the thing itself? Be honest, Warburton. Is it bad, now? Can you look at that picture, and say that it's worthless?"

"I never said anything of the kind."

"No, no! You're too deucedly good-natured. But I always detected what you were thinking, and I saw it didn't surprise you at all when the Academy muffs refused it."

"There you're wrong," cried Warburton. "I was really surprised."

"Confound your impudence! Well, you may think what you like. I maintain that the thing isn't half bad. It grows upon me. I see its merits more and more."

Franks was holding up the picture, eyeing it intently. "Sanctuary" represented the interior of an old village church. On the ground against a pillar, crouched a young and beautiful woman, her dress and general aspect indicating the last degree of vagrant wretchedness; worn out, she had fallen asleep in a most graceful attitude, and the rays of a winter sunset smote upon her pallid countenance. Before her stood the village clergyman, who had evidently just entered, and found her here; his white head was bent in the wonted attitude of clerical benevolence; in his face blended a gentle wonder and a compassionate tenderness.

"If that had been hung at Burlington House, Warburton, it would have been the picture of the year."

"I think it very likely."

"Yes, I know what you mean, you sarcastic old ruffian. But there's another point of view. Is the drawing good or not? Is the colour good or not? Of course you know nothing about it, but I tell you, for your information, I think it's a confoundedly clever bit of work. There remains the subject, and where's the harm in it? The incident's quite possible. And why shouldn't the girl be good-looking?"

"Angelic!"

"Well why not? There *are* girls with angelic faces. Don't I know one?"

Warburton, who had been sitting with a leg over the arm of his chair suddenly changed his position.

"That reminds me," he said. "I came across the Pomfrets in Switzerland."

"Where? When?"

"At Trient ten days ago. I spent three or four days with them. Hasn't Miss Elvan mentioned it?"

"I haven't heard from her for a long time," replied Franks. "Well, for more than a week. Did you meet them by chance?"

"Quite. I had a vague idea that the Pomfrets and their niece were somewhere in Switzerland."

"Vague idea!" cried the artist "Why, I told you all about it, and growled for five or six hours one evening here because I couldn't go with them."

"So you did," said Warburton, "but I'm afraid I was thinking of something else, and when I started for the Alps, I had really forgotten all about it. I made up my mind suddenly, you know. We're having a troublesome time in Ailie Street, and it was holiday now or never. By the bye, we shall have to wind up. Sugar spells ruin. We must get out of it whilst we can do so with a whole skin."

"Ah, really?" muttered Franks. "Tell me about that presently; I want to hear of Rosamund. You saw a good deal of her, of course?"

"I walked from Chamonix over the Col de Balme—grand view of Mont Blanc there! Then down to Trient, in the valley below. And there, as I went in to dinner at the hotel, I found the three. Good old Pomfret would have me stay awhile, and I was glad of the chance of long talks with him. Queer old bird, Ralph Pomfret."

"Yes, yes, so he is," muttered the artist, absently. "But Rosamund—was she enjoying herself?"

"Very much, I think. She certainly looked very well."

"Have much talk with her?" asked Franks, as if carelessly.

"We discussed you, of course. I forget whether our conclusion was favourable or not."

The artist laughed, and strode about the room with his hands in his pockets."

"You know what?" he exclaimed, seeming to look closely at a print on the wall. "I'm going to be married before the end of the year. On that point I've made up my mind. I went yesterday to see a house at Fulham—Mrs. Cross's, by the bye, it's to let at Michaelmas, rent forty-five. All but settled that I shall take it. Risk be hanged. I'm going to make money. What an ass I was to take that fellow's first offer for 'Sanctuary'! It was low water with me, and I felt bilious. Fifty guineas! Your fault, a good deal, you know; you made me think worse of it than it deserved. You'll see; Blackstaffe'll make a small fortune out of it; of course he has all the rights—idiot that I was! Well, it's too late to talk about that.—And I say, old man, don't take my growl too literally. I don't really mean that you were to blame. I should be an ungrateful cur if I thought such a thing."

"How's 'The Slummer' getting on?" asked Warburton good-humouredly.

"Well, I was going to say that I shall have it finished in a few weeks. If Blackstaffe wants 'The Slummer' he'll have to pay for it. Of course it must go to the Academy, and of course I shall keep all the rights—unless Blackstaffe makes a really handsome offer. Why, it ought to be worth five or six hundred to me at least. And that would start us. But I don't care, even if I only get half that, I shall be married all the same. Rosamund has plenty of pluck. I couldn't ask her to start life on a pound a week—about my average for the last two years; but with two or three hundred in hand, and a decent little house, like that of Mrs. Cross's, at a reasonable rent—well, we shall risk it. I'm sick of waiting. And it isn't fair to a girl—that's my view. Two years now; an engagement that lasts more than two years isn't likely to come to much good. You'll think my behaviour pretty cool, on one point. I don't forget, you old usurer, that I owe you something more than a hundred pounds——"

"Pooh!"

"Be poohed yourself! But for you, I should

have gone without dinner many a day; but for you, I should most likely have had to chuck painting altogether, and turn clerk or dock-labourer. But let me stay in your debt a little longer, old man. I can't put off my marriage any longer, and just at first I shall want all the money I can lay my hands on."

At this moment Mrs. Hopper entered with a lamp. There was a pause in the conversation. Franks lit a cigarette, and tried to sit still, but was very soon pacing the floor again. A tumbler of whisky and soda reanimated his flagging talk.

"No!" he exclaimed. "I'm not going to admit that 'Sanctuary' is cheap and sentimental, and all the rest of it. The more I think about it, the more convinced I am that it's nothing to be ashamed of. People have got hold of the idea that if a thing is popular it must be bad art. That's all rot. I'm going in for popularity. Look here! Suppose that's what I was meant for? What if it's the best I have in me to do? Shouldn't I be a jackass if I scorned to make money by what, for me, was good work, and preferred to starve whilst I turned out pretentious stuff that was worth nothing from my point of view?"

"I shouldn't wonder if you're right," said Warburton reflectively. "In any case, I know as much about art as I do about the differential calculus. To make money is a good and joyful thing as long as one doesn't bleed the poor. So go ahead, my son, and luck be with you!"

"I can't find my model yet for the Slummer's head. It mustn't be too like the 'Sanctuary' girl, but at the same time it must be a popular type of beauty. I've been haunting refreshment bars and florists' shops; lots of good material, but never *quite* the thing. There's a damsel at the Crystal Palace—but this doesn't interest you, you old misogynist."

"Old what?" exclaimed Warburton, with an air of genuine surprise.

"Have I got the word wrong? I'm not much of a classic——"

"The word's all right. But that's your idea of me, is it?"

The artist stood and gazed at his friend with an odd expression, as if a joke had been arrested on his lips by graver thought.

"Isn't it true?"

"Perhaps it is; yes, yes, I daresay."

And he turned at once to another subject.

CHAPTER III

THE year was 1886.

When at business, Warburton sat in a high, bare room, which looked upon little Ailie Street, in Whitechapel; the air he breathed had a taste and odour strongly saccharine. If his eye strayed to one of the walls, he saw a map of the West Indies; if to another, it fell upon a map of St. Kitts; if to the third, there was before him a plan of a sugar estate on that little island. Here he sat for certain hours of the solid day, issuing orders to clerks, receiving commercial callers, studying trade journals in sundry languages—often reading some book which had no obvious reference to the sugar-refining industry. It was not Will's ideal of life, but hither he had suffered himself to be led by circumstance, and his musings suggested no practicable issue into a more congenial world.

The death of his father when he was sixteen had left him with a certain liberty for shaping a career. What he saw definitely before him was a small share in the St. Kitts property of Messrs. Sherwood Brothers, a small share in the London business of the same firm, and a small sum of ready money—these things to be his when he attained his majority. His mother and sister, who lived in a little country house down in Huntingdonshire, were modestly but securely provided for, and Will might have gone quietly on with his studies till he could resolve upon a course in life. But no sooner was he freed from paternal restraint than the lad grew restive; nothing would please him but an adventure in foreign lands; and when it became clear that he was only wasting his time at school, Mrs. Warburton let him go to the West Indies, where a place was found for him in the house of Sherwood Brothers. At St. Kitts, Will remained till he was one-and-twenty. Long before that, he had grown heartily tired of his work, disgusted with the climate, and oppressed with home sickness, but pride forbade him to return until he could do so as a free man.

One thing this apprenticeship to life had taught him—that he was not made for subordination. "I don't care how poor I am," thus he wrote to his mother, "but I will be my own master. To be at other people's orders brings out all the bad in me; it makes me sullen and bearish, and all sorts of ugly things, which I certainly am not when my true self has play. So, you see, I must find some independent way of life. If I had to live by carrying round a Punch and Judy show, I should vastly prefer it to making a large income as somebody's servant."

Meanwhile, unfortunately for a young man of this temperament, his prospects had become less assured. There was perturbation in the sugar world; income from St. Kitts and from Whitechapel had sensibly diminished, and it seemed but too likely, would continue to do so. For some half-year Will lived in London, "looking about him," then he announced that Godfrey Sherwood, at present sole representative of Sherwood Brothers, had offered him an active partnership in Little Ailie Street, and that he had accepted it. He entered upon this position without zeal, but six months' investigation had taught him that to earn money without surrendering his independence was no very easy thing; he probably might wait a long time before an opening would present itself more attractive than this at the sugar-refinery.

Godfrey Sherwood was a schoolfellow of his, but some two or three years older; much good feeling existed between them, their tastes and tempers having just that difference in similarity which is the surest bond of friendship. Judged by his talk, Sherwood was all vigour, energy, fire; his personal habits, on the other hand, inclined to tranquillity and ease—a great reader, he loved the literature of romance and adventure, knew by heart authors such as Malory and Froissart, had on his shelves all the books of travel and adventure he could procure. As a boy he seemed destined to any life save that of humdrum commerce, of which he spoke with contempt and abhorrence; and there was no reason why he should not have gratified his desire of seeing the world, of leading what he called "the life of a man." Yet here he was, sitting each day in a counting-house in Whitechapel, with nothing behind him but a few rambles on the continent, and certainly with no immediate intention of going far afield. His father's death left him in sole command of the business, and his reasonable course would have been to retire from it as soon as possible, for foreign competition was making itself felt in the English trade, and many firms more solidly established than that in Little Ailie Street had either come to grief or withdrawn from the struggle. But Godfrey's inertia kept him in the familiar routine, with day-to-day postponement of practical decision. When Warburton came back from St. Kitts, and their friendship was renewed, Godfrey's talk gave full play to his imaginative energies. Yes, yes, the refining business was at a bad pass just now, but this was only temporary; those firms that could weather the storm for a year or two longer would enter upon a time of brilliant prosperity. Was it to be supposed that the Government would allow a great industry to perish out of mere regard for the fetish of Free Trade? City men with first-hand information declared that "measures" were being prepared; in one way or another, the English trade would be rescued and made triumphant over those bounty-fed foreigners.

"Hold on?" cried Sherwood. "Of course I mean to hold on. There's pleasure and honour in the thing. I enjoy the fight. I've had thoughts of getting into Parliament, to speak for sugar. One might do worse, you know. There'll be a dissolution next year, certain. First-rate fun, fighting a constituency. But in that case I must have a partner here—why that's an idea. How would it suit you? Why not join me?"

And so the thing came about. The terms which Godfrey offered were so generous that Will had to reduce them before he accepted: even thus, he found his income, at a stroke, all but doubled. Sherwood, to be sure, did not stand for Parliament, nor was anything definite heard about that sugar-protecting budget which he still believed in. In Little Ailie Street business steadily declined.

"It's a disgrace to England!" cried Godfrey. "Monstrous that not a finger should be lifted to save one of our most important industries. You, of course, are free to retire at any moment, Will. For my own part, here I stand, come what may.

If it's ruin, ruin let it be. I'll fight to the last. A man owes me ten thousand pounds. When I recover it, and I may any day—I shall put every penny into the business."

"Ten thousand pounds!" exclaimed Warburton in astonishment. "A trade debt, do you mean?"

"No, no. A friend of mine, son of a millionaire, who got into difficulties some time ago, and borrowed of me to clear himself. Good interest, and principal safe as Consols. In a year at most I shall have the money back, and every penny shall go into the business."

Will had his private view of the matter, and not seldom suffered a good deal of uneasiness as he saw the inevitable doom approach. But already it was too late to withdraw his share from the concern; that would have been merely to take advantage of Sherwood's generosity, and Will was himself not less chivalrous. In Godfrey's phrase, they continued "to fight the ship," and perhaps would have held out to the moment of sinking, had not the accession of the Liberals to power in the spring of this present year caused Sherwood so deep a disgust that he turned despondent and began to talk of surrender to hopeless circumstance.

"It's all up with us, Will. This Government spells ruin, and will count it one of its chief glories if we come to grief. But, by Heaven, they shan't have that joy. We'll square up, quietly, comfortably, with dignity. We'll come out of this fight with arms and baggage. It's still possible, you know. We'll sell the St. Kitts estate to the Germans. We'll find some one to buy us up here—the place would suit a brewer. And then—by Jove! we'll make jam."

"Jam?"

" Isn't it an idea ? Cheap sugar has done for the refiners, but it's a fortune for the jam trade. Why not put all we can realize into a jam factory ? We'll go down into the country ; find some delightful place where land is cheap ; start a fruit farm ; run up a building. Doesn't it take you, Will ? Think of going to business every day through lanes overhung with fruit-tree blossoms ! Better that than the filth and stench and gloom and uproar of Whitechapel—what ? We might found a village for our workpeople—the ideal village, perfectly healthy, every cottage beautiful. Eh ? What ? How does it strike you, Will ? "

" Pleasant. But the money ? "

" We shall have enough to start ; I think we shall. If not, we'll find a moneyed man to join us."

" What about that ten thousand pounds ? " suggested Warburton.

Sherwood shook his head.

" Can't get it just yet. To tell you the truth, it depends on the death of the man's father. No, but if necessary, some one will easily be found. Isn't the idea magnificent ? How it would rile the Government if they heard of it ! Ho, ho ! "

One could never be sure how far Godfrey was serious when he talked like this ; the humorous impulse so blended with the excitability of his imagination, that people who knew him little and heard him talking at large thought him something of a crack-brain. The odd thing was that, with all his peculiarities, he had many of the characteristics of a sound man of business ; indeed, had it been otherwise, the balance-sheets of the refinery must long ago have shown a disastrous deficit. As Warburton knew, things had been managed with no little prudence and sagacity; what he did not so clearly understand was that Sherwood had simply adhered to the traditions of the firm, following very exactly the path marked out for him by his father and his uncle, both notable traders. Concerning Godfrey's private resources, Warburton knew little or nothing; it seemed probable that the elder Sherwood had left a considerable fortune, which his only son must have inherited. No doubt, said Will to himself, this large reserve was the explanation of his partner's courage.

So the St. Kitts estate was sold, and, with all the deliberate dignity demanded by the fact that the Government's eye was upon them, Sherwood Brothers proceeded to terminate their affairs in Whitechapel. In July, Warburton took his three weeks' holiday, there being nothing better for him to do. And among the letters he found on his table when he returned, was one from Sherwood, which contained only these words:

"Great opportunity in view. Our fortunes are made!"

CHAPTER IV

WHEN Franks was gone, Warburton took up *The Art World*, which his friend had left, and glanced again at the photogravure of "Sanctuary." He knew, as he had declared, nothing about art, and judged pictures as he judged books, emotionally. His bent was to what is called the realistic point of view, and "Sanctuary" made him smile. But very good-naturedly; for he liked Norbert Franks, and believed he would do better things than this. Unless——?

The thought broke off with an uneasy interrogative.

He turned to the few lines of text devoted to the painter. Norbert Franks, he read, was still a very young man; "Sanctuary," now on exhibition at Birmingham, was his first important picture; hitherto he had been chiefly occupied with work in black and white. There followed a few critical comments, and prophecy of achievements to come.

Yes. But again the uneasy interrogative.

Their acquaintance dated from the year after Warburton's return from St. Kitts. Will had just established himself in his flat near Chelsea Bridge, delighted to be a Londoner, and was spending most of his leisure in exploration of London's vastness. He looked upon all his earlier years as wasted, because they had not been passed in the city on the Thames. The history of London, the multitudinous life of London as it lay about him, with marvels and mysteries in every highway and byway, occupied his mind, and wrought upon his imagination. Being a stout walker, and caring little for any other form of exercise, in his free hours he covered many a league of pavement. A fine summer morning would see him set forth, long before milk-carts had begun to rattle along the streets, and on one such expedition, as he stepped briskly through a poor district south of the river, he was surprised to see an artist at work, painting seriously, his easel in the dry gutter. He slackened his pace to have a glimpse of the canvas, and the painter, a young, pleasant-looking fellow, turned round and asked if he had a match. Able to supply this demand, Warburton talked whilst the other relit his pipe. It rejoiced him, he said, to see a painter engaged upon such a subject as this—a bit of squalid London's infinite picturesqueness.

The next morning Warburton took the same walk, and again found the painter at work. They talked freely; they exchanged invitations; and that same evening Norbert Franks climbed the staircase to Will's flat, and smoked his first pipe and drank his first whisky-and-soda in the pleasant room overlooking Ranelagh. His own quarters were in Queen's Road, Battersea, at no great distance. The two young men were soon seeing a great deal of each other. When their friendship had ripened through a twelvemonth, Franks, always impecunious, cheerily borrowed a five-pound note; not long after, he mirthfully doubled his debt; and this grew to a habit with him.

"You're a capitalist, Warburton," he remarked

one day, "and a generous fellow, too. Of course I shall pay what I owe you when I sell a big picture. Meanwhile, you have the gratification of supporting a man of genius, without the least inconvenience to yourself. Excellent idea of yours to strike up a friendship, wasn't it?"

The benefit was reciprocal. Warburton did not readily form intimacies; indeed Godfrey Sherwood had till now been almost the only man he called friend, and the peculiarity of his temper exposed him to the risk of being too much alone. Though neither arrogant nor envious, Will found little pleasure in the society of people who, from any point of view, were notably his superiors; even as he could not subordinate himself in money-earning relations, so did he become ill-at-ease, lose all spontaneity, in company above his social or intellectual level. Such a man's danger was obvious; he might, in default of congenial associates, decline upon inferiors; all the more that a softness of heart, a fineness of humanity, ever disposed him to feel and show special kindness for the poor, the distressed, the unfortunate. Sherwood's acquaintances had little attraction for him; they were mostly people who lived in a luxurious way, went in for sports, talked about the money market—all of which things fascinated Godfrey, though in truth he was far from belonging by nature to that particular world. With Franks, Will could be wholly himself, enjoying the slight advantage of his larger means, extending his knowledge without undue obligation, and getting all the good that comes to a man from the exercise of his kindliest feelings.

With less of geniality, because more occupied with himself, Norbert Franks resembled his new friend in a distaste for ordinary social pleasures and an enjoyment of the intimacies of life. He stood very much alone in the world, and from the age of eighteen he had in one way or another supported himself, chiefly by work on illustrated papers. His father, who belonged to what is called a good family, began life in easy circumstances, and gained some reputation as a connoisseur of art; imprudence and misfortune having obliged him to sell his collection, Mr. Franks took to buying pictures and bric-a-brac for profit, and during the last ten years of his life was associated in that capacity with a London firm. Norbert, motherless from infancy and an only child, received his early education at expensive schools, but, showing little aptitude for study and much for use of the pencil, was taken by his father at twelve years old to Paris, and there set to work under a good art-teacher. At sixteen he went to Italy, where he remained for a couple of years. Then, on a journey in the East, the elder Franks died. Norbert returned to England, learnt that a matter of fifty pounds was all his heritage, and pluckily turned to the task of keeping himself alive. Herein his foreign sketch-books proved serviceable, but the struggle was long and hard before he could house himself decently, and get to serious work as a painter. Later on, he was wont to say that this poverty had been the best possible thing for him, its enforced abstinences having come just at the time when he had begun to "wallow"—his word for any sort of excess; and "wallowing" was undoubtedly a peril to which Norbert's temper particularly exposed him. Short commons made him, as they have made many another youth, sober and chaste, at all events in practice; and when he began to lift up his head, a little; when, at the age of three-and-twenty, he earned what seemed to him at first the luxurious income of a pound or so a week; when, in short, the inclination to "wallow" might again have taken hold upon him, it was his chance to fall in love so seriously and hopefully that all the better features of his character were drawn out, emphasized, and, as it seemed, for good and all established in predominance.

Not long after his first meeting with Warburton, he one day received, through the publishers of a book he had illustrated, a letter signed "Ralph Pomfret," the writer of which asked whether "Norbert Franks" was the son of an old friend of whom he had lost sight for many years. By way of answer, Franks called upon his correspondent, who lived in a pleasant little house at Ashtead, in Surrey; he found a man of something less than sixty, with a touch of eccentricity in his thoughts and ways, by whom he was hospitably received, and invited to return whenever it pleased him. It was not very long before Franks asked permission to make the Pomfrets acquainted with his friend Warburton, a step which proved entirely justifiable. Together or separately, the two young men were often to be seen at Ashtead, whither they were attracted not only by the kindly and amusing talk of Ralph Pomfret, but at least as much by the grace and sweetness and sympathetic intelligence of the mistress of the house, for whom both entertained respect and admiration.

One Sunday afternoon, Warburton, tempted as usual by the thought of tea and talk in that delightful little garden, went out to Ashtead, and, as he pushed open the gate, was confused and vexed at the sight of strangers; there, before the house, stood a middle-aged gentleman and a young girl, chatting with Mrs. Pomfret. He would have turned away and taken himself off in disappointment, but that the clank of the gate had attracted attention, and he had no choice but to move forward. The strangers proved to be Mrs. Pomfret's brother and his daughter; they had been spending half a year in the south of France, and were here for a day or two before returning to their home at Bath. When he had recovered his equanimity, Warburton became aware that the young lady was fair to look upon. Her age seemed about two-and-twenty; not very tall, she bore herself with perhaps a touch of conscious dignity and impressiveness; perfect health, a warm complexion, magnificent hair, eyes that shone with gaiety and good-nature, made of Rosamund Elvan a living picture such as Will Warburton had not often seen; he was shy in her presence, and by no means did himself justice that afternoon. His downcast eyes presently noticed that she wore shoes of a peculiar kind—white canvas with soles of plaited cord; in the course of conversation he learnt that these were a memento of the Basque country, about which Miss Elvan talked with a very pretty enthusiasm. Will went away, after all, in a dissatisfied mood. Girls were to him merely a source of disquiet. "If she be not fair for me—" was his ordinary thought; and he had never yet succeeded in persuading himself that any girl, fair or not, was at all likely to conceive the idea of devoting herself to his happiness. In this matter, an excessive modesty subdued him. It had something to do with his holding so much apart from general society.

On the evening of the next day, there was a

thunderous knock at Warburton's flat, and in rushed Franks.

"You were at Ashtead yesterday," he cried.

"I was. What of that?"

"And you didn't come to tell me about the Elvans!"

"About Miss Elvan, I suppose you mean?" said Will.

"Well, yes, I do. I went there by chance this afternoon. The two men were away somewhere,—I found Mrs. Pomfret and that girl alone together. Never had such a delightful time in my life! But I say, Warburton, we must understand each other. Are you—do you—I mean, did she strike you particularly?"

Will threw back his head and laughed.

"You mean that?" shouted the other, joyously. "You really don't care—it's nothing to you?"

"Why, is it anything to *you*?"

"Anything? Rosamund Elvan is the most beautiful girl I ever saw, and the sweetest, and the brightest, and the altogether flooringest! And, by heaven and earth, I'm resolved to marry her!"

CHAPTER V

AS he sat musing, *The Art World* still in his hand, Warburton could hear his friend's voice ring out that audacious vow. He could remember, too, the odd little pang with which he heard it, a half spasm of altogether absurd jealousy. Of course the feeling did not last. There was no recurrence of it when he heard that Franks had again seen Miss Elvan before she left Ashtead; nor when he learnt that the artist had been spending a day or two at Bath. Less than a month after their first meeting, Franks won Rosamund's consent. He was frantic with exultation. Arriving with the news at ten o'clock one night, he shouted and maddened about Warburton's room until finally turned out at two in the morning. His circumstances being what they were, he could not hope for marriage yet awhile; he must work and wait. Never mind; see what work he would produce! Yet it appeared to his friend that all through the next twelvemonth he merely wasted time, such work as he did finish being of very slight value. He talked and talked, now of Rosamund, now of what he was *going* to do, until Warburton, losing patience, would cut him short with "Oh, go to Bath!"—an old cant phrase revived for its special appropriateness in this connection. Franks went to Bath far oftener than he could afford, money for his journey being generally borrowed from his long-enduring friend.

Rosamund herself had nothing, and but the smallest expectations should her father die. Two years before this, it had occurred to her that she should like to study art, and might possibly find in it a means of self-support. She was allowed to attend classes at South Kensington, but little came of this except a close friendship with a girl of her own age, by name Bertha Cross, who was following the art course with more serious purpose. When she had been betrothed for about a year, Rosamund chanced to spend a week in London at her friend's house, and this led to acquaintance between Franks and the Crosses. For a time, Warburton saw and heard less of the artist, who made confidantes of Mrs. Cross and her daughter, and spent many an evening with them talking, talking, talking about Rosamund; but this intimacy did not endure very long, Mrs. Cross being a person of marked peculiarities, which in the end overtried Norbert's temper. Only on the fourth story flat by Chelsea Bridge could the lover find that sort of sympathy which he really needed, solacing yet tonic. But for Warburton he would have worked even less. To Will it seemed an odd result of fortunate love that the artist, though in every other respect a better man than before, should have become, to all appearances, less zealous, less efficient, in his art. Had Rosamund Elvan the right influence on her lover; in spite of Norbert's lyric eulogy, had she served merely to confuse his aims, perhaps to bring him down to a lower level of thought?

There was his picture, "Sanctuary." Before he knew Rosamund, Franks would have scoffed at such a subject, would have howled at such treatment of it. There was notable distance between this and what Norbert was painting in that summer sunrise four years ago, with his portable easel in the gutter. And Miss Elvan admired "Sanctuary"—at least, Franks said she did. True, she also admired the picture of the pawnshop and the public-house; Will had himself heard her speak of it with high praise, and with impatient wonder that no purchaser could be found for it. Most likely she approved of everything Norbert did, and had no more serious criterion. Unless, indeed, her private test of artistic value were the financial result.

Warburton could not altogether believe that. Annoyance with the artist now and then inclined him to slighting thought of Rosamund; yet, on the whole, his view of her was not depreciatory. The disadvantage to his mind was her remarkable comeliness. He could not but fear that so much beauty must be inconsistent with the sterling qualities which make a good wife.

Will's eye fell on Sherwood's note, and he went to bed wondering what the project might be which was to make their fortune.

CHAPTER VI

HE had breakfasted, and was smoking his pipe as he wrote a letter, when Mrs. Hopper announced the visit, by appointment, of her brother-in-law, Allchin. There entered a short, sturdy, red-headed young fellow, in a Sunday suit of respectable antiquity; his features were rude, his aspect dogged; but a certain intelligence showed in his countenance, and a not unamiable smile responded to the bluff heartiness of Warburton's greeting. By original calling, Allchin was a grocer's assistant, but a troublesome temper had more than once set him adrift, the outcast of grocerdom, to earn a living as best he could by his vigorous thews, and it was in one of these intervals that, having need of a porter at the works, Warburton had engaged him, on Mrs. Hopper's petition. After a month or so of irreproachable service, Allchin fought with a foreman, and took his discharge. The same week, Mrs. Allchin presented him with their first child; the family fell into want; Mrs. Hopper (squeezed between door and jamb) drew her master's attention to the lamentable case, and help was of course forthcoming. Then, by good luck, Allchin was enabled to resume his vocation; he got a place at a grocer's in Fulham Road, and in a few weeks presented himself before his benefactor, bringing half-a-crown as a first instalment toward the discharge of his debt; for only on this condition had he accepted the money. Half a year elapsed without troublesome incident; the man made regular repayment in small sums; then came the disaster which Mrs. Hopper had yesterday announced.

"Well, Allchin," cried Warburton, "what's the latest?"

Before speaking, the other pressed his lips tightly together and puffed out his cheeks, as if it cost him an effort to bring words to the surface. His reply came forth with explosive abruptness

"Lost my place at Boxon's, sir."

"And how's that?"

"It happened last Saturday, sir. I don't want to make out as I wasn't at all to blame. I know as well as anybody that I've got a will of my own. But we're open late, as perhaps you know, sir, on Saturday night, and Mr. Boxon—well, it's only the truth—he's never quite himself after ten o'clock. I'd worked from eight in the morning to something past midnight—of course I don't think nothing of that, 'cause it's reg'lar in the trade. But—well, in come a customer, sir, a woman as didn't rightly know what she wanted; and she went out without buying, and Mr. Boxon he see it, and he come up to me and calls me the foulest name he could turn his tongue to. And so—well, sir, there was unpleasantness, as they say——"

He hesitated, Warburton eyeing him with a twinkle of subdued amusement.

"A quarrel, in fact, eh?"

"It did about come to that, sir!'

"You lost your temper, of course."

"That's about the truth, sir."

"And Boxon turned you out?"

Allchin looked hurt.

"Well, sir, I've no doubt he'd have liked to, but I was a bit beforehand with him. When I see him last, he was settin' on the pavement, sir, rubbin' his 'ead."

In spite of his inclination to laugh, Will kept a grave countenance.

"I'm afraid that kind of thing won't do, Allchin. You'll be in serious trouble one of these days."

"That's what my wife says, sir. I know well enough as it's hard on her, just after we've lost the baby—as perhaps Mrs. Hopper'll have told you, sir."

"I was very sorry to hear it, Allchin."

"Thank you, sir. You've always something kind to say. And I'm that vexed, because I was getting on well with paying my debts. But Mr. Boxon, sir, he's many a time made me that mad that I've gone out into the back yard and kicked the wall till my toes were sore, just to ease my feelings, like. To tell the truth, sir, I don't think he's ever rightly sober, and I've heard others say the same. And his business is fallin' off, something shockin'. Customers don't like to be insulted; that's only natural. He's always going down to Kempton Park, or Epsom, or some such place. They do say as he lost 'undreds of pounds at Kempton Park last week. It's my opinion the shop can't go on much longer. Well, sir, I thought I just ought to come and tell you the truth of things, and I won't disturb you no longer. I shall do my best to find another place."

Warburton's impulse was to offer temporary work in Little Ailie Street, but he remembered that the business was not in a position to increase expenses, and that the refinery might any day be closed.

"All right," he answered cheerily, "let me know how you get on."

When Allchin's heavy footsteps had echoed away down the stairs, Mrs. Hopper answered her master's call.

"I suppose they have a little money to go on with?" Warburton inquired. "I mean, enough for a week or so."

"Yes, I think they have that, sir. But I see how it'll be. My poor sister'll end in the work'us. Allchin'll never keep a place. Not that I can blame him, sir, for givin' it to that Boxon, 'cause every one says he's a brute."

"Well, just let me know if they begin to be in want. But of course Allchin can always get work as a porter. He must learn to keep his fists down, if he doesn't want to be perpetually out of employment."

"That's what I tell him, sir. And my poor sister, sir, she's never stopped talkin' to him, day or night you may say, ever since it happened——"

"Merciful Heavens!" groaned Warburton to himself.

CHAPTER VII

AT half-past nine he reached Little Ailie Street. "Mr. Sherwood not here yet, I suppose?" asked Will.

"Oh yes, he is, sir," replied the manager; "been here for half an hour."

Warburton went on to the senior partner's room. There sat Godfrey Sherwood bent over a book which, to judge from the smile upon his face, could have nothing to do with the sugar-refining question.

"How do, Will?" he exclaimed, with even more than his usual cheerfulness. "Did you ever read 'The Adventures of a Younger Son'? Oh, you must. Listen here. He's describing how he thrashed an assistant master at school; thrashed him, he says, till 'the sweat dropped from his brows like rain-drops from the eaves of a pig-sty!' Ho-ho-ho! What do you think of that for a comparison? Isn't it strong? By Jove! a bracing book! Trelawny, you know; the friend of Byron. As breezy a book as I know. It does one good."

Godfrey Sherwood was, as regards his visage, what is called a plain young man, but his smile told of infinite good-nature, and his voice, notwithstanding its frequent note of energy or zeal, had a natural softness of intonation which suggested other qualities than the practical and vigorous.

"Enjoyed your holiday?" he went on, rising,

stretching himself, and offering a box of cigarettes. "You look well. Done any summits? When we get our affairs in order, I must be off somewhere myself. Northward, I think. I want a little bracing cold. I should like to see Iceland. You know the Icelandic sagas? Magnificent! There's the saga of Grettir the Strong—by Jove! But come, this isn't business. I have news for you, real, substantial, hopeful news."

They seated themselves in roundbacked chairs, and Will lighted a cigarette.

"You know my thoughts were running on jam; jam is our salvation; of that I have long been convinced. I looked about, made a few inquiries, and by good luck, not long after you went off for your holiday, met just the man I wanted. You've heard of Applegarth's jams?"

Will said he had seen them advertised.

"Well, I came across Applegarth himself. I was talking to Linklater—and jams came up. 'You ought to see my friend Applegarth,' said he; and he arranged for us to meet. Applegarth happened to be in town, but he lives down in Somerset, and his factory is at Bristol. We all dined together at the Junior Carlton, and Applegarth and I got on so well that he asked me down to his place. Oxford man, clever, a fine musician, and an astronomer; has built himself a little observatory—magnificent telescope. By Jove! you should hear him handle the violin. Astonishing fellow! Not much of a talker; rather dry in his manner; but no end of energy, bubbling over with vital force. He began as a barrister, but couldn't get on, and saw his capital melting. 'Hang it!' said he, 'I must make some use of what money I have'; and he thought of jam. Brilliant idea! He began in a very modest way, down at Bristol, only aiming at local trade. But his jams were good ; the demand grew ; he built a factory ; profits became considerable. And now, he wants to withdraw from active business, keeping an interest. Wants to find some one who would run and extend the concern—put in a fair capital, and leave him to draw his income quietly. You see ? "

"Seems a good opportunity," said Warburton.

"Good ? It's simply superb. He took me over the works—a really beautiful sight, everything so admirably arranged. Then we had more private talk. Of course I spoke of you, said I could do nothing till we had consulted together. I didn't seem too eager—not good policy. But we've had some correspondence, and you shall see the letters."

He handed them to his partner. Warburton saw that there was a question of a good many thousand pounds.

"Of course," he remarked, "I could only stand for a very small part in this."

"Well, we must talk about that. To tell you the truth, Will," Sherwood continued, crossing his legs and clasping his hands behind his head, "I don't see my way to find the whole capital, and yet I don't want to bring in a stranger. Applegarth could sell to a company any moment, but that isn't his idea ; he wants to keep the concern in as few hands as possible. He has a first-rate manager ; the mere jam-making wouldn't worry us at all ; and the office work is largely a matter of routine. Will you take time to think about it ? "

The figures which Warburton had before him were decidedly stimulating ; they made a very pleasant contrast to the balance-sheets with which he had recently had to deal. He knew roughly what sum was at his disposal for investment; the winding-up of the business here could be completed at any moment, and involved no risk of surprises. But a thought had occurred to him which kept him silently reflecting for some minutes.

"I suppose," he said presently, "this affair has about as little risk as anything one could put money in?"

"I should say," Godfrey answered, with his man-of-business air, "that the element of risk is non-existent. What can be more solid than jam? There's competition to be sure; but Applegarth is already a good name throughout England, and in the West they swear by it. At Bristol, Exeter, Dorchester—all over there—Applegarth holds the field. Very seriously speaking, I see in this proposal nothing but sure and increasing gain."

"You know as well as I do," Will resumed, "how I stand. I have no resources of my own beyond what you are aware of. But I've been thinking——"

He broke off, stared at the window, drummed on the arm of his chair, Sherwood waiting with a patient smile.

"It's my mother and sister I have in mind," Will resumed. "That property of theirs; it brings them about a hundred and fifty pounds a year in cash, and three times that in worry. At any moment they might sell. A man at St. Neots offers four thousand pounds; I suspect more might be got if Turnbull, their lawyer, took the matter in hand. Suppose I advise them to sell and put the money in Applegarth?"

"By Jove!" cried Sherwood. "How could they do better? Splendid idea!"

"Yes—if all goes well. Bear in mind, on the other hand, that if they lost this money, they would have nothing to live upon, or as good as nothing. They draw some fifty pounds a year from another source, and they have their own house—that's all. Ought I to take this responsibility ?"

"I don't hesitate to guarantee," said Sherwood, with glowing gravity, "that in two years' time their four thousand pounds shall produce three times what it does now. Only think, my dear fellow! Jam—think what it means!"

For ten minutes Godfrey rhapsodised on the theme. Warburton was moved by his eloquence.

"I shall run down to St. Neots," said Will at length.

"Do. And then we'll both of us go down to Bristol. I'm sure you'll like Applegarth. By the bye, you never went in for astronomy, did you? I felt ashamed of my ignorance. Why, it's one of the most interesting subjects a man can study. I shall take it up. One might have a little observatory of one's own. Do you know Bristol at all? A beastly place, the town, but perfectly delightful country quite near at hand. Applegarth lives in an ideal spot—you'll see."

There was a knock at the door and the manager entered. Other business claimed their attention.

CHAPTER VIII

WARBURTON often returned from Whitechapel to Chelsea on foot, enjoying the long walk after his day in the office. This evening, a heavily clouded sky and sobbing wind told that rain was not far off; nevertheless, wishing to think hard, which he could never do so well as when walking at a brisk pace, he set off in the familiar direction —a straight cut across South London.

In Lower Kennington Lane he stopped, as his habit was, at a little stationer's shop, over which was the name Potts. During his last year in the West Indies, he had befriended an English lad whose health was suffering from the climate, and eventually had paid his passage to the United States, whither the young adventurer wished to go in pursuit of his fortune. Not long after he received a letter of thanks from the lad's father, and, on coming to London, he sought out Mr. Potts, whose gratitude and its quaint expression had pleased him. The acquaintance continued; whenever Warburton passed the shop he stepped in and made purchases—generally of things he did not in the least want. Potts had all the characteristics which were wont to interest Will, and touch his sympathies; he was poor, weak of body, humble-spirited, and of an honest, simple mind. Nothing more natural and cordial than Will's bearing as he entered and held out his hand to the shopkeeper. How was business ? Any news lately from Jack ? Jack, it seemed, was doing pretty well at Pittsburgh ; would Mr. Warburton care to read a long letter that had arrived from him a week ago ? To his satisfaction, Will found that the letter had enclosed a small sum of money, for a present on the father's birthday. Having, as usual, laden himself with newspapers, periodicals and notepaper, he went his way.

At grimy Vauxhall he crossed the river, and pursued his course along Grosvenor Road. Rain had begun to fall, and the driving of the wind obliged him to walk with the umbrella before his face. Happening to glance ahead, when not far from home, he saw, at a distance of twenty yards, a man whom he took for Norbert Franks. The artist was coming toward him, but suddenly he turned round about, and walked rapidly away, disappearing in a moment down a side street. Franks it certainly was ; impossible to mistake his figure, his gait ; and Warburton felt sure that the abrupt change of direction was caused by his friend's desire to avoid him. At the end of the byway he looked, and there was the familiar figure, marching with quick step into the rainy distance. Odd ! but perhaps it simply meant that Franks had not seen him.

He reached home, wrote some letters, made preparations for leaving town by an early train next morning, and dined with his customary appetite. Whilst smoking his after-dinner pipe, he thought again of that queer little incident in Grosvenor Road, and resolved of a sudden to go and see Franks. It still rained, so he took advantage of a passing hansom, and drove in a few minutes to the artist's lodging on the south side of Battersea

Park. The door was opened to him by the landlady, who smiled recognition.

"No, sir, Mr. Franks isn't at home, and hasn't been since after breakfast this morning. And I don't understand it; because he told me last night that he'd be working all day, and I was to get meals for him as usual. And at ten o'clock the model came—that rough man he's putting into the new picture, you know, sir; and I had to send him away, when he'd waited more than an hour."

Warburton was puzzled.

"I'll take my turn at waiting," he said. "Will you please light the gas for me in the studio?"

The studio was merely, in lodging-house language, the first floor front; a two-windowed room, with the advantage of north light. On the walls hung a few framed paintings, several unframed and unfinished, water-colour sketehes, studies in crayon, photographs, and so on. In the midst stood the easel, supporting a large canvas, the artist's work on which showed already in a state of hopeful advancement. "The Slummer" was his provisional name for this picture; he had not yet hit upon that more decorous title which might suit the Academy catalogue. A glance discovered the subject. In a typical London slum, between small and vile houses, which lowered upon the narrow way, stood a tall, graceful, prettily-clad young woman, obviously a visitant from other spheres; her one hand carried a book, and the other was held by a ragged, cripple child, who gazed up at her with a look of innocent adoration. Hard by stood a miserable creature with an infant at her breast, she too adoring the representative of health, wealth, and charity. Behind, a costermonger, out of work, sprawled on the curbstone, viewing the invader; he, with resentful eye, his lip suggestive of words unreportable. Where the face of the central figure should have shone, the canvas still remained blank.

"I'm afraid he's worried about *her*," said the landlady, when she had lit the gas, and stood with Warburton surveying the picture. "He can't find a model good-looking enough. I say to Mr. Franks why not make it the portrait of his own young lady? I'm sure *she's* good-looking enough for anything and——"

Whilst speaking, the woman had turned to look at a picture on the wall. Words died upon her lips; consternation appeared in her face; she stood with finger extended. Warburton, glancing where he was accustomed to see the portrait of Rosamund Elvan, also felt a shock. For, instead of the face which should have smiled upon him, he saw an ugly hole in the picture, the canvas having been violently cut, or rent with a blow.

"Hallo! What the deuce has he been doing?"

"Well, I never!" exclaimed the landlady. "It must be himself that's done it! What does *that* mean now, I wonder?"

Warburton was very uneasy. He no longer doubted that Franks had purposely avoided him this afternoon.

"I daresay," he added, with a pretence of carelessness, "the portrait had begun to vex him. He's often spoken of it discontentedly, and talked of painting another. It wasn't very good."

Accepting, or seeming to accept this explanation, the landlady withdrew, and Will paced thoughtfully about the floor. He was back in Switzerland, in the valley which rises to the glacier of Trient. Before him rambled Ralph Pomfret and his wife;

at his side was Rosamund Elvan, who listened with a flattering air of interest to all he said, but herself spoke seldom, and seemed, for the most part, preoccupied with some anxiety. He spoke of Norbert Franks; Miss Elvan replied mechanically, and at once made a remark about the landscape. At the time, he had thought little of this; now it revived in his memory, and disturbed him.

An hour passed. His patience was nearly at an end. He waited another ten minutes, then left the room, called to the landlady that he was going, and let himself out.

Scarcely had he walked half a dozen yards, when he stood face to face with Franks.

"Ah! Here you are! I waited as long as I could——"

"I'll walk with you," said the artist, turning on his heels.

He had shaken hands but limply. His look avoided Warburton's. His speech was flat, wearied.

"What's wrong, Franks?"

"As you've been in the studio, I daresay you know."

"I saw something that surprised me."

"*Did* it surprise you?" asked Norbert, in a half-sullen undertone.

"What do you mean by that?" said Will, with subdued resentment.

The rain had ceased; a high wind buffeted them as they went along the almost deserted street. The necessity of clutching at his hat might have explained Norbert's silence for a moment; but he strode on without speaking.

"Of course, if you don't care to talk about it," said Will, stopping short.

"I've been walking about all day," Franks

replied; "and I've got hell inside me; I'd rather not have met you to-night, that's the truth. But I can't let you go without asking a plain question. *Did* it surprise you to see that portrait smashed?"

"Very much. What do you hint at?"

"I had a letter this morning from Rosamund, saying she couldn't marry me, and that all must be over between us. Does *that* surprise you?"

"Yes, it does. Such a possibility had never entered my mind."

Franks checked his step, just where the wind roared at an unprotected corner.

"I've no choice but to believe you," he said, irritably. "And no doubt I'm making a fool of myself. That's why I shot out of your way this afternoon—I wanted to wait till I got calmer. Let's say good-night."

"You're tired out," said Warburton. "Don't go any farther this way, but let me walk back with you—I won't go in. I can't leave you in this state of mind. Of course I begin to see what you mean, and a wilder idea never got into any man's head. Whatever the explanation of what has happened, *I* have nothing to do with it."

"You say so, and I believe you."

"Which means, that you don't. I shan't cut up rough; you're not yourself, and I can make all allowances. Think over what I've said, and come and have another talk. Not to-morrow; I have to go down to St. Neots. But the day after, in the evening."

"Very well. Good-night."

This time they did not shake hands. Franks turned abruptly, with a wave of the arm, and walked off unsteadily, like a man in liquor. Observing this, Warburton said to himself that not improbably the artist had been trying to drown his misery, which might account for his strange delusion. Yet this explanation did not put Will's mind at ease. Gloomily he made his way homeward through the roaring night.

CHAPTER IX

TEN o'clock next morning saw him alighting from the train at St. Neots. A conveyance for which he had telegraphed awaited him at the station; its driver, a young man of his own age (they had known each other from boyhood), grinned his broadest as he ran toward Will on the platform, and relieved him of his bag.

"Well, Sam, how goes it? Everybody flourishing?—Drive first to Mr. Turnbull's office."

Mr. Turnbull was a grey-headed man of threescore, much troubled with lumbago, which made him stoop as he walked. He had a visage of extraordinary solemnity, and seemed to regard every one, no matter how prosperous or cheerful, with anxious commiseration. At the sight of Will, he endeavoured to smile, and his handshake, though the flabbiest possible, was meant for a cordial response to the young man's heartiness.

"I'm on my way to The Haws, Mr. Turnbull, and wanted to ask if you could come up and see us this evening?"

"Oh, with pleasure," answered the lawyer, his tone that of one invited to a funeral. "You may count on me."

"We're winding up at Sherwood's. I don't mean in bankruptcy; but that wouldn't be far off if we kept going."

"Ah! I can well understand that," said Mr.

Turnbull, with a gleam of satisfaction. Though a thoroughly kind man, it always brightened him to hear of misfortune, especially when he had himself foretold it; and he had always taken the darkest view of Will's prospects in Little Ailie Street.

"I have a project I should like to talk over with you——"

"Ah?" said the lawyer anxiously.

"As it concerns my mother and Jane——"

"Ah?" said Mr. Turnbull, with profound despondency.

"Then we shall expect you.—Will it rain, do you think?"

"I fear so. The glass is very low indeed. It wouldn't surprise me if we had rain through the whole month of August."

"Good Heavens! I hope not," replied Will laughing.

He drove out of the town again, in a different direction, for about a mile. On rising ground, overlooking the green valley of the Ouse, stood a small, plain, solidly-built house, sheltered on the cold side by a row of fine hawthorns, nearly as high as the top of its chimneys. In front, bordered along the road by hollies as impenetrable as a stone wall, lay a bright little flower garden. The Haws, originally built for the bailiff of an estate, long since broken up, was nearly a century old. Here Will's father was born, and here, after many wanderings, he had spent the greater part of his married life.

"Sam," said Will, as they drew up at the gate, "I don't think I shall pay for this drive. You're much richer than I am."

"Very good, sir," was the chuckling reply, for

Sam knew he always had to expect a joke of this kind from young Mr. Warburton. " As you please, sir."

" You couldn't lend me half-a-crown, Sam ? "

" I daresay I could, sir, if you really wanted it."

" Do then."

Will pocketed the half-crown, jumped off the trap, and took his bag.

" After all, Sam, perhaps I'd better pay. Your wife might grumble. Here you are."

He handed two shillings and sixpence in small change, which Sam took and examined with a grin of puzzlement.

" Well, what's the matter ? Don't you say thank you, nowadays ? "

" Yes, sir—thank you, sir—it's all right, Mr. Will."

" I should think it is indeed. Be here to-morrow morning, to catch the 6. 30 up train, Sam."

As Will entered the garden, there came forward a girl of something and twenty, rather short, square shouldered, firmly planted on her feet, but withal brisk of movement ; her face was remarkable for nothing but a grave good-humour. She wore a broad-brimmed straw hat, and her gardening gloves showed how she was occupied. Something of shyness appeared in the mutual greeting of brother and sister.

" Of course, you got my letter this morning ? " said Will.

" Yes."

" Mr. Turnbull is coming up to-night."

" I'm glad of that," said Jane thoughtfully, rubbing her gloves together to shake off moist earth.

"Of course he'll prophesy disaster, and plunge you both into the depths of discouragement. But I don't mind that. I feel so confident myself that I want some one to speak on the other side. He'll have to make inquiries, of course.—Where's mother?"

The question was answered by Mrs. Warburton herself, who at that moment came forth from the house; a tall, graceful woman, prematurely white-headed, and enfeebled by ill-health. Between her and Jane there was little resemblance of feature; Will, on the other hand, had inherited her oval face, arched brows and sensitive mouth. Emotion had touched her cheek with the faintest glow, but ordinarily it was pale as her hand. Nothing, however, of the invalid declared itself in her tone or language; the voice, soft and musical, might have been that of a young woman, and its vivacity was only less than that which marked the speech of her son.

"Come and look at the orange lilies," were her first words, after the greeting. "They've never been so fine."

"But notice Pompey first," said Jane. "He'll be offended in a minute."

A St. Bernard, who had already made such advances as his dignity permitted, stood close by Will, with eyes fixed upon him in grave and surprised reproach. The dog's name indicated a historical preference of Jane in her childhood; she had always championed Pompey against Cæsar, following therein her brother's guidance.

"Hallo, old Magnus!" cried the visitor, cordially repairing his omission. "Come along with us and see the lilies."

It was only when all the sights of the little garden

had been visited, Mrs. Warburton forgetting her weakness as she drew Will hither and thither, that the business for which they had met came under discussion. Discussion, indeed, it could hardly be called, for the mother and sister were quite content to listen whilst Will talked, and accept his view of things. Small as their income was, they never thought of themselves as poor; with one maid-servant and the occasional help of a gardener, they had all the comfort they wished for, and were able to bestow of their superfluity in vegetables and flowers upon less fortunate acquaintances. Until a year or two ago, Mrs. Warburton had led a life of ceaseless activity, indoors and out; such was the habit of her daughter, who enjoyed vigorous health, and cared little for sedentary pursuits and amusements. Their property, land and cottages hard by, had of late given them a good deal of trouble, and the proposal to sell had more than once been considered, but Mr. Turnbull, most cautious of counsellors, urged delay. Now, at length, the hoped-for opportunity of a good investment seemed to have presented itself; Will's sanguine report of what he had learnt from Sherwood was gladly accepted.

"It'll be a good thing for you as well," said Jane.

"Yes, it comes just in time. Sherwood knew what he was doing; now and then I've thought he was risking too much, but he's a clear-headed fellow. The way he has kept things going so long in Ailie Street is really remarkable."

"I daresay you had your share in that, Will," said Mrs. Warburton.

"A very small one; my work has never been more than routine. I don't pretend to be a man of business. If it had depended upon me, the concern would have fallen to pieces years ago, like so many others. House after house has gone down; our turn must have come very soon. As it is, we shall clear out with credit, and start afresh gloriously. By the bye, don't get any but Applegarth's jams in future."

"That depends," said Jane laughing, "if we like them."

In their simple and wholesome way of living, the Warburtons of course dined at midday, and Will, who rarely ate without appetite, surpassed himself as trencherman; nowhere had food such a savour for him as under this roof. The home-made bread and home-grown vegetables he was never tired of praising; such fragrant and toothsome loaves, he loudly protested, were to be eaten nowhere else in England. He began to talk of his holiday abroad, when all at once his countenance fell, his lips closed; in the pleasure of being "at home," he had forgotten all about Norbert Franks, and very unwelcome were the thoughts which attached themselves to this recollection of his days at Trient.

"What's the matter?" asked Jane, noticing his change of look.

"Oh, nothing—a stupid affair. I wrote to you about the Pomfrets and their niece. I'm afraid that girl is an idiot. She used the opportunity of her absence, I find, to break with Franks. No excuse whatever; simply sent him about his business."

"Oh!" exclaimed both the ladies, who had been interested in the artist's love story, as narrated to them, rather badly, by Will on former occasions.

"Of course, I don't know much about it. But it looks bad. Perhaps it's the best thing that could have happened to Franks, for it may mean that he hasn't made money fast enough to please her."

"But you gave us quite another idea of Miss Elvan," said his mother.

"Yes, I daresay I did. Who knows? I don't pretend to understand such things."

A little before sunset came Mr. Turnbull, who took supper at The Haws, and was fetched away by his coachman at ten o'clock. With this old friend, who in Will's eyes looked no older now than when he first knew him in early childhood, they talked freely of the Applegarth business, and Mr. Turnbull promised to make inquiries at once. Of course, he took a despondent view of jam. Jam, he inclined to think, was being overdone; after all, the country could consume only a certain quantity of even the most wholesome preserves, and a glut of jam already threatened the market. Applegarth? By the bye, did he not remember proceedings in bankruptcy connected with that unusual name? He must look into the matter. And, talking about bankruptcy—oh! how bad his lumbago was to-night!—poor Thomas Hart, of Three Ash Farm, was going to be sold up. Dear, dear! On every side, look where one would, nothing but decline and calamity. What was England coming to? Day by day he had expected to see the failure of Sherwood Brothers; how had they escaped the common doom of sugar refiners? Free trade, free trade; all very fine in theory, but look at its results on corn and sugar. For his own part he favoured a policy of moderate protection.

All this was not more than Will had foreseen. It would be annoying if Mr. Turnbull ultimately took an adverse view of his proposal; in that case, though his mother was quite free to manage her property as she chose, Will felt that he should not venture to urge his scheme against the lawyer's advice, and money must be sought elsewhere. A few days would decide the matter. As he went upstairs to bed, he dismissed worries from his mind.

The old quiet, the old comfort of home. Not a sound but that of pattering rain in the still night. As always, the room smelt of lavender, blended with that indescribable fragrance which comes of extreme cleanliness in an old country house. But for changed wall paper and carpet, everything was as Will remembered it ever since he could remember anything at all; the same simple furniture, the same white curtains, the same pictures, the same little hanging shelf, with books given to him in childhood. He thought of the elder brother who had died at school, and lay in the little churchyard far away. His only dark memory, that of the poor boy's death after a very short illness, before that other blow which made him fatherless.

The earlier retrospect was one of happiness unbroken; for all childish sorrows lost themselves in the very present sense of peace and love enveloping those far-away years. His parents' life, as he saw it then, as in reflection he saw it now, remained an ideal; he did not care to hope for himself, or to imagine, any other form of domestic contentment. As a child, he would have held nothing less conceivable than a moment's discord between father and mother, and manhood's meditation did but confirm him in the same view.

The mutual loyalty of kindred hearts and minds —that was the best life had to give. And Will's thoughts turned once more to Norbert Franks; he, poor fellow, doubtless now raging against the faithlessness which had blackened all his sky. In this moment of softened feeling, of lucid calm, Warburton saw Rosamund's behaviour in a new light. Perhaps she was not blameworthy at all, but rather deserving of all praise; for, if she had come to know, beyond doubt, that she did not love Norbert Franks as she had thought, then to break the engagement was her simple duty, and the courage with which she had taken this step must be set to her credit. Naturally, it would be some time before Franks himself took that view. A third person, whose vanity was not concerned, might moralise thus——

Will checked himself on an unpleasant thought. Was *his* vanity, in truth, unconcerned in this story? Why, then, had he been conscious of a sub-emotion, quite unavowable, which contradicted his indignant sympathy during that talk last night in the street? If the lover's jealousy were as ridiculous as he pretended, why did he feel what now he could confess to himself was an unworthy titillation, when Franks seemed to accuse him of some part in the girl's disloyalty? Vanity, that, sure enough; vanity of a very weak and futile kind. He would stamp the last traces of it out of his being. Happily it was but vanity, and no deeper feeling. Of this he was assured by the reposeful sigh with which he turned his head upon the pillow, drowsing to oblivion.

One unbroken sleep brought him to sunrise; a golden glimmer upon the blind in his return to consciousness told him that the rain was over, and tempted him to look forth. What he saw was decisive; with such a sky as that gleaming over the summer world, who could lie in bed? Will always dressed as if in a fury; seconds sufficed him for details of the toilet, which, had he spent minutes over them, would have fretted his nerves intolerably. His bath was one wild welter—not even the ceiling being safe from splashes; he clad himself in a brief series of plunges; his shaving might have earned the applause of an assembly gathered to behold feats of swift dexterity. Quietly he descended the stairs, and found the house-door already open; this might only mean that the servant was already up, but he suspected that the early riser was Jane. So it proved; he walked toward the kitchen garden, and there stood his sister, the sun making her face rosy.

"Come and help to pick scarlet runners," was her greeting, as he approached. "Aren't they magnificent?"

Her eyes sparkled with pleasure as she pointed to the heavy clusters of dark-green pods, hanging amid leaves and scarlet bloom.

"Splendid crop!" exclaimed Will, with answering enthusiasm.

"Doesn't the scent do one good?" went on his sister. "When I come into the garden on a morning like this, I have a feeling—oh, I can't describe it to you—perhaps you wouldn't understand——"

"I know," said Will, nodding.

"It's as if nature were calling out to me, like a friend, to come and admire and enjoy what she has done. I feel grateful for the things that earth offers me."

Not often did Jane speak like this; as a rule she was anything but effusive or poetical. But a peculiar animation shone in her looks this morning, and sounded in her voice. Very soon the reason was manifest; she began to speak of the Applegarth business, and declared her great satisfaction with it.

"There'll be an end of mother's worry," she said, "and I can't tell you how glad I shall be. It seems to me that women oughtn't to have to think about money, and mother hates the name of it; she always has done. Oh, what a blessing when it's all off our hands! We shouldn't care, even if the new arrangement brought us less."

"And it is certain to bring you more," remarked Will, "perhaps considerably more."

"Well, I shan't object to that; there are lots of uses for money; but it doesn't matter."

Jane's sincerity was evident. She dismissed the matter, and her basket being full of beans, seized a fork to dig potatoes.

"Here, let me do that," cried Will, interposing.

"You? Well then, as a very great favour."

"Of course I mean that. It's grand to turn up potatoes. What sort are these?"

"Pink-eyed flukes," replied Jane, watching him with keen interest. "We haven't touched them yet."

"Mealy, eh?"

"Balls of flour!"

Their voices joined in a cry of exultation, as the fork threw out even a finer root than they had expected. When enough had been dug, they strolled about, looking at other vegetables. Jane pointed to some Savoy seedlings, which she was going to plant out to-day. Then there sounded a joyous bark, and Pompey came bounding toward them.

"That means the milk-boy is here," said Jane. "Pompey always goes to meet him in the morning. Come and drink a glass—warm."

CHAPTER X

BACK at Chelsea, Will sent a note to Norbert Franks, a line or two without express reference to what had happened, asking him to come and have a talk. Three days passed, and there was no reply. Will grew uneasy; for, though the artist's silence perhaps meant only sullenness, danger might lurk in such a man's thwarted passion. On the fourth evening, just as he had made up his mind to walk over to Queen's Road, the familiar knock sounded. Mrs. Hopper had left; Will went to the door, and greeted his visitor in the usual way. But Franks entered without speaking. The lamplight showed a pitiful change in him; he was yellow and fishy-eyed, unshaven, disorderly in dress; indeed, so well did he look the part of the despairing lover that Warburton suspected a touch of theatric consciousness.

"If you hadn't come to-night," said Will, "I should have looked you up."

Franks lay limply in the armchair, staring blankly.

"I ought to have come before," he replied in low, toneless voice. "That night when I met you, I made a fool of myself. For one thing, I was drunk, and I've been drunk ever since."

"Ha! That accounts for your dirty collar," remarked Will, in his note of dry drollery.

"Is it dirty?" said the other, passing a finger

round his neck. "What does it matter? A little dirt more or less, in a world so full of it——"

Warburton could not contain himself; he laughed, and laughed again. And his mirth was contagious; Franks chuckled, unwillingly, dolefully.

"You are not extravagant in sympathy," said the artist, moving with fretful nervousness.

"If I were, would it do you any good, old fellow? Look here, are we to talk of this affair or not? Just as you like. For my part, I'd rather talk about 'The Slummer.' I had a look at it the other day. Uncommonly good, the blackguard on the curbstone, you've got him."

"You think so?" Franks sat a little straighter, but still with vacant eye. "Yes, not bad, I think. But who knows whether I shall finish the thing."

"If you don't," replied his friend, in a matter-of-fact tone, "you'll do something better. But I should finish it, if I were you. If you had the courage to paint in the right sort of face—the girl, you know."

"What sort of face, then?"

"Sharp-nosed, thin-lipped, rather anæmic, with a universe of self-conceit in the eye."

"They wouldn't hang it, and nobody would buy it. Besides, Warburton, you're wrong if you think the slummers are always that sort. Still, I'm not sure I shan't do it, out of spite. There's another reason, too—I hate beautiful women; I don't think I shall ever be able to paint another."

He sprang up, and paced, as of old, about the room. Will purposely kept silence.

"I've confessed," Franks began again, with effort, "that I made a fool of myself the other night. But I wish you'd tell me something about your time at Trient. Didn't you notice anything? Didn't anything make you suspect what she was going to do?"

"I never for a moment foresaw it," replied Will, with unemphasised sincerity.

"Yet she must have made up her mind whilst you were there. Her astounding hypocrisy! I had a letter a few days before, the same as usual——"

"Quite the same?"

"Absolutely!—Well, there was no difference that struck me. Then all at once she declares that for months she had felt her position false and painful. What a monstrous thing! Why did she go on pretending, playing a farce? I could have sworn that no girl lived who was more thoroughly honest in word and deed and thought. It's awful to think how one can be deceived. I understand now the novels about unfaithful wives, and all that kind of thing. I always said to myself—'Pooh, as if a fellow wouldn't know if his wife were deceiving him'! By Jove this has made me afraid of the thought of marriage. I shall never again trust a woman."

Warburton sat in meditation, only half smiling.

"Of course, she's ashamed to face me. For fear I should run after her, she wrote that they were just leaving Trient for another place, not mentioned. If I wrote, I was to address to Bath, and the letter would be forwarded. I wrote—of course a fool's letter; I only wish I'd never sent it. Sometimes I think I'll never try to see her again; sometimes I think I'll make her see me, and tell her the truth about herself. The only thing is—I'm half afraid—I've gone through torture enough; I don't want to begin again. Yet if I saw her——"

He took another turn across the room, then checked himself before Warburton.

"Tell me honestly what you think about it. I want advice. What's your opinion of her?"

"I have no opinion at all. I don't pretend to know her well enough."

"Well, but," persisted Franks, "your impression—your feeling. How does the thing strike you?"

"Why, disagreeably enough; that's a matter of course."

"You don't excuse her?" asked Norbert, his eyes fixed on the other.

"I can imagine excuses——"

"What? What excuse can there be for deliberate hypocrisy, treachery?"

"If it *was* deliberate," replied Warburton, "there's nothing to be said. In your position—since you ask advice—I should try to think that it wasn't, but that the girl had simply changed her mind, and went on and on, struggling with herself till she could stand it no longer. I've no taste for melodrama; quiet comedy is much more in my line—comedy ending with mutual tolerance and forgiveness. To be sure, if you feel you can't live without her, if you're determined to fight for her——"

"Fight with whom?" cried Franks.

"With *her*; then read Browning, and blaze away. It may be the best; who can tell? Only—on this point I am clear—no self-deception! Don't go in for heroics just because they seem fine. Settle with yourself whether she is indispensable to you or not.—Indispensable? why, no woman is that to any man; sooner or later, it's a matter of indifference. And if you feel, talking plainly with yourself, that the worst is over already, that it doesn't after all matter as much as you thought;

why, get back to your painting. If you can paint only ugly women, so much the better, I've no doubt."

Franks stood reflecting. Then he nodded.

"All that is sensible enough. But, if I give her up, I shall marry some one else straight away."

Then he abruptly said good-night, leaving Warburton not unhopeful about him, and much consoled by the disappearance of the shadow which had threatened their good understanding.

CHAPTER XI

THE Crosses, mother and daughter, lived at Walham Green. The house was less pleasant than another which Mrs. Cross owned at Putney, but it also represented a lower rental, and poverty obliged them to take this into account. When the second house stood tenantless, as had now been the case for half a year, Mrs. Cross' habitually querulous comment on life rose to a note of acrimony very afflictive to her daughter Bertha. The two bore as little resemblance to each other, physical or mental, as mother and child well could. Bertha Cross was a sensible, thoughtful girl, full of kindly feeling, and blest with a humorous turn that enabled her to see the amusing rather than the carking side of her pinched life. These virtues she had from her father. Poor Cross, who supplemented a small income from office routine by occasional comic journalism, and even wrote a farce (which brought money to a theatrical manager), made on his deathbed a characteristic joke. He had just signed his will, and was left alone with his wife. "I'm sure I've always wished to make your life happy," piped the afflicted woman. "And I yours," he faintly answered; adding, with a sad, kind smile, as he pointed to the testamentary document, "Take the will for the deed."

The two sons had emigrated to British Columbia,

and Bertha would not have been sorry to join her brothers there, for domestic labour on a farm, in peace and health, seemed to her considerably better than the quasi-genteel life she painfully supported. She had never dreamt of being an artist, but, showing some facility with the pencil, was sent by her father to South Kensington, where she met and made friends with Rosamund Elvan. Her necessity and her application being greater than Rosamund's, Bertha before long succeeded in earning a little money; without this help, life at home would scarcely have been possible for her. They might, to be sure, have taken a lodger, having spare rooms, but Mrs. Cross could only face that possibility if the person received into the house were "respectable" enough to be called a paying guest, and no such person offered. So they lived, as no end of "respectable" families do, a life of penury and seclusion, sometimes going without a meal that they might have decent clothing to wear abroad, never able to buy a book, to hear a concert, and only by painful sacrifice able to entertain a friend. When on a certain occasion, Miss Elvan passed a week at their house (Mrs. Cross approved of this friendship, and hoped it might be a means of discovering the paying guest), it meant for them a near approach to starvation during the month that ensued.

Time would have weighed heavily on Mrs. Cross but for her one recreation, which was perennial, ever fresh, constantly full of surprises and excitement. Poor as she was, she contrived to hire a domestic servant; to say that she "kept" one would come near to a verbal impropriety, seeing that no servant ever remained in the house for more than a few months, whilst it occasionally happened that the space of half a year would see a succession of some half dozen "generals." Underpaid and underfed, these persons (they varied in age from fourteen to forty) were of course incompetent, careless, rebellious, and Mrs. Cross found the sole genuine pleasure of her life in the war she waged with them. Having no reasonable way of spending her hours, she was thus supplied with occupation; being of acrid temper, she was thus supplied with a subject upon whom she could fearlessly exercise it; being remarkably mean of disposition, she saw in the paring-down of her servant's rations to a working minimum, at once profit and sport; lastly, being fond of the most trivial gossip, she had a never-failing topic of discussion with such ladies as could endure her society.

Bertha, having been accustomed to this domestic turbulence all her life long, for the most part paid no heed to it. She knew that if the management of the house were in her hands, instead of her mother's. things would go much more smoothly, but the mere suggestion of such a change (ventured once at a moment of acute crisis) had so amazed and exasperated Mrs. Cross, that Bertha never again looked in that direction. Yet from time to time a revolt of common sense forced her to speak, and as the only possible way, if quarrel were to be avoided, she began her remonstrance on the humorous note. Then when her mother had been wearying her for half an hour with complaints and lamentations over the misdoings of one Emma, Bertha as the alternative to throwing up her hands and rushing out of the house, began laughing to herself, whereat Mrs. Cross indignantly begged to be informed what there was so very amusing in a state of affairs which would assuredly bring her to her grave.

"If only you could see the comical side of it,

mother," replied Bertha. "It really has one, you know. Emma, if only you would be patient with her, is a well-meaning creature, and she says the funniest things. I asked her this morning if she didn't think she could find some way of remembering to put the salt on the table. And she looked at me very solemnly, and said, 'Indeed, I will, miss. I'll put it into my prayers, just after 'our daily bread.'"

Mrs. Cross saw nothing in this but profanity. She turned the attack on Bertha, who, by her soft way of speaking, simply encouraged the servants, she declared, in negligence and insolence.

"Look at it in this way, mother," replied the girl, as soon as she was suffered to speak. "To be badly served is bad enough, in itself; why make it worse by ceaseless talking about it, so leaving ourselves not a moment of peace and quiet? I'm sure I'd rather put the salt on the table myself at every meal, and think no more about it, than worry, worry, worry over the missing salt-cellars from one meal to the next. Don't you feel, dear mother, that it's shocking waste of life?"

"What nonsense you talk, child! Are we to live in dirt and disorder? Am I *never* to correct a servant, or teach her her duties? But of course everything *I* do is wrong. Of course *you* could do everything so very much better. That's what children are nowadays."

Whilst Mrs. Cross piped on, Bertha regarded her with eyes of humorous sadness. The girl often felt it a dreary thing not to be able to respect—nay, not to be able to feel much love for—her mother. At such times, her thought turned to the other parent, with whom, had he and she been left alone, she could have lived so happily, in so much mutual intelligence and affection. She sighed and moved away.

The unlet house was a very serious matter, and when one day Norbert Franks came to talk about it, saying that he would want a house very soon, and thought this of Mrs. Cross's might suit him, Bertha rejoiced no less than her mother. In consequence of the artist's announcement, she wrote to her friend Rosamund, saying how glad she was to hear that her marriage approached. The reply to this letter surprised her. Rosamund had been remiss in correspondence for the last few months; her few and brief letters, though they were as affectionate as ever, making no mention of what had formerly been an inexhaustible topic—the genius, goodness, and brilliant hopes of Franks. Now she wrote as if in utter despondency, a letter so confused in style and vague in expression, that Bertha could gather from it little or nothing except a grave doubt whether Franks' marriage was as near as he supposed. A week or two passed, and Rosamund again wrote—from Switzerland; again the letter was an unintelligible maze of dreary words, and a mere moaning and sighing, which puzzled Bertha as much as it distressed her. Rosamund's epistolary style, when she wrote to this bosom friend, was always pitched in a key of lyrical emotion, which now and then would have been trying to Bertha's sense of humour but for the sincerity manifest in every word; hitherto, however, she had expressed herself with perfect lucidity, and this sudden change seemed ominous of alarming things. Just when Bertha was anxiously wondering what could have happened,—of course inclined to attribute blame, if blame there were, to the artist rather than to his betrothed—a stranger came to inquire about the house to let.

It was necessary to ascertain at once whether Mr. Franks intended to become their tenant or not. Mrs. Cross wrote to him, and received the briefest possible reply, to the effect that his plans were changed.

"How vexatious!" exclaimed Mrs. Cross. "I had very much rather have let to people we know! I suppose he's seen a house that suits him better."

"I think there's another reason," said Bertha, after gazing for a minute or two at the scribbled, careless note. "The marriage is put off."

"And you knew that," cried her mother, "all the time, and never told me! And I might have missed twenty chances of letting. Really, Bertha, I never did see anything like you. There's that house standing empty month after month, and we hardly know where to turn for money, and you knew that Mr. Franks wouldn't take it, and yet you say not a word! How can you behave in such an extraordinary way? I think you really find pleasure in worrying me. Any one would fancy you wished to see me in my grave. To think that you knew all the time!"

CHAPTER XII

THERE passed a fortnight. Bertha heard nothing more of Miss Elvan, till a letter arrived one morning in an envelope, showing on the back an address at Teddington. Rosamund wrote that she had just returned from Switzerland, and was staying for a few days with friends; would it be possible for Bertha to come to Teddington the same afternoon, for an hour or two's talk? The writer had so much to say that could not be conveyed in a letter, and longed above all things to see Bertha, the only being in whom, at a very grave juncture in her life, she could absolutely confide. "We shall be quite alone—Mr. and Mrs. Capron are going to town immediately after lunch. This is a lovely place, and we shall have it to ourselves all the afternoon. So don't be frightened—I know how you hate strangers—but come, come, come!"

Bertha took train early in the afternoon. By an avenue of elms she passed into a large and beautiful garden, and so came to the imposing front door. Led into the drawing-room, she had time to take breath, and to gaze at splendours such as she had never seen before; then with soundless footfall, entered a slim, prettily-dressed girl who ran towards her, and caught her hands, and kissed her with graceful tenderness.

"My dear, dear old Bertha! What a happiness to see you again! How good of you to come!

Isn't it a lovely place? And the nicest people. You've heard me speak of Miss Anderton, of Bath. She is Mrs. Capron—married half a year ago. And they're just going to Egypt for a year, and—what do you think?—I'm going with them."

Rosamund's voice sunk and faltered. She stood holding Bertha's hands, and gazing into her face with eyes which grew large as if in a distressful appeal.

"To Egypt?"

"Yes. It was decided whilst I was in Switzerland. Mrs. Capron wants a friend to be with her; one who can help her in water-colours. She thought, of course, that I couldn't go; wrote to me just wishing it were possible. And I caught at the chance! Oh, caught at it!"

"That's what I don't understand," said Bertha.

"I want to explain it all. Come into this cosy corner. Nobody will disturb us except when they bring tea.—Do you know that picture of Leader's? Isn't it exquisite!—Are you tired, Bertha? You look so, a little. I'm afraid you walked from the station, and it's such a hot day. But oh, the loveliness of the trees about here! Do you remember our first walk together? You were shy, stiff; didn't feel quite sure whether you liked me or not. And I thought you—just a little critical. But before we got back again, I think we had begun to understand each other. And I wonder whether you'll understand me now. It would be dreadful if I felt you disapproved of me. Of course if you do, I'd much rather you said so. You will—won't you?"

She again fixed her eyes upon Bertha with the wide, appealing look.

"Whether I say it or not," replied the other,

"you'll see what I think. I never could help that."

"That's what I love in you! And that's what I've been thinking of, all these weeks of misery—your perfect sincerity. I've asked myself whether it would be possible for you to find yourself in such a position as mine; and how you would act, how you would speak. You're my ideal of truth and rightness, Bertha; I've often enough told you that."

Bertha moved uncomfortably, her eyes averted.

"Suppose you just tell me what has happened," she added quietly.

"Yes, I will. I hope you haven't been thinking it was some fault of *his*?"

"I couldn't help thinking that."

"Oh! Put that out of your mind at once. The fault is altogether mine. He has done nothing whatever—he is good and true, and all that a man should be. It's I who am behaving badly; so badly that I feel hot with shame now that I come to tell you. I have broken it off. I've said I couldn't marry him."

Their eyes met for an instant. Bertha looked rather grave, but with her wonted kindliness of expression; Rosamund's brows were wrinkled in distress, and her lips trembled.

"I've seen it coming since last Christmas," she continued, in a hurried, tremulous undertone. "You know he came down to Bath; that was our last meeting; and I felt that something was wrong. Ah, so hard to know oneself! I wanted to talk to you about it; but then I said to myself—what can Bertha do but tell me to know my own mind? And that's just what I couldn't come to,—to understand my own feelings. I was changing, I knew that.

I dreaded to look into my own thoughts, from day to day. Above all, I dreaded to sit down and write to him. Oh, the hateful falsity of those letters! —Yet what could I do, what could I do? I had no right to give such a blow, unless I felt that anything else was utterly, utterly impossible."

"And at last you did feel it?"

"In Switzerland—yes. It came like a flash of lightning. I was walking up that splendid valley —you remember my description—up toward the glacier. That morning I had had a letter, naming the very day for our marriage, and speaking of the house—your house at Putney—he meant to take. I had said to myself—'It must be; I can do nothing. I haven't the courage.' Then, as I was walking, a sort of horror fell upon me, and made me tremble; and when it passed I saw that, so far from not having the courage to break, I should never dare to go through with it. And I went back to the hotel, and sat down and wrote, without another moment's thought or hesitation."

"What else could you have done?" said Bertha, with a sigh of relief. "When it comes to horror and tremblings!"

There was a light in her eye which seemed the precursor of a smile; but her voice was not unsympathetic, and Rosamund knew that one of Bertha Cross' smiles was worth more in the way of friendship than another's tragic emotion.

"Have patience with me," she continued, "whilst I try to explain it all. The worst of my position is, that so many people will know what I have done, and so few of them, hardly any one, will understand why. One can't talk to people about such things. Even Winnie and father—I'm sure they don't really understand—though I'm afraid they're both rather glad. What a wretched thing it is to be misjudged. I feel sure, Bertha, that it's just this kind of thing that makes a woman sit down and write a novel —where she can speak freely in disguise, and do herself justice. Don't you think so ? "

" I shouldn't wonder," replied the listener, thoughtfully. " But does it really matter ? If you know you're only doing what you must do ? "

" But that's only how it seems to me. Another, in my place, would very likely see the must on the other side. Of course it's a terribly complicated thing—a situation like this. I haven't the slightest idea how one ought to be guided. One could argue and reason all day long about it—as I have done with myself for weeks past."

" Try just to tell me the reason which seems to you the strongest," said Bertha.

" That's very simple. I thought I loved him, and I find I don't."

" Exactly. But I hardly see how the change came about."

" I will try to tell you," replied Rosamund. " It was that picture, 'Sanctuary,' that began it. When I first saw it, it gave me a shock. You know how I have always thought of him—an artist living for his own idea of art, painting just as he liked, what pleased him, without caring for the public taste. I got enthusiastic ; and when I saw that he seemed to care for my opinion and my praise—of course all the rest followed. He told me about his life as an art student—Paris, Rome, all that ; and it was my ideal of romance. He was very poor, sometimes so poor that he hardly had enough to eat, and this made me proud of him, for I felt sure he could have got money if he would have condescended to do inferior work. Of course, as I too was poor, we could not think of marrying before his position improved. At last he painted 'Sanctuary.' He told me nothing about it. I came and saw it on the easel, nearly finished. And—this is the shocking thing—I pretended to admire it. I was astonished, pained—yet I had the worldliness to smile and praise. There's the fault of my chaacter. At that moment, truth and courage were wanted, and I had neither. The dreadful thing is to think that he degraded himself on my account. If I had said at once what I thought, he would have confessed—would have told me that impatience had made him untrue to himself. And from that day; oh, this is the worst of all, Bertha—he has adapted himself to what he thinks my lower mind and lower aims; he has consciously debased himself, out of thought for me. Horrible! Of course he believes in his heart that I was a hypocrite before. The astonishing thing is that this didn't cause him to turn cold to me. He must have felt that, but somehow he overcame it. All the worse! The very fact that he still cared for me shows how bad my influence has been. I feel that I have wrecked his life, Bertha—and yet I cannot give him my own, to make some poor sort of amends."

Bertha was listening wth a face that changed from puzzled interest to wondering confusion.

"Good gracious!" she exclaimed when the speaker ceased. "Is it possible to get into such entanglements of reasoning about what one thinks and feels? It's beyond me. Oh they're bringing the tea. Perhaps a cup of tea will clear my wits."

Rosamund at once began to speak of the landscape by Leader, which hung near them, and continued to do so even after the servant had withdrawn.

Her companion was silent, smiling now and then in an absent way. They sipped tea.

"The tea is doing me so much good," Bertha said, "I begin to feel equal to the most complicated reflections. And so you really believe that Mr. Franks is on the way to perdition, and that you are the cause of it?"

Rosamund did not reply. She had half averted her look; her brows were knit in an expression of trouble; she bit her lower lip. A moment passed, and——

"Suppose we go into the garden," she said, rising. "Don't you feel it a little close here?"

They strolled about the paths. Her companion, seeming to have dismissed from mind their subject of conversation, began to talk of Egypt, and the delight she promised herself there.

Presently Bertha reverted to the unfinished story.

"Oh, it doesn't interest you."

"Doesn't it indeed! Please go on. You had just explained all about 'Sanctuary'—which isn't really a bad picture at all."

"Oh, Bertha!" cried the other in pained protest. "That's your good nature. You never can speak severely of anybody's work. The picture is shameful, shameful! And its successor, I am too sure, will be worse still, from what I have heard of it. Oh, I can't bear to think of what it all means—Now that it's too late, I see what I ought to have done. In spite of everything and everybody I ought to have married him in the first year, when I had courage and hope enough to face any hardships. We spoke of it, but he was too generous. What a splendid thing to have starved with him—to have worked for him whilst he was working for art and fame, to have gone through all that together, and have come out triumphant! That was a life worth living. But to begin marriage at one's ease on the profits of pictures such as 'Sanctuary'—oh, the shame of it! Do you think I could face the friends who would come to see me?"

"How many friends," asked Bertha, "would be aware of your infamy? I credit myself with a little imagination. But I should never have suspected the black baseness which had poisoned your soul."

Again Rosamund bit her lip, and kept a short silence.

"It only shows," she said with some abruptness, "that I shall do better not to speak of it at all, and let people think what they like of me. If even *you* can't understand."

Bertha stood still, and spoke in a changed voice.

"I understand very well—or think I do. I'm perfectly sure that you could never have broken your engagement unless for the gravest reason—and for me it is quite enough to know that. Many a girl ought to do this, who never has the courage. Try not to worry about explanations, the thing is done, and there's an end of it. I'm very glad indeed you're going quite away; it's the best thing possible. When do you start?" she added.

"In three days.—Listen, Bertha, I have something very serious to ask of you. It is possible—isn't it?—that he may come to see you some day. If he does, or if by chance you see him alone, and if he speaks of me, I want you to make him think—you easily can—that what has happened is all for his good. Remind him how often artists have been spoilt by marriage, and hint—you surely could—that I am rather too fond of luxury, and that kind of thing."

Bertha wore an odd smile.

"Trust me," she replied, "I will blacken you most effectually."

"You promise? But, at the same time, you will urge him to be true to himself, to endure poverty——"

"I don't know about that. Why shouldn't poor Mr. Franks have enough to eat it he can get it?"

"Well—but you promise to help him in the other way? You needn't say very bad things; just a smile, a hint——"

"I quite understand," said Bertha, nodding.

CHAPTER XIII

WARBURTON had never seen Godfrey Sherwood so restless and excitable as during these weeks when the business in Little Ailie Street was being brought to an end, and the details of the transfer to Bristol were being settled. Had it not been inconsistent with all the hopeful facts of the situation, as well as with the man's temper, one would have thought that Godfrey suffered from extreme nervousness; that he lived under some oppressive anxiety, which it was his constant endeavour to combat with resolute high spirits. It seemed an odd thing that a man who had gone through the very real cares and perils of the last few years without a sign of perturbation, nay, with the cheeriest equanimity, should let himself be thrown into disorder by the mere change to a more promising state of things. Now and then Warburton asked himself whether his partner could be concealing some troublesome fact with regard to Applegarth's concern; but he dismissed the idea as too improbable; Sherwood was far too good a fellow, far too conscientious a man of business, to involve his friend in obvious risk—especially since it had been decided that Mrs. Warburton's and her daughter's money should go into the affair. The inquiries made by Mr. Turnbull had results so satisfactory that even the resolute pessimist could not but grudgingly admit his inability to discover storm-signals. Though a sense of responsibility made a new element in his life, which would not let him sleep quite so soundly as hitherto, Will persuaded himself that he had but to get to work, and all would be right.

The impression made upon him by Applegarth himself was very favourable. The fact that the jam manufacturer was a university man, an astronomer, and a musician, had touched Warburton's weak point, and he went down to Bristol the first time with an undeniable prejudice at the back of his mind; but this did not survive a day or two's intercourse. Applegarth recommended himself by an easy and humorous geniality of bearing which Warburton would have been the last man to resist; he talked of his affairs with the utmost frankness.

"The astonishing thing to me is," he said, "that I've made this business pay. I went into it on abstract principle. I knew nothing of business. At school, I rather think, I learnt something about 'single and double entry,' but I had forgotten it all—just as I find myself forgetting how to multiply and divide, now that I am accustomed to the higher mathematics. However, I had to earn a little money, somehow, and I thought I'd try jam. And it went by itself, I really don't understand it, mere good luck, I suppose. I hear of fellows who have tried business, and come shocking croppers. Perhaps they were classical men: nothing so hopeless as your classic. I beg your pardon; before saying that, I ought to have found out whether either of you is a classic."

The listeners both shook their heads, and laughed.

"So much the better. An astronomer, it is plain, may manufacture jam; a fellow brought up on Greek and Latin verses couldn't possibly."

They were together at Bristol for a week, then Sherwood received a telegram, and told Warburton that he must return to London immediately.

"Something that bothers you?" said Will, noting a peculiar tremor on his friend's countenance.

"No, no; a private affair; nothing to do with us. You stay on till Saturday? I might be back in twenty-four hours."

"Good. Yes; I want to have some more talk with Applegarth about that advertising proposal. I don't like to start with quite such a heavy outlay."

"Nor I either," replied Godfrey, his eyes wandering. He paused, bit the end of his moustache, and added. "By the bye, the St. Neots money will be paid on Saturday, you said?"

"I believe so. Or early next week."

"That's right. I want to get done. Queer how these details fidget me. Nerves! I ought to have had a holiday this summer. You were wiser."

The next day Warburton went out with Applegarth to his house some ten miles south of Bristol, and dined there, and stayed over night. It had not yet been settled where he and Sherwood should have their permanent abode; there was a suggestion that they should share a house which was to let not far from Applegarth's, but Will felt uneasy at the thought of a joint tenancy, doubting whether he could live in comfort with any man. He was vexed at having to leave his flat in Chelsea, which so thoroughly suited his habits and his tastes.

Warburton and his host talked much of Sherwood.

"When I first met him," said the jam-manufacturer, " he struck me as the queerest man of business—except myself—that I had ever seen. He talked about Norse sagas, witchcraft, and so on, and when he began about business, I felt uneasy. Of course I know him better now."

" There are not many steadier and shrewder men than Sherwood," remarked Will.

" I feel sure of that," replied the other. And he added, as if to fortify himself in the opinion: " Yes, I feel sure of it."

" In spite of all his energy, never rash."

" No, no; I can see that. Yet," added Applegarth, again as if for self-confirmation, " he *has* energy of an uncommon kind."

" That will soon show itself," replied Warburton, smiling. " He's surveying the field like a general before battle."

" Yes. No end of bright ideas. Some of them —perhaps—not immediately practicable."

" Oh, Sherwood looks far ahead."

Applegarth nodded, and for a minute or two each was occupied with his own reflections.

CHAPTER XIV

GODFREY having telegraphed that he must remain in town, Warburton soon joined him. His partner was more cheerful and sanguine than ever; he had cleared off numberless odds and ends of business; there remained little to be done before the day, a week hence, appointed for the signature of the new deed, for which purpose Applegarth would come to London. Mr. Turnbull, acting with his wonted caution, had at length concluded the sale of Mrs. Warburton's property, and on the day after his return, Will received from St. Neots a letter containing a cheque for four thousand pounds! All his own available capital was already in the hands of Sherwood; a sum not much greater in amount than that invested by his mother and sister. Sherwood, for his part, put in sixteen thousand, with regrets that it was all he had at command just now; before long, he might see his way greatly to increase their capital, but they had enough for moderate enterprise in the meanwhile.

Not half an hour after the post which brought him the cheque, Warburton was surprised by a visit from his friend.

"I thought you wouldn't have left home yet," said Godfrey, with a nervous laugh. "I had a letter from Applegarth last night, which I wanted you to see at once."

He handed it, and Will, glancing over the sheet, found only an unimportant discussion of a small detail.

"Well, that's all right," he said, "but I don't see that it need have brought you from Wimbledon to Chelsea before nine o'clock in the morning. Aren't you getting a little overstrung, old man?"

Godfrey looked it. His face was noticeably thinner than a month ago, and his eyes had a troubled fixity such as comes of intense preoccupation.

"Daresay I am," he admitted with a show of careless good-humour. "Can't get much sleep lately."

"But why? What the deuce is there to fuss about? Sit down and smoke a cigar. I suppose you've had breakfast?"

"No—yes, I mean, yes, of course, long ago."

Will did not believe the corrected statement. He gazed at his friend curiously and with some anxiety.

"It's an unaccountable thing that you should fret your gizzard out about this new affair, which seems all so smooth, when you took the Ailie Street worries without turning a hair."

"Stupid—nerves out of order," muttered Godfrey, as he crossed, uncrossed, recrossed his legs, and bit at a cigar, as if he meant to breakfast on it. "I must get away for a week or two as soon as we've signed."

"Yes, but look here." Warburton stood before him, hands on hips, regarding him gravely, and speaking with decision. "I don't quite understand you. You're not like yourself. Is there anything you're keeping from me?"

"Nothing—nothing whatever, I assure you, Warburton."

But Will was only half satisfied.

"You have no doubts of Applegarth?"

"Doubts!" cried the other. "Not a shadow of doubt of any sort, I declare and protest. No, no; it's entirely my own idiotic excitability. I can't account for it. Just don't notice it, there's a good fellow."

There was a pause. Will glanced again at Applegarth's note, whilst Sherwood went, as usual, to stand before the bookcase, and run his eye along the shelves.

"Anything new in my way?" he asked. "I want a good long quiet read.—Palgrave's *Arabia*! Where did you pick up that? One of the most glorious books I know. That and Layard's *Early Travels* sent me to heaven for a month, once upon a time. You don't know Layard? I must give it to you. The essence of romance! As good in its way as the *Arabian Nights*."

Thus he talked on for a quarter of an hour, and it seemed to relieve him. Returning to matters of the day, he asked, half abruptly:

"Have you the St. Neots cheque yet?"

"Came this morning."

"Payable to Sherwood Brothers, I suppose?" said Godfrey. "Right. It's most convenient so."

Will handed him the cheque, and he gazed at it as if with peculiar satisfaction. He sat smiling, cheque in one hand, cigar in the other, until Warburton asked what he was thinking over.

"Nothing—nothing. Well, I suppose I'd better take it with me; I'm on my way to the bank."

As Will watched the little slip of paper disappear into his friend's pocket-book, he had an unaccountable feeling of disquiet. Nothing could be more unworthy than distrust of Godfrey Sherwood; nothing less consonant with all his experience of the man; and, had the money been his, he would have handed it over as confidently as when, in fact, dealing with his own capital the other day. But the sense of responsibility to others was a new thing to which he could not yet accustom himself. It occurred to him for the first time that there was no necessity for accumulating these funds in the hands of Sherwood; he might just as well have retained his own money and this cheque until the day of the signing of the new deed. To be sure, he had only to reflect a moment to see the foolishness of his misgiving; yet, had he thought of it before——

He, too, was perhaps a little overstrung in the nerves. Not for the first time, he mentally threw a malediction at business, and all its sordid appurtenances.

A change came over Sherwood. His smile grew more natural; his eye lost its fixity; he puffed at his cigar with enjoyment.

"What news of Franks?" were his next words.

"Nothing very good," answered Will, frowning. "He seems to be still playing the fool. I've seen him only once in the last fortnight, and then it was evident he'd been drinking. I couldn't help saying a plain word or two, and he turned sullen. I called at his place last night, but he wasn't there; his landlady tells me he's been out of town several times lately, and he's done no work."

"Has the girl gone?"

"A week ago. I have a letter from Ralph Pomfret. The good old chap worries about this affair; so does Mrs. Pomfret. He doesn't say it plainly, but I suspect Franks has been behaving theatrically down at Ashstead; it's possible he went there in the same state in which I saw him last. Pomfret would have done well to punch his head, but I've no doubt they've stroked and patted and poor-fellow'd him—the very worst thing for Franks."

"Or for any man," remarked Sherwood.

"Worse for him than for most. I wish I had more of the gift of brutality; I see a way in which I might do him good; but it goes against the grain with me."

"That I can believe," said Godfrey, with his pleasantest look and nod.

"I was afraid he might somehow scrape together money enough to pursue her to Egypt. Perhaps he's trying for that. The Pomfrets want me to go down to Ashstead and have a talk with them about him. Whether he managed to see the girl before she left England, I don't know."

"After all, he *has* been badly treated," said Sherwood sympathetically.

"Well, yes, he has. But a fellow must have common sense, most of all with regard to women. I'm rather afraid Franks might think it a fine thing to go to the devil because he's been jilted. It isn't fashionable nowadays; there might seem to be a sort of originality about it."

They talked for a few minutes of business matters, and Sherwood briskly went his way.

Four days passed. Warburton paid a visit to the Pomfrets, and had from them a confirmation of all he suspected regarding Norbert Franks. The artist's behaviour at Ashstead had been very theatrical indeed; he talked much of suicide, preferably by the way of drink, and, when dissuaded from this, with a burst of tears—veritable tears—

begged Ralph Pomfret to lend him money enough to go to Cairo ; on which point, also, he met with kindliest opposition. Thereupon, he had raged for half an hour against some treacherous friend, unnamed. Who this could be, the Pomfrets had no idea. Warburton, though he affected equal ignorance, could not doubt but that it was himself, and he grew inwardly angry. Franks had been to Bath, and had obtained a private interview with Winifred Elvan, in which (Winifred wrote to her aunt) he had demeaned himself very humbly and pathetically, first of all imploring the sister's help with Rosamund, and, when she declared she could do nothing, entreating to be told whether or not he was ousted by a rival. Rather impatient with the artist's follies than troubled about his sufferings, Will came home again. He wrote a brief, not unfriendly letter to Franks, urging him to return to his better mind—the half-disdainful, half-philosophical resignation which he seemed to have attained a month ago. The answer to this was a couple of lines ; " Thanks. Your advice, no doubt, is well meant, but I had rather not have it just now. Don't let us meet for the present." Will shrugged his shoulders, and tried to forget all about the affair.

He did not see Sherwood, but had a note from him written in high spirits. Applegarth would be in town two days hence, and all three were to dine at his hotel. Having no occupation, Warburton spent most of his time in walking about London ; but these rambles did not give him the wonted pleasure, and though at night he was very tired, he did not sleep well. An inexplicable nervousness interfered with all his habits of mind and body. He was on the point of running down to

St. Neots, to get through the last day of intolerable idleness, when the morning post again brought a letter from Sherwood.

"Confound the fellow!" he muttered, as he tore open the envelope. "What else can he have to say? No infernal postponement, I hope——"

He read the first line and drew himself up like a man pierced with pain.

"My dear Warburton"—thus wrote his partner, in a hand less legible than of wont—"I have such bad news for you that I hardly know how to tell it. If I dared, I would come to you at once, but I simply have not the courage to face you until you know the worst, and have had time to get accustomed to it. It is seven o'clock; an hour ago I learnt that all our money is lost—all yours, all that from St. Neots, all mine—every penny I have. I have been guilty of unpardonable folly—how explain my behaviour? The truth is, after the settlement in Little Ailie Street, I found myself much worse off than I had expected. I went into the money market, and made a successful deal. Counting on being able to repeat this, I guaranteed the sixteen thousand for Bristol; but the second time I lost. So it has gone on; all these last weeks I have been speculating, winning and losing. Last Tuesday, when I came to see you, I had about twelve thousand, and hoped somehow to make up the deficiency. As the devil would have it, that same morning I met a City acquaintance, who spoke of a great *coup* to be made by any one who had some fifteen thousand at command. It meant an immediate profit of 25 per cent. Like a fool, I was persuaded—as you will see when I go into details, the thing looked horribly tempting. I put it all—every penny that lay at our bank in the name of Sherwood Bros. And now I learn that the house I trusted has smashed. It's in the papers this evening—Biggles, Thorpe and Biggles—you'll see it. I dare not ask you to forgive me. Of course I shall at once take steps to raise the money owing to you, and hope to be able to do that soon, but it's all over with the Bristol affair. I shall come to see you at twelve to-morrow.

"Yours,

"G. F. SHERWOOD."

CHAPTER XV

"AFTER all, there's something in presentiment."

This was the first thought that took shape in Will's whirling mind. The second was, that he might rationally have foreseen disaster. All the points of strangeness which had struck him in Sherwood's behaviour came back now with such glaring significance that he accused himself of inconceivable limpness in having allowed things to go their way—above all in trusting Godfrey with the St. Neots cheque. On this moment of painful lucidity followed blind rage. Why, what a grovelling imbecile was this fellow! To plunge into wild speculation, on the word of some City shark, with money not his own! But could one credit the story? Was it not more likely that Sherwood had got involved in some cunning thievery which he durst not avow? Perhaps he was a mere liar and hypocrite. That story of the ten thousand pounds he had lent to somebody—how improbable it sounded; why might he not have invented it, to strengthen confidence at a critical moment? The incredible baseness of the man! He, who knew well all that depended upon the safe investment of the St. Neots money—to risk it in this furiously reckless way. In all the records of City scoundrelism, was there a blacker case?

Raging thus, Warburton became aware that Mrs.

Hopper spoke to him. She had just laid breakfast, and, as usual when she wished to begin a conversation, had drawn back to the door, where she paused.

"That Boxon, the grocer, has had a bad accident, sir."

"Boxon ?—grocer ? "

"In the Fulham Road, sir ; him as Allchin was with."

"Ah ! "

Heedless of her master's gloomy abstraction, Mrs. Hopper continued. She related that Boxon had been at certain races where he had lost money and got drunk ; driving away in a trap, he had run into something, and been thrown out, with serious injuries, which might prove fatal.

"So much the worse for him," muttered Warburton. "I've no pity to spare for fools and blackguards."

"I should think not, indeed sir. I just mentioned it, sir, because Allchin was telling us about it last night. He and his wife looked in to see my sister, Liza, and they both said they never see such a change in anybody. And they said how grateful we ought to be to you, sir, and that I'm sure we are, for Liza'd never have been able to go away without your kindness."

Listening as if this talk sounded from a vague distance, Warburton was suddenly reminded of what had befallen himself ; for as yet he had thought only of his mother and sister. He was ruined. Some two or three hundred pounds, his private bank account, represented all he had in the world, and all prospect of making money had been taken away from him. Henceforth, small must be his charities. If he gained his own living, he must count himself lucky; nothing more difficult than for a man of his age and position, unexpectedly cut adrift, to find work and payment. By good fortune, his lease of this flat came to an end at Michaelmas, and already he had given notice that he did not mean to renew. Mrs. Hopper knew that he was on the point of leaving London, and not a little lamented it, for to her the loss would be serious indeed. Warburton's habitual generosity led her to hope for some signal benefaction ere his departure; perhaps on that account she was specially emphatic in gratitude for her sister's restoration to health.

"We was wondering, sir," she added, now having wedged herself between door and jamb, "whether you'd be so kind as to let my sister Liza see you just for a minute or two, to thank you herself, as I'm sure she ought? She could come any time as wouldn't be ill-convenient to you."

"I'm extremely busy, Mrs. Hopper," Will replied. "Please tell your sister I'm delighted to hear she's done so well at Southend, and I hope to see her some day; but not just now. By the bye, I'm not going out this morning, so don't wait, when you've finished."

By force of habit he ate and drank. Sherwood's letter lay open before him; he read it through again and again. But he could not fix his thoughts upon it. He found himself occupied with the story of Boxon, wondering whether Boxon would live or die. Boxon, the grocer—why, what an ass a man must be, a man with a good grocery business, to come to grief over drink and betting! Shopkeeping—what a sound and safe life it was; independent, as far as any money-earning life can be so. There must be a pleasure in counting the contents of one's till every night. Boxon! Of course, a mere brute. There came into Will's memory the picture of Boxon landed on the pavement one night, by Allchin's fist or toe—and of a sudden he laughed.

When he had half-smoked his pipe, comparative calmness fell upon him. Sherwood spoke of at once raising the money he owed, and, if he succeeded in doing so, much of the mischief would be undone. The four thousand pounds might be safely invested somewhere, and life at The Haws would go on as usual. But was it certain that Sherwood could "raise" such sums, being himself, as he declared, penniless? This disclosure showed him in an unpleasantly new light, as anything but the cautious man of business, the loyal friend, he had seemed to be. Who could put faith in a money-market gambler? Why, there was no difference to speak of between him and Boxon. And if his promise proved futile—what was to be done?

For a couple of hours, Will stared at this question. When the clock on his mantelpiece struck eleven, he happened to notice it, and was surprised to find how quickly time had passed. By the bye, he had never thought of looking at his newspaper, though Sherwood referred him to that source of information on the subject of Biggles, Thorpe and Biggles. Yes, here it was. A firm of brokers; unfortunate speculations; failure of another house—all the old story. As likely as not, the financial trick of a cluster of thieves. Will threw the paper aside. He had always scorned that cunning of the Stock Exchange, now he thought of it with fiery hatred.

Another hour passed in feverish waiting; then, just at mid-day, a knock sounded at the outer door.

Anything but a loud knock; anything but the confident summons of a friend. Will went to open. There stood Godfrey Sherwood, shrunk together like a man suffering from cold; he scarcely raised his eyes.

Will's purpose, on finding Sherwood at his door, was to admit him without a word, or any form of greeting; but the sight of that changed face and pitiful attitude overcame him; he offered a hand, and felt it warmly pressed.

They were together in the room; neither had spoken. Will pointed to a chair, but did not himself sit down.

"I suppose it's all true, Warburton," began the other in a low voice, "but I can't believe it yet. I seem to be walking in a nightmare; and when you gave me your hand at the door, I thought for a second that I'd just woke up."

"Sit down," said Will, "and let's have it out. Give me the details."

"That's exactly what I wish to do. Of course I haven't been to bed, and I've spent the night in writing out a statement of all my dealings for the past fifteen months. Here it is—and here are my pass-books."

Will took the paper, a half-sheet of foolscap, one side almost covered with figures. At a glance he saw that the statement was perfectly intelligible. The perusal of a few lines caused him to look up in astonishment.

"You mean to say that between last September and the end of the year you lost twenty-five thousand pounds?"

"I did."

"And you mean to say that you still went on with your gambling?"

"Things were getting bad in Ailie Street, you know."

"And you did your best to make them desperate."

Sherwood's head seemed trying to bury itself between his shoulders; his feet hid themselves under the chair, he held his hat in a way suggestive of the man who comes to beg.

"The devil of the City got hold of me," he replied, with a miserable attempt to look Warburton in the face.

"Yes," said Will, "that's clear. Then, a month ago, you really possessed only nine thousand pounds?"

"That was all I had left, out of nearly forty thousand."

"What astonishes me is, that you won from time to time."

"I did!" exclaimed Godfrey, with sudden animation. "Look at the fifth of February—that was a great day! It's that kind of thing that tempts a man on. Afterwards I lost steadily; but I might have won any day. And I had to make a good deal, if we were to come to terms with Applegarth. I nearly did it. I was as cautious as a man could be—content with small things. If only I hadn't been pressed for time! It was only the want of time that made me use your money. Of course, it was criminal. Don't think I wish to excuse myself for one moment. Absolutely criminal. I knew what was at stake. But I thought the thing was sure. It promised at the least twenty-five per cent. We should have started brilliantly at Bristol—several thousands for advertisement, beyond our estimate. I don't think the Biggles people were dishonest——"

"You don't *think* so!" interrupted Will, contemptuously. "If there's any doubt we know on which side it weighs. Just tell me the facts. What was the security?"

Sherwood replied with a brief, clear, and obviously honest account of the speculation into which he had been drawn. To the listener it seemed astounding that any responsible man should be lured by such gambler's chance; he could hardly find patience to point out the manifest risks so desperately incurred. And Sherwood admitted the full extent of his folly; he could only repeat that he had acted on an irresistible impulse, to be explained, though not defended, by the embarrassment in which he found himself.

"Thank Heaven, this is over!" he exclaimed at last, passing his handkerchief over a moist forehead. "I don't know how I got through last night. More than once, I thought it would be easier to kill myself than to come and face you. But there was the certainty that I could make good your loss. I may be able to do so very soon. I've written to——"

He checked himself on the point of uttering a name; then with eyes down, reflected for a moment.

"No, I haven't the right to tell you, though I should like to, to give you confidence. It's the story of the ten thousand pounds, you remember? When I lent that money, I promised never to let any one know. Even if I can't realise your capital at once, I can pay you good interest until the money's forthcoming. That would be the same thing to you?"

Warburton gave him a keen look, and said gravely—

"Let's understand each other, Sherwood. Have you any income at all?"

"None whatever now, except the interest on the ten thousand; and that—well, I'm sorry to say it hasn't been paid very regularly. But in future it must be—it *shall* be. Between two and three thousand are owing to me for arrears."

"It's a queer story."

"I know it is," admitted Godfrey. "But I hope you don't doubt my word?"

"No, I don't—What's to be done about Applegarth?"

"I must see him," replied Sherwood with a groan. "Of course you have no part in the miserable business. I must write at once, and then go and face him."

"Of course I shall go with you."

"You will? That's kind of you. Luckily he's a civilised man, not one of the City brutes one might have had to deal with."

"We must hope he'll live up to his reputation," said Warburton, with the first smile, and that no cheery one, which had risen to his lips during this interview.

From that point the talk became easier. All the aspects of their position were considered, without stress of feeling, for Will had recovered his self-control; and Sherwood, soothed by the sense of having discharged an appalling task, tended once more to sanguine thoughts. To be sure, neither of them could see any immediate way out of the gulf in which they found themselves; all hope of resuming business was at an end; the only practical question was, how to earn a living; but both were young men, and neither had ever known privation; it was difficult for them to believe all at once that they were really face to face with that grim necessity which they had thought of as conquering others, but never them. Certain unpleasant steps, however, had at once to be taken. Sherwood must give up his house at Wimbledon; Warburton must look about for a cheap lodging into which to remove at Michaelmas. Worse still, and more urgent, was the duty of making known to Mrs. Warburton what had happened.

"I suppose I must go down at once," said Will gloomily.

"I see no hurry," urged the other. "As a matter of fact, your mother and sister will lose nothing. You undertook to pay them a minimum of three per cent. on their money, and that you can do; I guarantee you that, in any case."

Will mused. If indeed it were possible to avoid the disclosure—— ? But that would involve much lying, a thing, even in a good cause, little to his taste. Still, when he thought of his mother's weak health, and how she might be affected by the news of this catastrophe, he began seriously to ponder the practicability of well-meaning deception. That, of course, must depend upon their difficulties with Applegarth remaining strictly private; and even so, could Mr. Turnbull's scent for disaster be successfully reckoned with?

"Don't do anything hastily, Warburton, I beg of you," continued the other. "Things are never so bad as they look at first sight. Wait till I have seen—you know who. I might even be able to—but it's better not to promise. Wait a day or two, at all events."

And this Warburton resolved to do; for, if the worst came to the worst, he had some three hundred pounds of his own still in the bank, and so could assure, for two years at all events, the income of which his mother and Jane had absolute need. For himself, he should find some way of earning bread and cheese ; he could no longer stand on his dignity, and talk of independence, that was plain.

When at length his calamitous partner had gone, he made an indifferent lunch on the cold meat he found in Mrs. Hopper's precincts, and then decided that he had better take a walk ; to sit still and brood was the worst possible way of facing such a crisis. There was no friend with whom he could discuss the situation ; none whose companionship would just now do him any particular good. Better to walk twenty miles, and tire himself out, and see how things looked after a good night's sleep. So he put on his soft hat, and took his walking-stick, and slammed the door behind him. Some one was coming up the stairs ; sunk in his own thoughts he paid no heed, even when the other man stood in front of him. Then a familiar voice claimed his attention.

"Do you want to cut me, Warburton ?"

CHAPTER XVI

WARBURTON stopped, and looked into the speaker's face, as if he hardly recognised him.

"You're going out," added Franks, turning round. "I won't keep you."

And he seemed about to descend the stairs quickly. But Will at length found voice.

"Come in. I was thinking of something, and didn't see you."

They entered, and passed as usual into the sitting-room, but not with the wonted exchange of friendly words. The interval since their last meeting seemed to have alienated them more than the events which preceded it. Warburton was trying to smile, but each glance he took at the other's face made his lips less inclined to relax from a certain severity rarely seen in them; and Franks succeeded but ill in his attempt to lounge familiarly, with careless casting of the eye this way and that. It was he who broke silence.

"I've found a new drink—gin and laudanum. First rate for the nerves."

"Ah!" replied Warburton gravely. "My latest tipple is oil of vitriol with a dash of strychnine. Splendid pick-me-up."

Franks laughed loudly, but unmirthfully.

"No, but I'm quite serious," he continued. "It's the only thing that keeps me going. If

I hadn't found the use of laudanum in small doses, I should have tried a very large one before now."

His language had a note of bravado, and his attitude betrayed the self-conscious actor, but there was that in his countenance which could only have come of real misery. The thin cheeks, heavy-lidded and bloodshot eyes, ill-coloured lips, made a picture anything but agreeable to look upon; and quite in keeping with it was the shabbiness of his garb. After an intent and stern gaze at him, Will asked bluntly:

"When did you last have a bath?"

"Bath? Good God—how do I know?"

And again Franks laughed in the key of stage recklessness.

"I should advise a Turkish," said Will, "followed by rhubarb of the same country. You'd feel vastly better next day."

"The remedies," answered Franks, smiling disdainfully, "of one who has never been through moral suffering."

"Yet efficacious, even morally, I can assure you. And, by the bye, I want to know when you're going to finish 'The Slummer.'"

"Finish it? Why, never! I could as soon turn to and build a bridge over the Thames."

"What do you mean? I suppose you have to earn your living?"

"I see no necessity for it. What do I care, whether I live or not?"

"Well, then, I am obliged to ask whether you feel it incumbent upon you—to pay your debts?"

The last words came out with a jerk, after a little pause which proved what it cost Warburton to speak them. To save his countenance, he assumed an unnatural grimness of feature, staring

Franks resolutely in the face. And the result was the artist's utter subjugation; he shuffled, dropped his head, made confused efforts to reply.

"Of course I shall do so—somehow," he muttered at length.

"Have you any other way—honest way—except by working?"

"Very well, then, I'll find work. Real work. Not that cursed daubing, which it turns my stomach to think of."

Warburton paused a moment, then said kindly:

"That's the talk of a very sore and dazed man. Before long, you'll be yourself again, and you'll go back to your painting with an appetite. And the sooner you try the better. I don't particularly like dunning people for money, as I think you know, but, when you can pay that debt of yours, I shall be glad. I've had a bit of bad luck since last we saw each other."

Franks gazed in heavy-eyed wonder, uncertain whether to take this as a joke or not.

"Bad luck? What sort of bad luck?"

"Why, neither on the turf nor at Monte Carlo. But a speculation has gone wrong, and I'm adrift. I shall have to leave this flat. How I'm going to keep myself alive, I don't know yet. The Bristol affair is of course off. I'm as good as penniless, and a hundred pounds or so will come very conveniently, whenever you can manage it."

"Are you serious, Warburton?"

"Perfectly."

"You've really lost everything? You've got to leave this flat because you can't afford it?"

"That, my boy, is the state of the case."

"By Jove! No wonder you didn't see me as I came upstairs. What the deuce! You in Queer

Street! I never dreamt of such a thing as a possibility. I've always thought of you as a flourishing capitalist—sound as the Mansion House. Why didn't you begin by telling me this? I'm about as miserable as a fellow can be, but I should never have bothered you with my miseries.—Warburton in want of money? Why, the idea is grotesque; I can't get hold of it. I came to you as men go to a bank. Of course, I meant to pay it all, some day, but you were so generous and so rich, I never thought there would be any hurry. I'm astounded—I'm floored!"

With infinite satisfaction, Warburton saw the better man rising again in his friend, noted the change of countenance, of bearing, of tone.

"You see," he said, with a nod and a smile, "that you've no choice but to finish 'The Slummer!'"

Franks looked about him uneasily, fretfully.

"Either that—or something else," he muttered.

"No—*that*! It'll bring you two or three hundred pounds without much delay."

"I daresay it would. But if you knew how I loathe and curse the very sight of the thing—Why I haven't burnt it I don't know."

"Probably," said Will, "because in summer weather you take your gin and laudanum cold."

This time the artist's laugh was more genuine.

"The hideous time I have been going through!" he continued. "It's no use trying to give you an idea of it. Of course you'd say it was all damned foolery. Well, I shan't go through it again, that's one satisfaction. I've done with women. One reason why I loathe the thought of going on with that picture is because I still have the girl's head to put in. But I'll do it. I'll go back and get to work at once. If I can't find a model, I'll fake the head—get it out of some woman's paper where the fashions are illustrated ; that'll do very well. I'll go and see how the beastly thing looks. It's turned against the wall, and I wonder I haven't put my boot through it."

CHAPTER XVII

WARBURTON waited for a quarter of an hour after the artist had gone, then set out for his walk. The result of this unexpected conversation with Franks was excellent ; the foolish fellow seemed to have recovered his common sense. But Will felt ashamed of himself. Of course he had acted solely with a view to the other's good, seeing no hope but this of rescuing Franks from the slough in which he wallowed ; nevertheless, he was stung with shame. For the first time in his life he had asked repayment of money lent to a friend. And he had done the thing blunderingly, without tact. For the purpose in view, it would have been enough to speak of his own calamity ; just the same effect would have been produced on Franks. He saw this now, and writhed under the sense of his grossness. The only excuse he could urge for himself was that Franks' behaviour provoked and merited rough handling. Still, he might have had perspicacity enough to understand that the artist was not so sunk in squalor as he pretended.

"Just like me," he growled to himself, with a nervous twitching of the face. "I've no presence of mind. I see the right thing when it's too late, and when I've made myself appear a bounder. How many thousand times have I blundered in this way! A man like me ought to live alone—as I've a very fair chance of doing in future."

His walk did him no good, and on his return

he passed a black evening. With Mrs. Hopper, who came as usual to get dinner for him, he held little conversation; in a few days he would have to tell her what had befallen him, or invent some lie to account for the change in his arrangements, and this again tortured Will's nerves. In one sense of the word, no man was less pretentious; but his liberality of thought and behaviour consisted with a personal pride which was very much at the mercy of circumstance. Even as he could not endure subjection, so did he shrink from the thought of losing dignity in the eyes of his social inferiors. Mere poverty and lack of ease did not frighten him at all; he had hardly given a thought as yet to that aspect of misfortune. What most of all distressed his imagination (putting aside thought of his mother and sister) was the sudden fall from a position of genial authority, of beneficent command, with all the respect and gratitude and consideration attaching thereto. He could do without personal comforts, if need were, but it pained him horribly to think of being no longer a patron and a master. With a good deal more philosophy than the average man, and vastly more benevolence, he could not attain to the humility which would have seen in this change of fortune a mere surrender of privileges perhaps quite unjustifiable. Social grades were an inseparable part of his view of life; he recognised the existence of his superiors—though resolved to have as little to do with them as possible, and took it as a matter of course that multitudes of men should stand below his level. To imagine himself an object of pity for Mrs. Hopper and Allchin and the rest of them wrought upon his bile, disordered his digestion.

He who had regarded so impatiently the trials

of Norbert Franks now had to go through an evil time, with worse results upon his temper, his health, and whole being, than he would have thought conceivable. For a whole fortnight he lived in a state of suspense and forced idleness, which helped him to understand the artist's recourse to gin and laudanum. The weather was magnificent, but for him no sun rose in the sky. If he walked about London, he saw only ugliness and wretchedness, his eyes seeming to have lost the power of perceiving other things. Every two or three days he heard from Sherwood, who wrote that he was doing his utmost, and continued to hold out hope that he would soon have money: but these letters were not reassuring. The disagreeable interview with Applegarth had passed off better than might have been expected. Though greatly astonished, and obviously in some doubt as to the facts of the matter, Applegarth behaved as a gentleman, resigned all claims upon the defaulters, and brought the affair to a decent close as quickly as possible. But Warburton came away with a face so yellow that he seemed on the point of an attack of jaundice. For him to be the object of another man's generous forbearance was something new and intolerable. Before parting with Sherwood, he spoke to him bitterly, all but savagely. A few hours later, of course, repentance came upon him, and he wrote to ask pardon. An evil time.

At length Sherwood came to Chelsea, having written to ask for a meeting. Will's forebodings were but too well justified. The disastrous man came only to say that all his efforts had failed. His debtor for ten thousand pounds was himself in such straits that he could only live by desperate expedients, and probably would not be able to pay a penny of interest this year.

"Happily," said Sherwood, "his father's health is breaking. One is obliged to talk in this brutal way, you know. At the father's death it will be all right ; I shall then have my legal remedy, if there's need of it. To take any step of that sort now would be ruinous ; my friend would be cut off with a shilling, if the affair came to his father's ears."

"So this is how we stand," said Warburton, grimly. "It's all over."

Sherwood laid on the table a number of bank-notes, saying simply :

"There's two hundred and sixty pounds—the result of the sale of my furniture and things. Will you use that and trust me a little longer ?"

Warburton writhed in his chair.

"What have you to live upon ?" he asked with eyes downcast.

"Oh, I shall get on all right. I've one or two ideas."

"But this is all the money you have ?"

"I've kept about fifty pounds," answered the other, "out of which I can pay my debts—they're small—and the rent of my house for this quarter."

Warburton pushed back the notes.

"I can't take it—you know I can't."

"You must."

"How the devil are you going to live ?" cried Will, in exasperation.

"I shall find a way," replied Sherwood with an echo of his old confident tone. "I need a little time to look about me, that's all, There's a relative of mine, an old fellow who lives comfortably in North Wales, and who invites me down every two or three years. The best thing will be for me to go and spend a short time with him, and get my nerves into order—I'm shaky, there's no disguising it. I haven't exhausted all the possibilities of raising money; there's hope still in one or two directions; if I get a little quietness and rest I shall be able to think things out more clearly. Don't you think this justifiable?"

As to the money he remained inflexible. Very reluctantly Warburton consented to keep this sum, giving a receipt in form.

"You haven't said anything to Mrs. Warburton yet?" asked Sherwood nervously.

"Not yet," muttered Will.

"I wish you could postpone it a little longer. Could you—do you think—without too much strain of conscience? Doesn't it seem a pity—when any day may enable me to put things right?"

Will muttered again that he would think of it; that assuredly he preferred not to disclose the matter if it could decently be kept secret. And on this Sherwood took his leave, going away with a brighter face than he had brought to the interview; whilst Will remained brooding gloomily, his eyes fixed on the bank-notes, in an unconscious stare.

Little of a man of business as he was, Warburton knew very well that things at the office were passing in a flagrantly irregular way: he knew that any one else in his position would have put this serious affair into legal hands, if only out of justice to Sherwood himself. More than once he had thought of communicating with Mr. Turnbull, but shame withheld him. It seemed improbable, too, that the solicitor would connive at keeping his friends at The Haws ignorant of what had befallen them, and with every day that passed Will felt more disposed to hide that catastrophe, if by any means that were possible. Already he had half committed himself to this deception, having written to his mother (without mention of any other detail) that he might, after all, continue to live in London, where Applegarth's were about to establish a warehouse. The question was how, if he put aside all the money he had for payment of pretended dividend to his mother and sister, how, in that case, was he himself to live? At the thought of going about applying for clerk's work, or anything of that kind, cold water flowed down his back; rather than that, he would follow Allchin's example, and turn porter—an independent position compared with bent-backed slavery on an office-stool. Some means of earning money he must find without delay. To live on what he had, one day longer than could be helped, would be sheer dishonesty. Sherwood might succeed in bringing him a few hundreds—of the ten thousand Will thought not at all, so fantastic did the whole story sound—but that would be merely another small instalment of the sum due to the unsuspecting victims at St. Neots. Strictly speaking, he owned not a penny; his very meals to-day were at the expense of his mother and Jane. This thought goaded him. His sleep became a mere nightmare; his waking, a dry-throated misery.

In spite of loathing and dread, he began to read the thick-serried columns of newspaper advertisement, Wanted! Wanted! Wanted! Wants by the thousand; but many more those of the would-be employed than those of the would-be employers, and under the second heading not one in a hundred that offered him the slightest hint or hope. Wanted! Wanted. To glance over these columns is like listening to the clamour of a hunger-driven multitude; the ears sing, the head turns giddy. After a quarter of an hour of such search, Will flung the paper aside, and stamped like a madman about his room. A horror of life seized him; he understood, with fearful sympathy, the impulse of those who, rather than be any longer hustled in this howling mob dash themselves to destruction.

He thought over the list of his friends. Friends —what man has more than two or three? At this moment he knew of no one who wished him well who could be of the slightest service. His acquaintances were of course more numerous. There lay on his table two invitations just received—the kind of invitation received by every man who does not live the life of a hermit. But what human significance had they? Not a name rose in his mind which symbolised helpfulness. True, that might be to some extent his own fault; the people of whom he saw most were such as needed, not such as could offer, aid. He thought of Ralph Pomfret. There, certainly, a kindly will would not be lacking, but how could he worry with his foolish affairs a man on whom he had no shadow of claim? No: he stood alone. It was a lesson in social science such as reading could never have afforded him. His insight into the order of a man's world had all at once been marvellously quickened, the scope of his reflections incredibly extended. Some vague consciousness of this now and then arrested him in his long purposeless walks; he began to be aware of seeing common things with new eyes. But the perception was akin to fear; he started and looked nervously about, as if suddenly aware of some peril.

One afternoon he was on his way home from a westward trudge, plodding along the remoter part of Fulham Road, when words spoken by a woman whom he passed caught his ears.

" See ' ere! The shutters is up. Boxon must be dead."

Boxon? How did he come to know that name? He slackened his pace, reflecting. Why, Boxon was the name of the betting and drinking grocer, with whom Allchin used to be. He stopped, and saw a group of three or four women staring at the closed shop. Didn't Mrs. Hopper say that Boxon had been nearly killed in a carriage accident? Doubtless he was dead.

He walked on, but before he had gone a dozen yards, stopped abruptly, turned, crossed to the other side of the road, and went back till he stood opposite the closed shop. The name of the tradesman in great gilt letters proved that there was no mistake. He examined the building; there were two storys above the shop; the first seemed to be used for storage; white blinds at the windows of the second showed it to be inhabited. For some five minutes Will stood gazing and reflecting; then, with head bent as before, he pursued his way.

When he reached home, Mrs. Hopper regarded him compassionately; the good woman was much disturbed by the strangeness of his demeanour lately, and feared he was going to be ill.

" You look dre'ful tired, sir," she said. " I'll make you a cup of tea at once. It 'll do you good."

" Yes, get me some tea," answered Warburton, absently. Then, as she was leaving the room, he asked, " Is it true that the grocer Boxon is dead?"

" I was going to speak of it this morning, sir," replied Mrs. Hopper, " but you seemed so busy. Yes, sir, he's died—died the day before yesterday, they say, and it'd be surprising to hear as anybody's sorry."

" Who'll take his business?" asked Warburton.

"We was talking about that last night, sir, me and my sister Liza, and the Allchins. It's fallen off a great deal lately, what else could you expect? since Boxon got into his bad ways. But anybody as had a little money might do well there. Allchin was saying he wished he had a few 'undreds."

"A few hundred would be enough?" interrupted the listener, without noticing the look of peculiar eagerness on Mrs. Hopper's face.

"Allchin thinks the goodwill can be had for about a 'undred, sir; and the rent, it's only eighty pounds——"

"Shop and house?"

"Yes, sir; so Allchin says. It isn't much of a 'ouse, of course."

"What profits could be made, do you suppose, by an energetic man?"

"When Boxon began, sir," replied Mrs. Hopper, with growing animation, "he used to make—so Allchin says—a good five or six 'undred a year. There's a good deal of profit in the grocery business, and Boxon's situation is good; there's no other grocer near him. But of course—as Allchin says—you want to lay out a good deal at starting——"

"Yes, yes, of course, you must have stock." said Will carelessly. "Bring me some tea at once, Mrs. Hopper."

It had suddenly occurred to him that Allchin might think of trying to borrow the capital wherewith to start this business, and that Mrs. Hopper might advise her brother-in-law to apply to him for the loan.

But this was not at all the idea which had prompted Will's inquiries.

CHAPTER XVIII

ANOTHER week went by. Warburton was still living in the same restless way, but did not wear quite so gloomy a countenance; now and then he looked almost cheerful. That was the case when one morning he received a letter from Sherwood. Godfrey wrote that, no sooner had he arrived at his relative's in North Wales than he was seized with a violent liver-attack, which for some days prostrated him; he was now recovering, and better news still, had succeeded in borrowing a couple of hundred pounds. Half of this sum he sent to Warburton; the other half he begged to be allowed to retain, as he had what might prove a very fruitful idea for the use of the money—details presently. To this letter Will immediately replied at some length. The cheque he paid into his account, which thus reached a total of more than six hundred pounds.

A few days later, after breakfast as usual, he let his servant clear the table, then said with a peculiar smile.

"I want to have a little talk with you, Mrs. Hopper. Please sit down."

To seat herself in her master's presence went against all Mrs. Hopper's ideas of propriety. Seeing her hesitate, Will pointed steadily to a chair, and the good woman, much flurried, placed herself on the edge of it.

"You have noticed," Warburton resumed, "that I haven't been quite myself lately. There was a good reason for it. I've had a misfortune in business; all my plans are changed; I shall have to begin quite a new life—a different life altogether from that I have led till now."

Mrs. Hopper seemed to have a sudden pain in the side. She groaned under her breath, staring at the speaker pitifully.

"There's no need to talk about it, you know," Will went on with a friendly nod. "I tell you, because I'm thinking of going into a business in which your brother-in-law could help me, if he cares to."

He paused. Mrs. Hopper kept her wide eyes on him.

"Allchin'll be very glad to hear of that, sir. What am I saying? Of course I don't mean he'll be glad you've had misfortune, sir, and I'm that sorry to hear it, I can't tell you. But it does just happen as he's out of work, through that nasty temper of his. Not," she corrected herself hastily, "as I ought to call him nasty-tempered. With a good employer, I'm sure he'd never get into no trouble at all."

"Does he still wish to get back into the grocery business?"

"He'd be only too glad, sir, But, of course, any place as *you* offered him——"

"Well, it happens," said Warburton, "that it is the grocery business I'm thinking about."

"You, sir?" gasped Mrs. Hopper.

"I think I shall take Boxon's shop."

"*You*, sir? Take a grocer's shop?—You mean, you'd put Allchin in to manage it?"

"No, I don't, Mrs. Hopper," replied Will,

smiling mechanically. "I have more than my own living to earn ; other people are dependent upon me ; so I must make as much money as possible. I can't afford to pay a manager. I shall go behind the counter myself, and Allchin, if he cares for the place, shall be my assistant."

The good woman could find no words to express her astonishment.

"Suppose you have a word with Allchin, and send him to see me this evening? I say again, there's no need to talk about the thing to anybody else. We'll just keep it quiet between us."

"You can depend upon me, sir," declared Mrs. Hopper. "But did you *hever!* It's come upon me so sudden like. And what'll Allchin say! Why, he'll think I'm having a game with him."

To this point had Will Warburton brought himself, urged by conscience and fear. Little by little, since the afternoon when he gazed at Boxon's closed shop, had this purpose grown in his mind, until he saw it as a possibility—a desirability—a fact. By shopkeeping, he might hope to earn sufficient for supply of the guaranteed income to his mother and sister, and at the same time be no man's servant. His acquaintance with Allchin enabled him to disregard his lack of grocery experience ; with Allchin for an assistant, he would soon overcome initial difficulties. Only to Godfrey Sherwood had he communicated his project. "What difference is there," he wrote, "between selling sugar from an office in Whitechapel, and selling it from behind a counter in Fulham Road?" And Sherwood—who was still reposing in North Wales—wrote a long, affectionate, admiring reply. "You are splendid! What energy! What courage! I could almost say that I don't regret my criminal recklessness, seeing that it has given the occasion for such a magnificent display of character." He added, "Of course it will be only for a short time. Even if the plans I am now working out—details shortly—come to nothing (a very unlikely thing), I am sure to recover my ten thousand pounds in a year or so."—"Of course," he wrote in a postscript, "I breathe no word of it to any mortal."

This letter—so are we made—did Warburton good. It strengthened him in carrying through the deception of his relatives and of Mr. Turnbull, for he saw himself as *splendide mendax.* In Sherwood's plans and assurances he had no shadow of faith, but Sherwood's admiration was worth having, and it threw a gilding upon the name of grocer. Should he impart the secret to Norbert Franks? That question he could not decide just yet. In any case, he should tell no one else; all other acquaintances must be content—if they cared to inquire—with vague references to an "agency," or something of the sort. Neither his mother nor Jane ever came to London; for them, his change of address to a poorer district would have no significance. In short, London, being London, it seemed perfectly feasible to pass his life in a grocer's shop without the fact becoming known to any one from whom he wished to conceal it.

The rent of the shop and house was eighty-five pounds—an increase upon that paid by Boxon. "Plant" was estimated at a hundred and twenty-five; the stock at one hundred and fifty, and the goodwill at a round hundred. This made a total of four hundred and sixty pounds, leaving Warburton some couple of hundred for all the expenses of his start. The landlord had consented to do certain repairs, including a repainting of the shop, and this work had already begun. Not a day must be lost. Will knew that the first half-year would decide his fate as a tradesman. Did he come out at the end of six months with sufficient profit to pay a bare three per cent. on the St. Neots money, all would be safe and well. If the balance went against him, why then the whole battle of life was lost, and he might go hide his head in some corner even more obscure.

Of course he counted largely on the help of Allchin. Allchin, though pig-headed and pugnacious, had a fair knowledge of the business, to which he had been bred, and of business matters in general always talked shrewdly. Unable, whatever his own straits, to deal penuriously with any one, Will had thought out a liberal arrangement, whereby all the dwelling part of the house should be given over, rent free, to Allchin and his wife, with permission to take one lodger; the assistant to be paid a small salary, and a percentage on shop takings when they reached a certain sum per month. This proposal, then, he set before the muscular man on his presenting himself this afternoon. Allchin's astonishment at the story he had heard from Mrs. Hopper was not less than that of the woman herself. With difficulty persuaded to sit down, he showed a countenance in which the gloom he thought decorous struggled against jubilation on his own account: and Warburton had not talked long before his listener's features irresistibly expanded in a happy grin.

"How would something of this kind suit you?" asked Will.

"Me, sir?" Allchin slapped his leg. "You ask how it suits *me*?"

His feelings were too much for him. He grew very red, and could say no more.

"Then suppose we settle it so. I've written out the terms of your engagement. Read and sign."

Allchin pretended to read the paper, but obviously paid no attention to it. He seemed to be struggling with some mental obstacle.

"Something you want to alter?" asked Warburton.

"Why, sir, you've altogether forgot as I'm in your debt. It stands to reason as you must take that money out before you begin to pay me anything."

"Oh, we won't say anything more about that trifle. We're making a new beginning. But look here, Allchin, I don't want you to quarrel with me, as you do with every one else——"

"With *you*, sir? Ho, ho!"

Allchin guffawed, and at once looked ashamed of himself.

"I quarrel," he added, "with people as are insulting, or as try to best me. It goes against my nature, sir, to be insulted and to be bested."

They talked about the details of the business, and presently Allchin asked what name was to be put up over the shop.

"I've thought of that," answered Will. "What do you say to—*Jollyman*?"

The assistant was delighted; he repeated the name a dozen times, snorting and choking with appreciation of the joke. Next morning, they met again, and went together to look at the shop. Here Allchin made great play with his valuable qualities. He pointed out the errors and negligencies of the late Boxon, declared it a scandal that a business such as this should have been allowed to fall off, and was full of ingenious ideas for a brilliant opening. Among other forms of inexpensive advertisement, he suggested that, for the first day, a band should be engaged to play in the front room over the shop, with the windows open ; and he undertook to find amateur bandsmen who would undertake the job on very moderate terms.

Not many days elapsed before the old name had disappeared from the house front, giving place to that of Jollyman. Whilst this was being painted up, Allchin stood on the opposite side of the way, watching delightedly.

" When I think as the name used to be Boxon," he exclaimed to his employer, " why, I can't believe as any money was ever made here. Boxon ! Why, it was enough to drive customers away ! If you ever heard a worse name, sir, for a shopkeeper, I should be glad to be told of it. But *Jollyman !* Why, it'll bring people from Putney, from Battersea, from who knows how far. Jollyman's Teas, Jollyman's sugar— can't you *hear* 'em saying it, already ? It's a fortune in itself, that name. Why, sir, if a grocer called Boxon came at this moment, and offered to take me into partnership on half profits, I wouldn't listen to him—there ! "

Naturally, all this did not pass without many a pang in Warburton's sensitive spots. He had set his face like brass, or tried to do so ; but in the night season he could all but have shed tears of humiliation, as he tossed on his comfortless pillow. The day was spent in visits to wholesale grocery establishments, in study of trade journals, in calculating innumerable petty questions of profit and loss. When nausea threatened him : when an all but horror of what lay before him assailed his mind; he thought fixedly of The Haws, and made a picture to himself of that peaceful little home devastated by his own fault. And to think that all this sweat and misery arose from the need of gaining less than a couple of hundred pounds a year! Life at The Haws, a life of refinement and goodness and tranquillity such as can seldom be found, demanded only that—a sum which the wealthy vulgar throw away upon the foolish amusement of an hour. Warburton had a tumultuous mind in reflecting on these things; but the disturbance was salutary, bearing him through trials of nerve and patience and self-respect which he could not otherwise have endured.

Warburton had now to find cheap lodgings for himself, unfurnished rooms in some poor quarter not too far from the shop.

At length, in a new little street of very red brick, not far from Fulham Palace Road at the Hammersmith end, he came upon a small house which exhibited in its parlour window a card inscribed: "Two unfurnished rooms to be let to single gentlemen only." The precision of this notice made him hopeful, and a certain cleanliness of aspect in the woman who opened to him was an added encouragement; but he found negotiations not altogether easy. The landlady, a middle-aged widow, seemed to regard him with some peculiar suspicion; before even admitting him to the house, she questioned him closely as to his business, his present place of abode, and so on, and Warburton was all but turning away in impatience, when at last she drew aside, and cautiously invited him to enter. Further acquaintance with Mrs. Wick led him to understand that the cold, misgiving in her eye, the sour rigidity of her lips, and her generally repellant manner, were characteristics which meant nothing in particular—save as they resulted from a more or less hard life amid London's crowd; at present, the woman annoyed him, and only the clean freshness of her vacant rooms induced him to take the trouble of coming to terms with her.

"There's one thing I must say to you quite plain, to begin with," remarked Mrs. Wick, whose language, though not disrespectful, had a certain bluntness. "I can't admit female visitors—not on any excuse."

Speaking thus, she set her face at its rigidest and sourest, and stared past Warburton at the wall. He, unable to repress a smile, declared his perfect readiness to accept this condition of tenancy.

"Another thing," pursued the landlady, "is that I don't like late hours." And she eyed him as one might a person caught in flagrant crapulence at one o'clock a.m.

"Why, neither do I," Will replied. "But for all that, I may be obliged to come home late now and then."

"From the theatre, I suppose?"

"I very seldom go to the theatre." (Mrs. Wick looked sanguine for an instant, but at once relapsed into darker suspicion than ever.) "But as to my hour of returning home, I must have entire liberty."

The woman meditated, profound gloom on her brows.

"You haven't told me," she resumed, shooting a glance of keen distrust, "exactly what your business may be."

"I am in the sugar line," responded Will.

"Sugar? You wouldn't mind giving me the name of your employers?"

The word so rasped on Warburton's sensitive

temper that he seemed about to speak angrily. This the woman observed, and added at once:

"I don't doubt but that you're quite respectable, sir, but you can understand as I have to be careful who I take into my house."

"I understand that, but I must ask you to be satisfied with a reference to my present landlord. That, and a month's payment in advance, ought to suffice."

Evidently it did, for Mrs. Wick, after shooting one or two more of her sharpest looks, declared herself willing to enter into discussion of details. He required attendance, did he? Well it all depended upon what sort of attendance he expected; if he wanted cooking at late hours.—Warburton cut short these anticipatory objections, and made known that his wants were few and simple: plain breakfast at eight o'clock, cold supper on the table when he came home, a mid-day meal on Sundays, and the keeping of his rooms in order; that was all. After morose reflection, Mrs. Wick put her demand for rooms and service at a pound a week, but to this Warburton demurred. It cost him agonies to debate such a matter; but, as he knew very well, the price was excessive for unfurnished lodgings, and need constrained him. He offered fifteen shillings, and said he would call for Mrs. Wick's decision on the morrow. The landlady allowed him to go to the foot of the stairs, then stopped him.

"I wouldn't mind taking fifteen shillings," she said, "if I knew it was for a permanency."

"I can't bind myself more than by the month."

"Would you be willing to leave a deposit?"

So the matter was settled, and Warburton arranged to enter into possession that day week.

Without delay the shop repairs were finished, inside and out; orders for stock were completed; in two days—as a great bill on the shutters announced—"Jollyman's Grocery Stores" would be open to the public. Allchin pleaded strongly for the engagement of the brass band; it wouldn't cost much, and the effect would be immense. Warburton shrugged, hesitated, gave way, and the band was engaged.

CHAPTER XIX

ROSAMUND ELVAN was what ladies call a good correspondent. She wrote often, she wrote at length, and was satisfied with few or brief letters in reply. Scarcely had she been a week at Cairo, when some half dozen sheets of thin paper, covered with her small swift writing, were dispatched to Bertha Cross, and, thence onwards, about once a fortnight such a letter arrived at Walham Green. Sitting by a fire kept, for economical reasons, as low as possible, with her mother's voice sounding querulously somewhere in the house, and too often a clammy fog at the window, Bertha read of Egyptian delights and wonders, set glowingly before her in Rosamund's fluent style. She was glad of the letters, for they manifested a true affection, and were in every way more interesting than any others that she received; but at times they made the cheerless little house seem more cheerless still, and the pang of contrast between her life and Rosamund's called at such moments for all Bertha's sense of humour to make it endurable.

Not that Miss Elvan represented herself as happy. In her very first letter she besought Bertha not to suppose that her appreciation of strange and beautiful things meant forgetfulness of what must be a lifelong sorrow. "I am often worse than depressed. I sleep very badly, and in the night I often shed wretched tears. Though I did only what conscience compelled me to do, I suffer all the miseries of remorse. And how can I wish that it should be otherwise? It is better, surely, to be capable of such suffering, than to go one's way in light-hearted egoism. I'm not sure that I don't sometimes *encourage* despondency. You can understand that? I know you can, dear Bertha, for many a time I have detected the deep feeling which lies beneath your joking way." Passages such as this Bertha was careful to omit when reading from the letters to her mother. Mrs. Cross took very little interest in her daughter's friend, and regarded the broken engagement with no less disapproval than surprise; but it would have gravely offended her if Bertha had kept this correspondence altogether to herself.

"I suppose," she remarked, on one such occasion, "we shall never again see Mr. Franks."

"He would find it rather awkward to call, no doubt," replied Bertha.

"I shall *never* understand it!" Mrs. Cross exclaimed, in a vexed tone, after thinking awhile. "No doubt there's something you keep from me."

"About Rosamund? Nothing whatever, I assure you, mother."

"Then you yourself don't know all, that's *quite* certain."

Mrs. Cross had made the remark many times, and always with the same satisfaction. Her daughter was content that the discussion should remain at this point; for the feeling that she had said something at once unpleasant and unanswerable made Mrs. Cross almost good humoured for at least an hour.

Few were the distressful lady's sources of comfort, but one sure way of soothing her mind and temper, was to suggest some method of saving money, no matter how little. One day in the winter, Bertha passing along the further part of Fulham Road, noticed a new-looking grocer's, the window full of price tickets, some of them very attractive to a housekeeper's eye; on returning home she spoke of this, mentioning figures which moved her mother to a sour effervescence of delight. The shop was rather too far away for convenience, but that same evening Mrs. Cross went to inspect it, and came back quite flurried with what she had seen.

"I shall most certainly deal at Jollyman's," she exclaimed. "What a pity we didn't know of him before! Such a gentlemanly man—indeed, *quite* a gentleman. I never saw a shopkeeper who behaved so nicely. So different from Billings—a man I have always thoroughly disliked, and his coffee has been getting worse and worse. Mr. Jollyman is quite willing to send even the smallest orders. Isn't that nice of him—such a distance! Billings was quite insolent to me the day before yesterday, when I asked him to send; yet it was nearly a two-shilling order. Never go into that shop again, Bertha. It's really quite a pleasure to buy of Mr. Jollyman; he knows how to behave; I really almost felt as if I was talking to some one of our own class. Without his apron, he must be a thorough gentleman."

Bertha could not restrain a laugh.

"How thoughtless of him to wear an apron at all!" she exclaimed merrily. "Couldn't one suggest to him discreetly, that *but* for the apron——"

"Don't be ridiculous, Bertha!" interrupted her mother. "You always make nonsense of what one says. Mr. Jollyman is a shopkeeper, and it's just because he doesn't forget that, after all, that his behaviour is so good. Do you remember that horrid Stokes, in King's Road? There was a man who thought himself too good for his business, and in reality was nothing but an underbred, impertinent creature. I can hear his 'Yes, Mrs. Cross—no, Mrs. Cross—thank you, Mrs. Cross'—and once, when I protested against an overcharge, he cried out, 'Oh, my *dear* Mrs. Cross!' The insolence of that man! Now, Mr. Jollyman——"

It was not long before Bertha had an opportunity of seeing this remarkable shopkeeper, and for once she was able to agree with her mother. Mr. Jollyman bore very little resemblance to the typical grocer, and each visit to his shop strengthened Bertha's suspicion that he had not grown up in this way of life. It cost her some constraint to make a very small purchase of him, paying a few coppers, and still more when she asked him if he had nothing cheaper than this or that; all the more so that Mr. Jollyman seemed to share her embarrassment, lowering his voice as if involuntarily, and being careful not to meet her eye. One thing Bertha noticed was that, though the grocer invariable addressed her mother as "madam," in speaking to *her* he never used the grocerly "miss"; and when, by chance, she heard him bestow this objectionable title upon a servant girl who was making purchases at the same time, Bertha not only felt grateful for the distinction, but saw in it a fresh proof of Mr. Jollyman's good breeding.

The winter passed, and with the spring came events in which Bertha was interested. Mr. Elvan, who for his health's sake spent the winter in the south-west of France, fell so ill early in the year that Rosamund was summoned from Egypt. With all speed she travelled to St. Jean de Luz.

When she arrived, her father was no longer in danger; but there seemed no hope of his being able to return to England for some months, so Rosamund remained with him and her sister, and was soon writing to her friend at Walham Green in a strain of revived enthusiasm for the country of the Basques. A postscript to one of these letters, written in the middle of May, ran as follows: "I hear that N. F. has a picture in the Academy called 'A Ministering Angel,' and that it promises to be one of the most popular of the year. Have you seen it?" To this, Rosamund's correspondent was able to reply that she had seen "N.F's" picture, and that it certainly was a good deal talked about; she added no opinion as to the merits of the painting, and, in her next letter, Miss Elvan left the subject untouched. Bertha was glad of this. "A Ministering Angel" seemed to her by no means a very remarkable production, and she liked much better to say nothing about it than to depreciate the painter; for to do this would have been like seeking to confirm Rosamund in her attitude towards Norbert Franks, which was not at all Bertha's wish.

A few weeks later, Rosamund returned to the topic. "N. F's picture," she wrote, "is evidently a great success—and you can imagine how I feel about it. I saw it, you remember, at an early stage, when he called it 'The Slummer,' and you remember too, the effect it had upon me. Oh, Bertha, this is nothing less than a soul's tragedy! When I think what he used to be, what I hoped of him, what he hoped for himself! Is it not dreadful that he should have fallen so low, and in so short a time! A popular success! Oh, the shame of it, the bitter shame!"

At this point, the reader's smile threatened laughter. But, feeling sure that her friend, if guilty of affectation, was quite unconscious of it, she composed her face to read gravely on.

"A soul's tragedy, Bertha, and *I* the cause of it. One can see now, but too well, what is before him. All his hardships are over, and all his struggles. He will become a popular painter—one of those whose name is familiar to the crowd, like—" instances were cited. "I can say, with all earnestness, that I had rather have seen him starved to death. Poor, poor N. F.! Something whispers to me that perhaps I was always under an illusion about him. *Could* he so rapidly sink to this, if he were indeed the man I thought him? Would he not rather have—oh, have done *anything*?—Yet this may be only a temptation of my lower self, a way of giving ease to my conscience. Despair may account for his degradation. And when I remember that a word, one word, from me, at the right moment, would have checked him on the dangerous path! When I saw 'Sanctuary,' why had I not the courage to tell him what I thought? No, I became the accomplice of his suicide, and I, alone, am the cause of this wretched disaster.—Before long he will be rich. Can you imagine N. F. *rich*? I shudder at the thought."

The paper rustled in Bertha's hand; her shoulders shook; she could no longer restrain the merry laugh. When she sat down to answer Rosamund, a roguish smile played about her lips.

"I grieve with you"—thus she began—"over the shocking prospect of N. F.'s becoming *rich*. Alas! I fear the thing is past praying for; I can all but see the poor young man in a shiny silk hat and an overcoat trimmed with the most expensive fur. His Academy picture is everywhere produced; a large photogravure will soon be published; all day long a crowd stands before it at Burlington House, and his name—shall we ever again dare to speak it?—is on the lips of casual people in train and 'bus and tram. How shall I write on such a painful subject? You see that my hand is unsteady. Don't blame yourself too much. The man capable of becoming rich *will* become so, whatever the noble influences which endeavour to restrain him. I suspect—I feel all but convinced—that N. F. could not help himself; the misfortune is that his fatal turn for money-making did not show itself earlier, and so warn you away. I don't know whether I dare send you a paragraph I have cut from yesterday's *Echo*. Yet I will—it will serve to show you that—as you used to write from Egypt—all this is Kismet."

The newspaper cutting showed an item of news interesting alike to the fashionable and the artistic world. Mr. Norbert Franks, the young painter whose Academy picture had been so much discussed, was about to paint the portrait of Lady Rockett, recently espoused wife of Sir Samuel Rockett, the Australian millionaire. As every one knew, Lady Rockett had made a brilliant figure in the now closing Season, and her image had been in all the society journals. Mr. Franks might be congratulated on this excellent opportunity for the display of his admirable talent as an exponent of female beauty.—"Exponent" was the word.

CHAPTER XX

IN these summer days, whilst Norbert Franks was achieving popularity, success in humbler guise came to the humorous and much-enduring artist at Walham Green. For a year or two, Bertha Cross had spent what time she could spare upon the illustration of a quaint old story-book, a book which had amused her own childhood, and still held its place in her affection. The work was now finished; she showed it to a publisher of her acquaintance, who at once offered to purchase it on what seemed to Bertha excellent terms. Of her own abilities she thought very modestly indeed, and had always been surprised when any one consented to pay—oftener in shillings than in pounds—for work which had cost her an infinity of conscientious trouble; now, however, she suspected that she had done something not altogether bad, and she spoke of it in a letter to Rosamund Elvan, still in the country of the Basques.

"As you know," Rosamund replied, "I have never doubted that you would make a success one day, for you are wonderfully clever, and only need a little more self-confidence in making yourself known. I wish *I* could feel anything like so sure of earning money. For I shall have to, that is now certain. Poor father, who gets weaker and weaker, talked to us the other day about what we could expect after his death; and it will be only just a little sum for each of us, nothing like enough to invest and live upon. I am working at my water-colours, and I have been trying pastel—there's no end of good material here. When the end comes—and it can't be long—I must go to London, and see whether my things have any market value. I don't like the prospect of life in a garret on bread and water—by myself, that is. You know how joyfully, gladly, proudly, I would have accepted it, under *other* circumstances. If I had real talent myself—but I feel more than doubtful about that. I pray that I may not fall too low. Can I trust you to overwhelm me with scorn, if I seem in danger of doing vulgar work?"

Bertha yielded to the temptations of a later summer rich in warmth and hue, and made little excursions by herself into the country, leaving home before her mother was up in the morning, and coming back after sunset. Her sketching materials and a packet of sandwiches were but a light burden; she was a good walker; and the shilling or two spent on the railway, which formerly she could not have spared, no longer frightened her.

In this way, one morning of September, she went by early train as far as Epsom, walked through the streets, and came into that high-banked lane which leads up to the downs. Blackberries shone thick upon the brambles, and above, even to the very tops of the hedge-row trees, climbed the hoary clematis. Glad in this leafy solitude, Bertha rambled slowly on. She made no unpleasing figure against the rural background, for she was straight and slim, graceful in her movements, and had a face from which no one would have turned indifferently, so bright was it with youthful enjoyment and with older thought.

Whilst thus she lingered, a footstep approached, that of a man who was walking in the same direction. When close to her, this pedestrian stopped, and his voice startled Bertha with unexpected greeting. The speaker was Norbert Franks.

"How glad I am to see you!" he exclaimed, in a tone and with a look which vouched for his sincerity. "I ought to have been to Walham Green long ago. Again and again I meant to come. But this is jolly; I like chance meetings. Are you often down here in Surrey?"

With amusement Bertha remarked the evidence of prosperity in Franks' dress and bearing; he had changed notably since the days when he used to come to their little house to talk of Rosamund, and was glad of an indifferent cup of tea. He seemed to be in very fair health, his countenance giving no hint of sentimental sorrows.

Franks noticed a bunch of tinted leafage which she was carrying, and spoke of its beauty.

"Going to make use of them, no doubt. What are you working at just now?"

Bertha told of her recent success with the illustrated story-book, and Franks declared himself delighted. Clearly, he was in the mood to be delighted with everything. Between his remarks, which were uttered in the sprightliest tone, he hummed phrases of melody.

"Your Academy picture was a great success," said Bertha, discreetly watching him as she spoke.

"Yes, I suppose it was," he answered, with a light-hearted laugh. "Did you see it?— And what did you think of it?—No, seriously; I should like your real opinion. I know you *have* opinions."

"You meant it to be successful," was Bertha's reply.

"Well, yes, I did. At the same time I think some of the critics—the high and mighty ones, you know—were altogether wrong about it. Perhaps, on the whole, you take their view?"

"Oh no, I don't," answered his companion, cheerfully. "I thought the picture very clever, and very true."

"I'm delighted! I've always maintained that it was perfectly true. A friend of mine—why, you remember me speaking of Warburton—Warburton wanted me to make the Slummer ugly. But why? It's just the prettiest girls—of that kind—who go slumming nowadays. Still, you are quite right. I did mean it to be 'successful.' I *had* to make a success, that's the fact of the matter. You know what bad times I was having. I got sick of it, that's the truth. Then, I owed money, and money that had to be paid back, one way or another. Now I'm out of debt, and see my way to live and work in decent comfort. And I maintain that I've done nothing to be ashamed of."

Bertha smiled approvingly.

"I've just finished a portrait—a millionaire's wife, Lady Rockett," went on Franks. "Of course it was my Slummer that got me the job. Women have been raving about that girl's head; and it isn't bad, though I say it. I had to take a studio at a couple of days' notice—couldn't ask Lady Rockett to come and sit at that place of mine in Battersea; a shabby hole. She isn't really anything out of the way, as a pretty woman; but I've made her—well, you'll see it at some exhibition this winter, if you care to. Pleased? Isn't she pleased! And her husband, the podgy old millionaire baronet, used to come every day and stare in delight. To tell you the truth, I think it's rather a remarkable bit of painting. I didn't quite know I could turn out anything so *chic*. I shouldn't be surprised if I make a specialty of women's portraits. How many men can flatter, and still keep a good likeness? That's what I've done. But wait till you see the thing."

Bertha was bubbling over with amusement; for, whilst the artist talked, she thought of Rosamund's farewell entreaty, that she would do her best, if occasion offered, to strengthen Norbert Franks under his affliction, even by depreciatory comment on the faithless girl; there came into her mind, too, those many passages of Rosamund's letters where Franks was spoken of in terms of profoundest compassion mingled with dark remorse. Perhaps her smile, which quivered on the verge of laughter, betrayed the nature of her thought. Of a sudden, Franks ceased to talk; his countenance changed, overcast with melancholy; and when, after some moments' silence, Bertha again spoke of the landscape, he gave only a dull assent to her words.

"And it all comes too late," fell from him, presently. "Too late."

"Your success?"

"What's the good of it to me?" He smote his leg with the rattan he was swinging. "A couple of years ago, money would have meant everything. Now—what do I care about it!"

Bertha's surprise obliged her to keep an unnaturally solemn visage.

"Don't you think it'll grow upon you," she said, 'if you give it time?"

"Grow upon me? Why, I'm only afraid it may. That's just the danger. To pursue success—vulgar success—when all the better part has gone out of life——"

He ended on a sigh, and again whacked his leg with the stick.

"But" urged his companion, as though gravely, "isn't it easy *not* to pursue success? I mean if it really makes you uncomfortable. There are so many kinds of work in art which would protect you against the perils of riches."

Franks was watching her as she spoke.

"Miss Cross" he said, "I suspect you are satirical. I remember you used to have a turn that way. Well, well, never mind; I don't expect you to understand me."

They had passed out of Ashtead Park and were now ascending by the lane which leads up to Epsom Common.

"I suppose we are both going the same way," said Franks, who had recovered all his cheerfulness. "There's a train at something after five, if we can catch it. Splendid idea of yours to have a whole day's walking. I don't walk enough. Are you likely to be going again before long?"

Bertha replied that she never made plans beforehand. Her mood and the weather decided an excursion.

"Of course. That's the only way. Well, if you'll let me, I must come to Walham Green, one of these days. How's Mrs. Cross? I ought to have asked before, but I never do the right thing.—Have you any particular day for being at home?—All right. If you had had, I should have asked you to let me come on some other. I don't care much, you know, for general society; and ten to one, when I do come I shall be rather gloomy. Old memories, you know.—Really very jolly, this meeting with you. I should have done the walk to Epsom just as a constitutional, without enjoying it a bit. As it is——"

CHAPTER XXI

IT was a week or two after the day in Surrey, that Bertha Cross, needing a small wooden box in which to pack a present for her brothers in British Columbia, bethought herself of Mr. Jollyman. The amiable grocer could probably supply her want, and she went off to the shop. There the assistant and an errand boy were unloading goods just arrived by cart, and behind the counter, reading a newspaper—for it was early in the morning—stood Mr. Jollyman himself. Seeing the young lady enter, he smiled and bowed; not at all with tradesmanlike emphasis, but rather, it seemed to Bertha, like a man tired and absent-minded, performing a civility in the well-bred way. The newspaper thrown aside, he stood with head bent and eyes cast down, listening to her request.

"I think I have something that will do very well," he replied. "Excuse me for a moment."

From regions behind the shop, he produced a serviceable box just of the right dimensions.

"It will do? Then you shall have it in about half an hour."

"I'm ashamed to trouble you," said Bertha "I could carry it——"

"On no account. The boy will be free in a few minutes."

"And I owe you—?" asked Bertha, purse in hand.

"The box has no value," replied Mr. Jollyman, with that smile, suggestive of latent humour, which always caused her to smile responsively. "And at the same time," he continued, a peculiar twinkle in his eyes, "I will ask you to accept one of these packets of chocolate. I am giving one to-day to every customer—to celebrate the anniversary of my opening shop."

"Thank you very much," said Bertha. And, on an impulse, she added: "I will put it with what I am sending in the box—a present for two brothers of mine who are a long way off, in Canada."

His hands upon the counter, his body bent forward, Mr. Jollyman looked her for a moment in the face. A crease appeared on his forehead, as he said slowly and dreamily:

"Canada? Do they like their life out there?"

"They seem to enjoy it, on the whole. But it evidently isn't an easy life."

"Not many kinds of life are" rejoined the grocer. "But the open air—the liberty——"

"Oh yes, that must be the good side of it," assented Bertha.

"On a morning like this——"

Mr. Jollyman's eyes wandered to a gleam of sunny sky visible through the shop window. The girl's glance passed quickly over his features, and she was on the point of saying something; but discretion interposed. Instead of the too personal remark, she repeated her thanks, bent her head with perhaps a little more than the wonted graciousness, and left the shop.

The grocer stood looking toward the doorway. His countenance had fallen. Something of bitterness showed in the hardness of his lips.

CHAPTER XXII

JUST a year since the day when Allchin's band played at the first floor windows above Jollyman's new grocery stores.

From the very beginning, business promised well. He and his assistant had plenty of work; there was little time for meditation; when not serving customers, he was busy with practical details of grocerdom, often such as he had not foreseen, matters which called for all his energy and ingenuity. A gratifying aspect of the life was that, day by day, he handled his returns in solid cash. Jollyman's gave no credit; all goods had to be paid for on purchase or delivery; and to turn out the till when the shop had closed—to make piles of silver and mountains of copper, with a few pieces of gold beside them—put a cheering end to the day's labour. Warburton found himself clinking handfuls of coin, pleased with the sound. Only at the end of the first three months, the close of the year, did he perceive that much less than he had hoped of the cash taken could be reckoned as clear profit. He had much to learn in the cunning of retail trade, and it was a kind of study that went sorely against the grain with him. Happily, at Christmas time came Norbert Franks (whom Will had decided *not* to take into his confidence) and paid his debt of a hundred and twenty pounds. This set things right for the moment. Will was able to pay a three-and-a-half per cent. dividend to his mother and sister, and to fare ahead hopefully.

He would rather not have gone down to The Haws that Christmastide, but feared that his failure to do so might seem strange. The needful prevarication cost him so many pangs that he came very near to confessing the truth ; he probably would have done so, had not his mother been ailing, and, it seemed to him, little able to bear the shock of such a disclosure. So the honest deception went on. Will was supposed to be managing a London branch of the Applegarth business. Great expenditure on advertising had to account for the smallness of the dividend at first. No one less likely than the ladies at The Haws to make trouble in such a matter. They had what sufficed to them, and were content with it. Thinking over this in shame-faced solitude, Warburton felt a glow of proud thankfulness that his mother and sister were so unlike the vulgar average of mankind—that rapacious multitude, whom nothing animates but a chance of gain, with whom nothing weighs but a commercial argument. A new tenderness stirred within him, and resolutely he stamped under foot the impulses of self-esteem, of self-indulgence, which made his life hard to bear.

It was with a hard satisfaction that he returned to the shop, and found all going on in the usual way, Allchin grinning a hearty welcome as he weighed out sugar. Will's sister talked of the scents of her garden, how they refreshed and inspirited her ; to him, the odour of the shop—new-roasted coffee predominated to-day—had its invigorating effect ; it meant money, and money meant life, the peaceful, fruitful life of those dear to him. He scarcely gave himself time to eat dinner, laid for him, as usual, by Mrs. Allchin, in the sitting-room behind the shop; so eager was he to get on his apron, and return to profitable labour.

At first, he had endured a good deal of physical fatigue. Standing for so many hours a day wearied him much more than walking would have done, and with bodily exhaustion came at times a lowness of spirits such as he had never felt. His resource against this misery was conversation with Allchin. In Allchin he had a henchman whose sturdy optimism and gross common sense were of the utmost value. The brawny assistant, having speedily found a lodger according to the agreement, saw himself in clover, and determined that, if *he* could help it, his fortunes should never again suffer eclipse. He and his wife felt a reasonable gratitude to the founder of their prosperity—whom, by the bye, they invariably spoke of as "Mr. Jollyman"—and did their best to smooth for him the unfamiliar path he was treading.

The success with which Warburton kept his secret, merely proved how solitary most men are amid the crowds of London, and how easy it is for a Londoner to disappear from among his acquaintances whilst continuing to live openly amid the city's roar. No one of those who cared enough about him to learn that he had fallen on ill-luck harboured the slightest suspicion of what he was doing; he simply dropped out of sight, except for the two or three who, in a real sense of the word, could be called his friends. The Pomfrets, whom he went to see at very long intervals, supposed him to have some sort of office employment, and saw nothing in his demeanour to make them anxious about him. As for Norbert Franks, why, he was very busy, and came not oftener than once a month to his friend's obscure lodgings; he asked no intrusive questions, and, like the Pomfrets, could only suppose that Warburton had found a clerkship somewhere. They were not quite on the old terms, for each had gone through a crisis of life, and was not altogether the same as before; but their mutual liking subsisted. Obliged to retrench his hospitality, Warburton never seemed altogether at his ease when Franks was in his room; nor could he overcome what seemed to him the shame of having asked payment of a debt from a needy friend, notwithstanding the fact, loudly declared by Franks himself, that nothing could have been more beneficial to the debtor's moral health. So Will listened rather than talked, and was sometimes too obviously in no mood for any sort of converse.

Sherwood he had not seen since the disastrous optimist's flight into Wales; nor had there come any remittance from him since the cheque for a hundred pounds. Two or three times, however, Godfrey had written—thoroughly characteristic letters—warm, sanguine, self-reproachful. From Wales he had crossed over to Ireland, where he was working at a scheme for making a fortune out of Irish eggs and poultry. In what the "work" consisted, was not clear, for he had no money, beyond a small loan from his relative which enabled him to live; but he sent a sheet of foolscap covered with computations whereby his project was proved to be thoroughly practical and vastly lucrative.

Meanwhile, he had made one new acquaintance, which was at first merely a source of amusement to him, but little by little became something more. In the winter days, when his business was new, there one day came into the shop a rather sour-lipped and querulous-voiced lady, who after much discussion of prices, made a modest purchase and asked that the goods might be sent for her. On hearing her name—Mrs. Cross—the grocer smiled, for he remembered that the Crosses of whom he knew from Norbert Franks, lived at Walham Green, and the artist's description of Mrs. Cross tallied very well with the aspect and manner of this customer. Once or twice the lady returned ; then, on a day of very bad weather, there came in her place a much younger and decidedly more pleasing person, whom Will took to be Mrs. Cross's daughter. Facial resemblance there was none discoverable ; in bearing, in look, in tone, the two were different as women could be ; but at the younger lady's second visit, his surmise was confirmed, for she begged him to change a five-pound note, and, as the custom is in London shops, endorsed it with her name—" Bertha Cross." Franks had never spoken much of Miss Cross ; " rather a nice sort of girl, " was as far as his appreciation went. And with this judgment Will at once agreed ; before long, he would have inclined to be more express in his good opinion. Before summer came, he found himself looking forward to the girl's appearance in the shop, with a sense of disappointment when—as generally happened—Mrs. Cross came in person. The charm of the young face lay for him in its ever-present suggestion of a roguishly winsome smile, which made it difficult not to watch too intently the play of her eyes and lips. Then, her way of speaking, which was altogether her own. It infused with a humorous possibility the driest, most matter-of-fact remarks, and Will had to guard himself against the temptation to reply in a corresponding note.

" I suppose you see no more of those people—what's their name—the Crosses ? " he let fall, as if casually, one evening when Franks had come to see him "

" Lost sight of them altogether," was the reply. " Why do you ask ? "

" I happened to think of them," said Will ; and turned to another subject.

CHAPTER XXIII

WAS he to be a grocer for the rest of his life? —This question, which at first scarcely occurred to him, absorbed as he was in the problem of money-earning for immediate needs, at length began to press and worry. Of course he had meant nothing of the kind; his imagination had seen in the shop a temporary expedient; he had not troubled to pursue the ultimate probabilities of the life that lay before him, but contented himself with the vague assurance of his hopeful temper. Yet where was the way out? To save money, to accumulate sufficient capital for his release, was an impossibility, at all events within any reasonable time. And for what windfall could he look? Sherwood's ten thousand pounds hovered in his memory, but no more substantial than any fairy-tale. No man living, it seemed to him, had less chance of being signally favoured by fortune. He had donned his apron and aproned he must remain.

Suppose, then, he so far succeeded in his business as to make a little more than the household at St. Neots required; suppose it became practicable to—well, say, to think of marriage, of course on the most modest basis; could he quite see himself offering to the girl he chose the hand and heart of a grocer? He laughed. It was well to laugh; merriment is the great digestive, and an unspeakable boon to the man capable of it in all but every situation;

but what if *she* also laughed, and not in the sympathetic way? Worse still, what if she could ***not*** laugh, but looked wretchedly embarrassed, confused, shamed? That would be a crisis it needed some philosophy to contemplate.

For the present, common sense made it rigorously plain to him that the less he thought of these things, the better. He had not a penny to spare. Only by exercising an economy which in the old days would have appalled him, could he send his mother and sister an annual sum just sufficient to their needs. He who scorned and loathed all kinds of parsimony had learnt to cut down his expenditure at every possible point. He still smoked his pipe; he bought newspapers; he granted himself an excursion, of the cheapest, on fine Sundays; but these surely were necessities of life. In food and clothing and the common expenses of a civilised man, he pinched remorselessly; there was no choice. His lodgings cost him very little; but Mrs. Wick, whose profound suspiciousness was allied with imperfect honesty, now and then made paltry overcharges in her bill, and he was angry with himself for his want of courage to resist them. It meant only a shilling or two, but retail trade had taught him the importance of shillings. He had to remind himself that, if he was poor, his landlady was poorer still, and that in cheating him she did but follow the traditions of her class. To debate an excess of sixpence for paraffin, of ninepence for bacon, would have made him flush and grind his teeth for hours afterwards; but he noticed the effect upon himself of the new habit of niggardliness—how it disposed him to acerbity of temper. No matter how pure the motive, a man cannot devote his days to squeezing out pecuniary profits without some moral detriment.

Formerly this woman, Mrs. Wick, with her gimlet eyes, and her leech lips, with her spyings and eaves-droppings, with her sour civility, her stinted discharge of obligations, her pilferings and mendacities, would have rather amused than annoyed him. "Poor creature, isn't it a miserable as well as a sordid life. Let her have her pickings, however illegitimate, and much good may they do her." Now he too often found himself regarding her with something like animosity, whereby, to be sure, he brought himself to the woman's level. Was it not a struggle between him and her for a share of life's poorest comforts? When he looked at it in that light, his cheeks were hot.

A tradesman must harden himself. Why, in the early months, it cost him a wrench somewhere to take coppers at the counter from very poor folk who perhaps made up the odd halfpenny in farthings, and looked at the coins reluctantly as they laid them down. More than once, he said, "Oh never mind the ha'penny," and was met with a look—not of gratitude but of blank amazement. Allchin happened to be a witness of one such incident, and, in the first moment of privacy, ventured a respectful yet a most energetic, protest. "It's the kindness of your 'eart, sir, and if anybody knows how much of that you have, I'm sure it's me, and I ought to be the last to find fault with it. But that'll never do behind the counter, sir, never! Why, just think. The profit on what that woman bought was just three farthings." He detailed the computation. "And there you've been and given her a whole ha'penny, so that you've only one blessed farthing over on the whole transaction! That ain't business, sir; that's charity; and Jollyman's ain't a charitable institution. You really must not, sir. It's unjust to yourself." And Will, with an uneasy shrug, admitted his folly. But he was ashamed to the core. Only in the second half-year did he really accustom himself to disregard a customer's poverty. He had thought the thing out, faced all its most sordid aspects. Yes, he was fighting with these people for daily bread; he and his could live only if his three farthings of profit were plucked out of that toil-worn hand of charwoman or sempstress. Accept the necessity, and think no more of it. He was a man behind the counter; he saw face to face the people who supported him. With this exception had not things been just the same when he sat in the counting-house at the sugar refinery? It was an unpleasant truth, which appearances had formerly veiled from him.

With the beginning of his second winter came a new anxiety, a new source of bitter and degrading reflections. At not more than five minutes' walk away, another grocer started business; happily no great capitalist, but to all appearances a man of enterprise who knew what he was about. Morning and evening, Warburton passed the new shop and felt his very soul turn sour in the thought that he must do what in him lay to prevent that man from gaining custom; if he could make his business a failure, destroy all his hopes, so much the better. With Allchin, he held long and eager conferences. The robust assistant was of course troubled by no scruples; he warmed to the combat, chuckled over each good idea for the enemy's defeat; every nerve must be strained for the great Christmas engagement; as much money as possible must be spent in making a brave show. And it was only by pausing every now and then to remember *why* he stood here, in what cause he was so debasing the manner of his life, that Warburton could find strength to go through such a trial of body and of spirit. When, the Christmas fight well over, with manifest triumph on his side he went down for a couple of days to St. Neots, once more he had his reward. But the struggle was telling upon his health; it showed in his face, in his bearing. Mother and sister spoke uneasily of a change they noticed; surely he was working too hard; what did he mean by taking no summer holiday? Will laughed.

"Business, business! A good deal to do at first, you know. Things'll be smoother next year."

And the comfort, the quiet, the simple contentment of that little house by the Ouse, sent him back to Fulham Road, once more resigned, courageous.

Naturally, he sometimes contrasted his own sordid existence with the unforeseen success which had made such changes in the life of Norbert Franks. It was more than three months since he and Franks had met, when, one day early in January, he received a note from the artist. "What has become of you? I haven't had a chance of getting your way—work and social foolery. Could you come and lunch with me here, on Sunday, alone, like the old days? I have a portrait to show you." So on Sunday, Warburton went to his friend's new studio, which was in the Holland Park region. Formerly it was always he who played the host, and he did not like this change of positions; but Franks, however sensible of his good luck, and inclined at times to take himself rather seriously, had no touch of the snob in his temper; when with him, Will generally lost sight of unpleasant things in good-natured amusement. To-day, however, grocerdom lay heavily on his soul. On the return journey from St. Neots he had caught a cold, and a week of sore throat behind the counter—a week too, of quarrel with a wholesale house which had been cheating him—left his nerves in a bad state. For reply to the artist's cordial greeting he could only growl inarticulately.

"Out of sorts?" asked the other, as they entered the large well-warmed studio "You look rather bad."

"Leave me alone," muttered Warburton.

"All right. Sit down here and thaw yourself."

But Will's eye had fallen on a great canvas, showing the portrait of a brilliant lady who reclined at ease and caressed the head of a great deer-hound. He went and stood before it.

"Who's that?"

"Lady Caroline—I told you about her—don't you think it's rather good?"

"Yes. And for that very reason I'm afraid it's bad."

The artist laughed.

"That's good satire on the critics. When anything strikes them as good—by a new man, that is—they're ashamed to say so, just because they never dare trust their own judgment.—But it *is* good, Warburton; uncommonly good. If there's a weak point, it's doggy; I can't come the Landseer. Still, you can see it's meant for a doggy, eh?"

"I guessed it," replied Will, warming his hands.

"Lady Caroline is superb," went on Franks, standing before the canvas, head aside and hands in his pocket. "This is my specialty, old boy—lovely woman made yet lovelier, without loss of likeness. She'll be the fury of the next Academy.—See that something in the eyes, Warburton? Don't know how to call it. My enemies call it claptrap. But they can't do the trick, my boy, they can't do it. They'd give the end of their noses if they could."

He laughed gaily, boyishly. How well he was looking! Warburton, having glanced at him, smiled with a surly kindness.

"All your doing, you know," pursued Franks, who had caught the look and the smile. "You've made me. But for you I should have gone to the devil. I was saying so yesterday to the Crosses."

"The Crosses?"

Will had sharply turned his head, with a curious surprise.

"Don't you remember the Crosses?" said Franks, smiling with a certain embarrassment, "Rosamund's friends at Walham Green. I met them by chance not long ago, and they wanted me to go and see them. The old lady's a bore, but she can be agreeable when she likes; the girl's rather clever—does pictures for children's books, you know. She seems to be getting on better lately. But they are wretchedly poor. I was saying to them—oh, but that reminds me of something else. You haven't seen the Pomfrets lately?"

"No."

"Then you don't know that Mr. Elvan's dead?"

"No."

"He died a month ago, over there in the South of France. Rosamund has gone back to Egypt, to stay with that friend of hers at Cairo. Mrs. Pomfret hints to me that the girls will have to find a way of earning their living; Elvan has left practically nothing. I wonder whether——"

He smiled and broke off.

"Whether what?" asked the listener.

"Oh, nothing. What's the time?"

"Whether *what*?" repeated Warburton, savagely.

" Well—whether Rosamund doesn't a little regret ? "

" Do *you* ? " asked Will, without looking round.

" I ? Not for a moment, my dear boy ! She did me the greatest possible kindness—only *you* even did me a greater. At this moment I should have been cursing and smoking cheap tobacco in Battersea—unless I had got sick of it all and done the *hic jacet* business, a strong probability. Never did a girl behave more sensibly. Some day I hope to tell her so ; of course when she has married somebody else. Then I'll paint her portrait, and make her the envy of a season—by Jove, I will ! Splendid subject, she'd be. . . . When I think of that beastly so-called portrait that I put my foot through, the day I was in hell ! Queer how one develops all at a jump. Two years ago I could no more paint a woman's portrait than I could build a cathedral. I caught the trick in the Slummer, but didn't see all it meant till Blackstaffe asked me to paint Lady Rockett.—Rosamund ought to have given me the sack when she saw that daub, meant for her. Good little girl ; she held as long as she could. Oh, I'll paint her divinely, one of these days."

The soft humming of a gong summoned them to another room, where lunch was ready. Never had Warburton showed such lack of genial humour at his friend's table. He ate mechanically, and spoke hardly at all. Little by little, Franks felt the depressing effect of this companionship. When they returned to the studio, to smoke by the fireside, only a casual word broke the cheerless silence.

" I oughtn't to have come to-day," said Will, at length, half apologetically. " I feel like a bear with a sore head. I think I'm going."

"Shall I come and see you some evening?" asked the other in his friendliest tone.

"No—I mean not just yet.—I'll write and ask you."

And Will went out into the frosty gloom.

CHAPTER XXIV

BY way of Allchin, who knew all the gossip of the neighbourhood, Warburton learnt that his new competitor in trade was a man with five children and a wife given to drink ; he had been in business in another part of London, and was suspected to have removed with the hope that new surroundings might help his wife to overcome her disastrous failing. A very respectable man, people said ; kind husband, good father, honest dealer. But Allchin reported, with a twinkle of the eye, that all his capital had gone in the new start, and it was already clear that his business did not thrive.

"We shall starve him out ! " cried the assistant, snapping his thumb and finger.

"And what'll become of him then ? " asked Will.

"Oh, that's for him to think about," replied Allchin. "Wouldn't he starve us, if he could, sir ? "

And Warburton, brooding on this matter, stood appalled at the ferocity of the struggle amid which he lived, in which he had his part. Gone was all his old enjoyment of the streets of London. In looking back upon his mood of that earlier day, he saw himself as an incredibly ignorant and careless man ; marvelled at the lightness of heart which had enabled him to find amusement in rambling over this vast slaughter-strewn field of battle. Picturesque, forsooth ! Where was its picturesqueness for that struggling, soon-to-be-defeated tradesman, with his tipsy wife, and band of children who looked to him for bread? "And I myself am crushing the man—as surely as if I had my hand on his gullet and my knee on his chest! Crush him I must; otherwise, what becomes of that little home down at St. Neots—dear to me as his children are to him. There's no room for both of us; he has come too near; he must pay the penalty of his miscalculation. Is there not the workhouse for such people?" And Will went about repeating to himself. "There's the work-house—don't I pay poor-rates?—the workhouse is an admirable institution."

He lay awake many an hour of these winter nights, seeing in vision his own life and the life of man. He remembered the office in Little Ailie Street; saw himself and Godfrey Sherwood sitting together, talking, laughing, making a jest of their effort to support a doomed house. Godfrey used to repeat legends, sagas, stories of travel, as though existence had not a care, or the possibility of one; and he, in turn, talked about some bit of London he had been exploring, showed an old map he had picked up, an old volume of London topography. The while, world-wide forces, the hunger-struggle of nations, were shaking the roof above their heads. Theoretically they knew it. But they could escape in time; they had a cosy little corner preserved for themselves, safe from these pestilent worries. Fate has a grudge against the foolishly secure. If he laughed now, it was in self-mockery.

The night of London, always rife with mysterious sounds, spoke dreadfully to his straining ear. He heard voices near and far, cries of pain or of misery, shouts savage or bestial; over and through all, that low, far-off rumble or roar, which never for a moment ceases, the groan, as it seemed, of suffering multitudes. There tripped before his dreaming eyes a procession from the world of wealth and pleasure, and the amazement with which he viewed it changed of a sudden to fiery wrath; he tossed upon the bed, uttered his rage in a loud exclamation, felt his heart pierced with misery which brought him all but to tears. Close upon astonishment and indignation followed dread. Given health and strength, he might perhaps continue to hold his own in this merciless conflict; perhaps, only; but what if some accident, such as befalls this man or that in every moment of time, threw him among the weaklings? He saw his mother, in her age and ill-health, reduced to the pittance of the poorest; his sister going forth to earn her living; himself, a helpless burden upon both.—Nay, was there not rat-poison to be purchased?

How—he cried within himself—how, in the name of sense and mercy, is mankind content to live on in such a world as this? By what devil are they hunted, that, not only do they neglect the means of solace suggested to every humane and rational mind, but, the vast majority of them spend all their strength and ingenuity in embittering the common lot? Overwhelmed by the hateful unreason of it all, he felt as though his brain reeled on the verge of madness.

Every day, and all the day long, the shop, the counter. Had he chosen, he might have taken a half-holiday, now and then; on certain days Allchin was quite able, and abundantly willing, to manage alone; but what was the use? To go to a distance was merely to see with more distinctness the squalor of his position. Never for a moment was he tempted to abandon this work; he saw no hope whatever of earning money in any other way, and money he must needs earn, as long as he lived. But the life weighed upon him with a burden such as he had never imagined. Never had he understood before what was meant by the sickening weariness of routine; his fretfulness as a youth in the West Indies seemed to him now inconceivable. His own master? Why, he was the slave of every kitchen wench who came into the shop to spend a penny; he trembled at the thought of failing to please her, and so losing her custom. The grocery odours, once pleasant to him, had grown nauseating. And the ever repeated tasks, the weighing, parcel making, string cutting; the parrot phrases a thousand times repeated; the idiot bowing and smiling—how these things gnawed at his nerves, till he quivered like a beaten horse. He tried to console himself by thinking that things were now at the worst; that he was subduing himself, and would soon reach a happy, dull indifference; but in truth it was with fear that he looked forward—fear of unknown possibilities in himself; fear that he might sink yet more wretchedly in his own esteem.

For the worst part of his suffering was self-scorn. When he embarked upon this strange enterprise, he knew, or thought he knew, all the trials to which he would be exposed, and not slight would have been his indignation had any one ventured to hint that his character might prove unequal to the test. Sherwood's letter had pleased him so much, precisely because it praised his resolve as courageous, manly. On manliness of spirit, Will had always piqued himself; it was his pride that he carried a heart equal to any lot imposed upon him by duty. Yet little more than a twelvemonth of shopkeeping had so undermined his pluck, enfeebled his temper, that he could not regard himself in the glass without shame. He tried to explain it by failure of health. Assuredly his physical state had for months been declining and the bad cold from which he had recently suffered seemed to complete his moral downfall. In this piercing and gloom-wrapped month of February, coward thoughts continually beset him. In his cold lodgings, in the cold streets, in the draughts of the shop, he felt soul and body shrink together, till he became as the meanest of starveling hucksters.

Then something happened, which rescued him for awhile from this haunting self. One night, just at closing time—a night of wild wind and driven rain—Mrs. Hopper came rushing into the shop, her face a tale of woe. Warburton learnt that her sister "Liza," the ailing girl whom he had befriended in his comfortable days, had been seized with lung hemorrhage, and lay in a lamentable state; the help of Mrs. Allchin was called for, and any other that might be forthcoming. Two years ago Will would have responded to such an appeal as this with lavish generosity; now, though the impulse of compassion blinded him for a moment to his changed circumstances, he soom remembered that his charity must be that of a poor man, of a debtor. He paid for a cab, that the two women might speed to their sister through the stormy night as quickly as possible, and he promised to think of what could be done for the invalid—with the result that he lost a night's sleep in calculating what sum he might spare. On the morrow came the news he had expected; the doctor suggested Brompton Hospital, if admission could be obtained; home treatment at this time of the year, and in the patient's circumstances, was not likely to be of any good. Warburton took the matter in hand, went about making inquiries, found that there must necessarily be delay. Right or wrong, he put his hand in his pocket, and Mrs. Hopper was enabled to nurse her sister in a way otherwise impossible. He visited the sick-room, and for half an hour managed to talk as of old, in the note of gallant sympathy and encouragement. Let there be no stint of fire, of food, of anything the doctor might advise. Meanwhile, he would ask about other hospitals—do everything in his power. As indeed he did, with the result that in a fortnight's time, the sufferer was admitted to an institution to which, for the nonce, Warburton had become a subscriber.

He saw her doctor. "Not much chance, I'm afraid. Of course, if she were able to change climate—that kind of thing. But, under the circumstances——"

And through a whole Sunday morning Will paced about his little sitting-room, not caring to go forth, nor caring to read, caring for nothing at all in a world so full of needless misery. "Of course, if she were able to change climate—" Yes, the accident of possessing money; a life to depend upon that! In another station—though, as likely as not, with no moral superiority to justify the privilege—the sick woman would be guarded, soothed, fortified by every expedient of science, every resource of humanity. Chance to be poor, and not only must you die when you need not, but must die with the minimum of comfort, the extreme of bodily and mental distress. This commonplace struck so forcibly upon Will's imagination, that it was as a new discovery to him. He stood amazed, bewildered—as men of any thinking power are wont to do when experience makes real to them the truisms of life. A few coins, or pieces of printed paper to signify all that! An explosion of angry laughter broke the mood.

Pacing, pacing, back and fro in the little room, for hour after hour, till his head whirled, and his legs ached. Out of doors there was fitfully glinting sunshine upon the wet roofs; a pale blue now and then revealed amid the grey rack. Two years ago he would have walked twenty miles on a day like this, with eyes for nothing but the beauty and joy of earth. Was he not—he suddenly asked himself—a wiser man now than then? Did he not see into the truth of things; whereas, formerly, he had seen only the deceptive surface? There should be some solace in this reflection, if he took it well to heart.

Then his mind wandered away to Norbert Franks, who at this moment was somewhere enjoying himself. This afternoon he might be calling upon the Crosses. Why should that thought be disagreeable? It was, as he perceived, not for the first time. If he pictured the artist chatting side by side with Bertha Cross, something turned cold within him. By the bye, it was rather a long time since he had seen Miss Cross; her mother had been doing the shopping lately. She might come, perhaps, one day this week; the chance gave him something to look forward to.

How often had he called himself a fool for paying heed to Bertha Cross's visits?

CHAPTER XXV

AGAIN came springtime, and, as he stood behind the counter, Warburton thought of all that was going on in the world he had forsaken. Amusements for which he had never much cared haunted his fancy; feeling himself shut out from the life of grace and intellect, he suffered a sense of dishonour, as though his position resulted from some personal baseness, some crime. He numbered the acquaintances he had dropped, and pictured them as mentioning his name—if ever they did so—with cold disapproval. Godfrey Sherwood had ceased to write; it was six months since his last letter, in which he hinted a fear that the Irish enterprise would have to be abandoned for lack of capital. Even Franks, good fellow as he was, seemed to grow lukewarm in friendship. The painter had an appointment for a Sunday in May at Will's lodgings, to smoke and talk, but on the evening before he sent a telegram excusing himself. Vexed, humiliated, Warburton wasted the Sunday morning, and only after his midday meal yielded to the temptation of a brilliant sky, which called him forth. Walking westward, with little heed to distance or direction, he presently found himself at Kew; on the bridge he lingered awhile, idly gazing at boats, and, as he thus leaned over the parapet, the sound of a voice behind him fell startlingly upon his ear. He turned, just in time to catch a glimpse of the features which that voice had brought before his mind's eye, Bertha Cross was passing, with her mother. Probably they had not seen him. And even if they had, if they had recognised him—did he flatter himself that the Crosses would give any sign in public of knowing their grocer?

With his eyes on the graceful figure of Bertha, he slowly followed. The ladies were crossing Kew Green; doubtless they would enter the Gardens to spend the afternoon there. Would it not be pleasant to join them, to walk by Bertha's side, to talk freely with her, forgetting the counter, which always restrained their conversation? Bertha was nicely dressed, though one saw that her clothes cost nothing. In the old days, if he had noticed her at all she would have seemed to him rather a pretty girl of the lower middle class, perhaps a little less insignificant than her like; now she shone for him against a background of "customers," the one in whom he saw a human being of his own kind, and who, within the imposed limits, had given proof of admitting his humanity. He saw her turn to look at her mother, and smile; a smile of infinite kindness and good-humour. Involuntarily his own lips responded; he walked on smiling—smiling.

They passed through the gates; he, at a distance of a dozen yards, still followed. There was no risk of detection; indeed he was doing no harm; even a grocer might observe, from afar off, a girl walking with her mother. But, after strolling for a quarter of an hour, they paused beside a bench, and there seated themselves. Mrs. Cross seemed to be complaining of something; Bertha seemed to soothe her. When he was near enough to be aware of this Will saw that he was too near. He turned abruptly on his heels, and—stood face to face with Norbert Franks.

"Hallo!" exclaimed the painter, with an air of embarrassment. "I thought that was your back!"

"Your engagement was here?" asked Will bluntly, referring to the other's telegram of excuse.

"Yes. I was obliged to——"

He broke off, his eyes fixed on the figures of Bertha and her mother.

"You were obliged——?"

"You see the ladies there," said Franks in a lower voice, "there, on the seat? It's Mrs. Cross and her daughter—you remember the Crosses? I called to see them yesterday, and only Mrs. Cross was at home, and—the fact is, I as good as promised to meet them here, if it was fine."

"Very well," replied Warburton carelessly, "I won't keep you."

"Go, but——"

Franks was in great confusion. He looked this way and that, as if seeking for an escape. As Will began to move away, he kept at his side.

"Look here, Warburton, let me introduce you to them. They're very nice people; I'm sure you'd like them; do let me——"

"Thank you, no. I don't want any new acquaintances."

"Why? Come along old man," urged the other. "You're getting too grumpy; you live too much alone. Just to please me——"

"No!" answered Will, resolutely, walking on.

"Very well—just as you like. But, I say, should I find you at home this evening? Say, nine o'clock. I particularly want to have a talk."

"Good. I'll be there," replied Will, and so, with knitted brows strode away.

Very punctually did the visitor arrive that evening. He entered the room with that same look of embarrassment which he had worn during the brief colloquy at Kew; he shook hands awkwardly, and, as he seated himself, talked about the fall of temperature since sunset, which made a fire agreeable. Warburton, ashamed of the sullenness he could not overcome, rolled this way and that in his chair, holding the poker and making lunges with it at a piece of coal which would not break.

"That was a lucky chance," began Franks at length, "our meeting this afternoon."

"Lucky? Why?"

"Because it has given me the courage to speak to you about something. Queerest chance I ever knew that you should be there close by the Crosses."

"Did they ask who I was?" inquired Warburton after a violent lunge with the poker, which sent pieces of coal flying into the room.

"They didn't happen to see me whilst I was talking with you. But, in any case," added Franks, "they wouldn't have asked. They're well-bred people, you know—really ladies. I suspect you've had a different idea of them. Wasn't that why you wouldn't let me introduce you?"

"Not at all," answered Will, with a forced laugh. "I've no doubt of their ladyhood."

"The fact of the matter is," continued the other, crossing and uncrossing, and re-crossing his legs in nervous restlessness, "that I've been seeing them now and then since I told you I was going to call there. You guess why? It isn't Mrs. Cross, depend upon it."

"Mrs. Cross's tea, perhaps?" said Will, with a hard grin.

"Not exactly. It's the worst tea I ever tasted. I must advise her to change her grocer."

Warburton exploded in a roar of laughter, and cried, as Franks stared wonderingly at him:

"You'll never make a better joke in your life than that."

"Shows what I can do when I try," answered the artist. "However, the tea *is* shockingly bad."

"What can you expect for one and sevenpence halfpenny per pound?" cried Will.

"How do *you* know what she pays?"

Warburton's answer was another peal of merriment.

"Well, I shouldn't wonder," Franks went on. "The fact is, you know, they're very poor. It's a miserable sort of a life for a girl like Bertha Cross. She's clever, in her way; did you ever see any of her work? Children's book-illustrating? It's more than passable, I assure you. But of course she's wretchedly paid. Apart from that, a really nice girl."

"So this is what you had to tell me?" said Warburton, in a subdued voice, when the speaker hesitated.

"I wanted to talk about it, old man, that's the truth."

Franks accompanied these words with a shy smiling look of such friendly appeal that Will felt his hard and surly humour begin to soften, and something of the old geniality stirring under the dull weight that had so long oppressed him.

"I suppose it's settled," he asked, staring at the fire.

"Settled? How?"

"When it comes to meetings at Kew Gardens—"

"Oh don't misunderstand," exclaimed Franks nervously, "I told you that it was with the mother I made the appointment—not with Bertha herself. I'm quite sure Bertha never heard a word of it."

"Well, it comes to the same thing."

"Not at all! I half wish it did."

"Half?" asked Warburton, with a quick glance.

"Can't you see that I haven't really made up my mind," said Franks, fidgeting in his chair. "I'm not sure of myself—and I'm still less sure of her. It's all in the air. I've been there perhaps half a dozen times—but only like any other acquaintance. And, you know, she isn't the kind of girl to meet one half way. I'm sorry you don't know her. You'd be able to understand better.—Then, you see, there's something a little awkward in her position and mine. She's the intimate friend of—of the other one, you know; at least, I suppose she still is; of course we haven't said anything about that. It makes misunderstandings very possible. Suppose she thought I made friends with her in the hope of getting round to the other again? You see how difficult it is to judge her behaviour—to come to any conclusion."

"Yes, I see," Warburton let fall, musingly.

"And, even if I were sure of understanding *her*—there's myself. Look at the position, now. I suppose I may call myself a successful man; well on the way to success, at all events. Unless fortune plays me a dirty trick, I ought soon to be making my three or four thousand a year; and there's the possibility of double that. Think what that means, in the way of opportunity. Once or twice. when I was going to see the Crosses, I've pulled myself up and asked what the deuce I was doing—but I went all the same. The truth is, there's something about Bertha—I wish you knew her, Warburton; I really wish you did. She's the kind of girl any man might marry. Nothing brilliant about her —but—well, I can't describe it. As different as could be from—the other. In fact, it isn't easy to see how they became such close friends. Of course, she knows all about me—what I'm doing, and so on. In the case of an ordinary girl in her position, it would be irresistible; but I'm not at all sure that *she* looks at it in that way. She behaves to one—well, in the most natural way possible. Now and then I rather think she makes fun of me."

Warburton allowed a low chuckle to escape him.

"Why do you laugh?—I don't mean that she does it disagreeably. It's her way to look at things on the humorous side—and I rather like that. Don't you think it a good sign in a girl?"

"That depends," muttered Will.

"Well, that's how things are. I wanted to tell you. There's nobody else I should think of talking to about it."

Silence hung between them for a minute or two.

"You'll have to make up your mind pretty soon, I suppose," said Warburton at length, in a not unpleasant voice.

"That's the worst of it. I don't want to be in a hurry—it's just what I don't want."

"Doesn't it occur to you," asked Will, as if a sudden idea had struck him, "that perhaps she's no more in a hurry than you are?"

"It's possible. I shouldn't wonder. But if I seem to be playing the fool——?"

"That depends on yourself.—But," Will added,

with a twinkle in his eye, " there's just one piece of advice I should like to offer you."

" Let me have it," replied the other eagerly. " Very good of you, old man, not to be bored."

" Don't," said Warburton, in an impressive undertone, " don't persuade Mrs. Cross to change her grocer."

CHAPTER XXVI

THIS conversation brought Warburton a short relief. Laughter, even though it come from the throat rather than the midriff, tends to dispel morbid humours, and when he woke next morning, after unusually sound sleep, Will had a pleasure in the sunlight such as he had not known for a long time. He thought of Norbert Franks, and chuckled; of Bertha Cross, and smiled. For a day or two the toil of the shop was less irksome. Then came sordid troubles which again overcast the sky. Acting against his trusty henchman's advice, Will had made a considerable purchase of goods from a bankrupt stock; and what seemed to be a great bargain was beginning to prove a serious loss. Customers grumbled about the quality of articles supplied to them out of this unlucky venture, and among the dissatisfied was Mrs. Cross, who came and talked for twenty minutes about some tapioca that had been sent to her, obliging Mr. Jollyman to make repeated apologies and promises that such a thing should never occur again. When the querulous-voiced lady at length withdrew, Will was boiling over with rage.

"Idiot!" he exclaimed, regardless of the fact that Allchin overheard him.

"You see, sir," remarked the assistant. "It's just as I said; but I couldn't persuade you."

Will held his lips tight and stared before him.

"There'll be a net loss of ten pounds on that

transaction," pursued Allchin. "It's a principle of honest business, never buy a bankrupt stock. But you wouldn't listen to me, sir——"

"That'll do, Allchin, that'll do!" broke in the master, quivering with the restraint he imposed upon himself. "Can't you see I'm not in a mood for that sort of thing?"

This same day, there was a leakage of gas on the premises, due to bad workmanship in some new fittings which had cost Will more than he liked. Then the shop awning gave way, and fell upon the head of a passer-by, who came into the shop swearing at large and demanding compensation for his damaged hat. Sundry other things went wrong in the course of the week, and by closing-time on Saturday night Warburton's nerves were in a state of tension which threatened catastrophe. He went to bed at one o'clock; at six in the morning, not having closed his eyes for a moment, he tumbled out again, dressed with fury, and rushed out of the house.

It was a morning of sunny showers; one moment the stones were covered with shining moisture, and the next were steaming themselves dry under unclouded rays. Heedless whither he went, so he did but move quickly enough, Will crossed the river, and struck southward, till he found himself by Clapham Junction. The sun had now triumphed; the day would be brilliant. Feeling already better for his exercise, he stood awhile reflecting, and decided at length to go by rail into the country. He might perhaps call on the Pomfrets at Ashtead; that would depend upon his mood. At all events he would journey in that direction.

It was some three months since he had seen the Pomfrets. He had a standing invitation to the pleasant little house, where he was always received with simple, cordial hospitality. About eleven o'clock, after a ramble about Ashtead Common, he pushed open the garden wicket, and knocked at the door under the leafy porch. So quiet was the house, that he half feared he would find nobody at home; but the servant at once led him in, and announced him at the door of her master's sanctum.

"Warburton?" cried a high, hearty voice, before he had entered. "Good fellow. Every day this week I've been wanting to ask you to come; but I was afraid; it's so long since we saw you, I fancied you must have been bored the last time you were here."

A small, thin, dry-featured man, with bald occiput and grizzled beard, Ralph Pomfret sat deep in an easy chair, his legs resting on another. Humour and kindliness twinkled in his grey eye. The room, which was full of books, had a fair view of meadows, and hill. Garden perfumes floated in at the open window.

"Kind fellow, to come like this," he went on. "You see that the old enemy has a grip on me. He pinches, he pinches. He'll get at my vitals one of these days, no doubt. And I've not even the satisfaction of having got my gout in an honourable way. If it had come to me from a fine old three-bottle ancestor! But I, who never had a grandfather, and hardly tasted wine till I was thirty years old—why, I feel ashamed to call myself gouty. Sit down, my wife's at church. Strange thing that people still go to church—but they do, you know. Force of habit, force of habit. Rosamund's with her."

"Miss Elvan?" asked Warburton, with surprise.

"Ah, yes; I forgot you didn't know she was here. Came back with those friends of hers from Egypt a week ago. She has no home in England now; don't know where she will decide to live."

"Have you seen Norbert lately?" continued Mr. Pomfret, all in one breath. "He's too busy to come out to Ashtead, perhaps too prosperous. But no, I won't say that; I won't really think it. A good lad, Norbert—better, I suspect, than his work. There's a strange thing now; a painter without enthusiasm for art. He used to have a little; more than a little; but it's all gone. Or so it seems to me."

"He's very honest about it," said Warburton. "Makes no pretences—calls his painting a trick, and really feels surprised, I'm sure, that he's so successful."

"Poor Norbert! A good lad, a good lad. I wonder—do you think if I wrote a line, mentioning, by the way, that Rosamund's here, do you think he'd come?"

The speaker accompanied his words with an intimate glance. Will averted his eyes, and gazed for a moment at the sunny landscape.

"How long will Miss Elvan stay?" he asked.

"Oh, as long as she likes. We are very glad to have her."

Their looks met for an instant.

"A pity, a pity!" said Ralph, shaking his head and smiling. "Don't *you* think so?"

"Why, yes. I've always thought so."

Will knew that this was not strictly the truth. But in this moment he refused to see anything but the dimly suggested possibility that Franks might meet again with Rosamund Elvan, and again succumb to her charm.

"Heaven forbid!" resumed Ralph, "that one should interfere where lives are at stake! Nothing of that, nothing of that. You are as little disposed for it as I am. But simply to acquaint him with the fact——?"

"I see no harm. If I met him——?"

"Ah! To be sure. It would be natural to say——"

"I owe him a visit," remarked Will.

They talked of other things. All at once Warburton had become aware that he was hungry; he had not broken his fast to-day. Happily, the clock on the mantelpiece pointed towards noon. And at this moment there sounded voices within the house, followed by a tap at the study door which opened, admitting Mrs. Pomfret. The lady advanced with hospitable greeting; homely of look and speech, she had caught her husband's smile, and something of his manner —testimony to the happiness of a long wedded life. Behind her came the figure of youth and grace which Warburton's eyes expected; very little changed since he last saw it, in the Valley of Trient, Warburton was conscious of an impression that the young lady saw him again with pleasure. In a minute or two, Mrs. Pomfret and her niece had left the room, but Warburton still saw those pure, pale features, the emotional eyes and lips, the slight droop of the head to one side. Far indeed—so he said within himself—from his ideal; but, he easily understood, strong in seductiveness for such a man as Franks, whom the old passion had evidently left lukewarm in his thought of other women.

The bell gave a welcome summons to lunch—or dinner, as it was called in this household of simple traditions. Helped by his friend's arm, Ralph managed to hobble to table; he ate little, and talked throughout the meal in his wonted vein of cheerful reflection. Will enjoyed everything that was set before him; the good, wholesome food, which did credit to Mrs. Pomfret's housekeeping, had a rare savour after months of dining in the little parlour behind his shop, varied only by Mrs. Wick's cooking on Sundays. One thing, however, interfered with his ease; seated opposite to Rosamund Elvan, he called to mind the fact that his toilet this morning had been of the most summary description; he was unshaven, and his clothing was precisely what he had worn all yesterday at the counter. The girl's eyes passed observantly over him now and then; she was critical of appearances, no doubt. That his aspect and demeanour might be in keeping, he bore himself somewhat bluffly, threw out brief, blunt phrases, and met Miss Elvan's glance with a confident smile. No resentment of this behaviour appeared in her look or speech; as the meal went on, she talked more freely, and something of frank curiosity began to reveal itself in her countenance as she listened to him.

Ralph Pomfret having hobbled back to his study chair, to doze, if might be, for an hour or two, the others presently strolled out into the garden, where rustic chairs awaited them on the shadowy side.

"You have your pipe, I hope?" said the hostess, as Warburton stretched himself out with a sigh of content.

"I have."

"And matches?"

"Yes—No! The box is empty."

"I'll send you some. I have one or two things to see to indoors."

So Will and Rosamund sat alone, gazing idly

at the summer sky, hearing the twitter of a bird, the hum of insects, whilst the scents of flower and leaf lulled them to a restful intimacy. Without a word of ceremony, Will used the matches that were brought him, and puffed a cloud into the warm air. They were talking of the beauties of this neighbourhood, of the delightful position of the house.

"You often come out to see my uncle, I suppose," said Rosamund.

"Not often, I'm seldom free, and not always in the humour."

"Not in the humour for *this* ?"

"It sounds strange, doesn't it ?" said Will, meeting her eyes. "When I'm here, I want to be here always; winter or summer, there's nothing more enjoyable—in the way of enjoyment that does only good. Do you regret Egypt ?"

"No, indeed. I shall never care to go there again."

"Or the Pyrenees ?"

"Have you seen them yet ?" asked Rosamund.

Will shook his head.

"I remember your saying," she remarked, "you would go for your next holiday to the Basque country."

"Did I ? Yes—when you had been talking much about it. But since then I've had no holiday."

"No holiday—all this time ?"

Rosamund's brows betrayed her sympathy.

"How long is it since we were together in Switzerland ?" asked Will, dreamily, between puffs. "This is the second summer, isn't it ? One loses count of time, there in London. I was saying to Franks the other day——"

He stopped, but not abruptly; the words seemed to murmur away as his thoughts wandered. Rosamund's eyes were for a moment cast down. But for a moment only; then she fixed them upon him in a steady, untroubled gaze.

"You were saying to Mr. Franks——?"

The quiet sincerity of her voice drew Warburton's look. She was sitting straight in the cane chair, her hands upon her lap, with an air of pleasant interest.

"I was saying—oh, I forget—it's gone."

"Do you often see him?" Rosamund inquired in the same calmly interested tone.

"Now and then. He's a busy man, with a great many friends—like most men who succeed."

"But you don't mean, I hope, that he cares less for his friends of the old time, before he succeeded?"

"Not at all," exclaimed Will, rolling upon his chair, and gazing at the distance. "He's the same as ever. It's my fault that we don't meet oftener. I was always a good deal of a solitary, you know, and my temper hasn't been improved by ill-luck."

"Ill-luck?"

Again there was sympathy in Rosamund's knitted brow; her voice touched a note of melodious surprise and pain.

"That's neither here nor there. We were talking of Franks. If anything, he's improved, I should say. I can't imagine any one bearing success better—just the same bright, good-natured, sincere fellow. Of course, he enjoys his good fortune—he's been through hard times."

"Which would have been harder still, but for a friend of his," said Rosamund, with eyes thoughtfully drooped.

Warburton watched her as she spoke. Her look and her voice carried him back to the Valley of Trient; he heard the foaming torrent; saw the dark fir-woods, felt a cool breath from the glacier. Thus had Rosamund been wont to talk; then, as now, touching his elementary emotions, but moving his reflective self to a smile.

"Have you seen Miss Cross since you came back?" he asked, as if casually.

"Oh, yes. If I stay in England, I hope to live somewhere near her. Perhaps I shall take rooms in London, and work at water-colours and black-and-white. Unless I go to the Basque country, where my sister is. Don't you think, Mr. Warbuton, one might make a lot of drawings in the Pyrenees, and then have an exhibition of them in London? I have to earn my living, and I must do something of that kind."

Whilst Will was shaping his answer Mrs. Pomfret came toward them from the house, and the current of the conversation was turned. Presently Ralph summoned his guest to the book-room, where they talked till the kindly hour of tea. But before setting out for his homeward journey, Warburton had another opportunity of exchanging words with Miss Elvan in the garden.

"Well, I shall hear what you decide to do," he said, bluffly. "If you go to the Pyrenees—but I don't think you will."

"No, perhaps not. London rather tempts me," was the girl's dreamy reply.

"I'm glad to hear it."

"I must get Bertha's advice—Miss Cross'."

Will nodded. He was about to say something, but altered his mind; and so the colloquy ended.

CHAPTER XXVII

TOWARD ten o'clock that evening, Warburton alighted from a train at Notting Hill Gate, and walked through heavy rain to the abode of Norbert Franks. With satisfaction, he saw the light at the great window of his studio, and learnt from the servant who admitted him that Franks had no company. His friend received him with surprise, so long was it since Warburton had looked in unexpectedly.

"Nothing amiss?" said Franks, examining the hard-set face, with its heavy eyes, and cheeks sunken.

"All right. Came to ask for news, that's all."

"News? Ah, I understand. There's no news."

"Still reflecting?"

"Yes. Keeping away, just to see how I like it. Sensible that, don't you think?"

Warburton nodded. The conversation did not promise much vivacity, for Franks looked tired, and the visitor seemed much occupied with his own thoughts. After a few words about a canvas which stood on the easel—another woman the artist was boldly transforming into loveliness—Will remarked carelessly that he had spent the day at Ashtead.

"By Jove, I ought to go and see those people," said Franks.

"Better wait a little, perhaps," returned the

other with a smile. "Miss Elvan is with them."

"Ah! Lucky you told me—not that it matters much," added Franks, after a moment's reflection, "at all events as far as I'm concerned. But it might be a little awkward for her. How long is she staying?"

Will told all he knew of Miss Elvan's projects. He went on to say that she seemed to him more thoughtful, more serious, than in the old time; to be sure, she had but recently lost her father, and the subduing influence of that event might have done her good.

"You had a lot of talk?" said Franks.

"Oh, we gossiped in the garden. Poor old Pomfret has his gout, and couldn't come out with us. What do you think, by the bye, of her chance of living by art? She says she'll have to."

"By that, or something else, no doubt," Franks replied disinterestedly. "I know her father had nothing to leave, nothing to make an income."

"Are her water-colours worth anything?"

"Not much, I'm afraid, I can't quite see her living by anything of that sort. She's the amateur, pure and simple. Now, Bertha Cross—there's the kind of girl who does work and gets paid for it. In her modest line, Bertha is a real artist. I do wish you knew her, Warburton."

"So you have said a good many times," remarked Will. "But I don't see how it would help you. I know Miss Elvan, and——"

He paused, as if musing on a thought.

"And what?" asked Franks impatiently.

"Nothing—except that I like her better than I used to."

As he spoke, he stood up.

"Well, I can't stay. It's raining like the devil

I wanted to know whether you'd done anything decisive, that's all."

"I'll let you know when I do," answered Franks, suppressing a yawn. "Good-night, old man."

For a fortnight, Warburton led his wonted life, shut off as usual from the outer world. About this time, Allchin began to observe with anxiety the change in his master's aspect and general behaviour.

"I'm afraid you're not feeling quite yourself, sir," he said at closing time one night. "I've noticed lately you don't seem quite well."

"Have you? Well, perhaps you are right. But it doesn't matter."

"If you'll excuse *me*, sir," returned the assistant, "I'm afraid it does matter. I hope, sir, you won't think I speak disrespectful, but I've been noticing that you didn't seem to care about waiting on customers lately."

"You've noticed that?"

"I have, sir, if the truth must be told. And I kept saying to myself as it wasn't like you. What I'm afraid of, sir, if you don't mind me saying it, is that the customers themselves are beginning to notice it. Mrs. Gilpin said to me yesterday—'What's come to Mr. Jollyman?' she says. 'He hasn't a civil word for me!' she says. Of course, I made out as you'd been suffering from a bad 'eadache, and I shouldn't wonder if that's the truth, sir."

Warburton set his teeth and said nothing.

"You wouldn't like to take just a little 'oliday, sir?" returned Allchin. "This next week, I could manage well enough. It might do you good, sir, to have a mouthful of sea air—"

"I'll think about it," broke in the other abruptly.

He was going away without another word, but, in crossing the shop, he caught his henchman's eye fixed on him with a troublous gaze. Self-reproach checked his steps.

"You're quite right, Allchin," he said in a confidential tone. "I'm not quite up to the mark, and perhaps I should do well to take a holiday. Thank you for speaking about it."

He walked home, and there, on his table, he found a letter from Franks, which he eagerly tore open. "I have as good as decided," wrote the artist. "Yesterday, I went to Ashtead, and saw R. We met like old friends—just as I wished. Talked as naturally as you and I. I suspect—only suspect of course—that she knows of my visits to Walham Green, and smiles at them! Yes, as you say, I think she has improved—decidedly. The upshot of it all is that I shall call on the Crosses again, and, when an opportunity offers, try my chance. I think I am acting sensibly, don't you?"

After reading this, Will paced about his room for an hour or two. Then he flung himself into bed, but got no sleep until past dawn. Rising at the usual hour, he told himself that this would not do; to live on in this way was mere moral suicide; he resolved to run down to St. Neots, whence, if his mother were capable of the journey, she and Jane might go for a week or two to the seaside. So, having packed his travelling bag, he walked to the shop, and arranged with Allchin for a week's absence, greatly to the assistant's satisfaction. Before noon he was at The Haws. But the idea of a family expedition to the seaside could not be carried out: Mrs. Warburton was not strong enough to leave home, and Jane had just invited a friend to come and spend a week with them. Disguising as best he could his miserable state of mind and body, Will stayed for a couple of days. The necessity for detailed lying about his affairs in London—lying which would long ago have been detected, but for the absolute confidence of his mother and sister, and the retired habits of their life—added another cause of unrest to those already tormenting him, and he was glad to escape into solitude. Though with little faith in the remedy, he betook himself to a quiet spot on the coast of Norfolk, associated with memories of holiday in childhood, and there for the rest of the time he had allowed himself did what a man could do to get benefit from sea and sky.

And in these endless hours of solitude there grew upon him a perception of the veritable cause of his illness. Not loss of station, not overwork, not love; but simply the lie to which he was committed. There was the root of the matter. Slowly, dimly, he groped toward the fact that what rendered his life intolerable was its radical dishonesty. Lived openly, avowedly, it would have involved hardships indeed, but nothing of this dull wretchedness which made the world a desert. He began to see how much better, how much easier, it would have been to tell the truth two years ago. His mother was not so weak-minded a woman as to be stricken down by loss of money; and as for Sherwood, his folly merited more than the unpleasantness that might have resulted to him from disclosure. Grocerdom with a clear conscience would have been a totally different thing from grocerdom surreptitiously embraced. Instead of slinking into a corner for the performance of an honourable act, he should have declared it, frankly, unaffectedly, to all who had any claim upon him. At once, the enterprise became amusing, interesting. If it disgraced him with any of his acquaintances, so much the worse for them; all whose friendship was worth having would have shown only the more his friends; as things stood, he was ashamed, degraded, not by circumstances, but by himself.

To undo it all—? To proclaim the truth—? Was it not easy enough? He had proved now that his business would yield income sufficient for his mother and sister, as well as for his own needs; the crisis was surmounted; why not cast off this load of mean falsehood, which was crushing him to the ground? By Heaven! he would do so.

Not immediately. Better wait till he had heard from Jane that their mother was a little stronger, which would probably be the case in a week or two. But (he declared in his mind) the resolve was taken. At the first favourable moment he would undo his folly. Before taking this step, he must of course announce it to Godfrey Sherwood; an unpleasant necessity; but no matter.

He walked about the beach in a piping wind, waved his arms, talked to himself, now and then raised a great shout. And that night he slept soundly.

CHAPTER XXVIII

HE got back to Fulham Road in time for the press of Saturday night. Allchin declared that he looked much better, and customers were once more gratified by Mr. Jollyman's studious civility. On Sunday morning he wrote a long letter to Sherwood, which, for lack of other address, he sent to the care of Godfrey's relative in Wales. This was something done. In the afternoon he took a long walk, which led him through the Holland Park region. He called to see Franks, but the artist was not at home ; so he left a card asking for news. And the next day brought Franks' telegraphic reply. "Nothing definite yet. Shall come to see you late one of these evenings. I have not been to Walham Green." Though he had all but persuaded himself that he cared not at all, one way or the other, this message did Warburton good. Midway in the week, business being slack, he granted himself a half holiday, and went to Ashtead, merely in friendliness to Ralph Pomfret—so he said to himself.

From Ashtead station to the Pomfrets' house was a good twenty minutes' walk. As he strode along, eyes upon the ground, Will all at once saw the path darkened by a shadow ; he then became conscious of a female figure just in front of him, and heedlessly glancing at the face, was arrested by a familiar smile.

"You were coming to see us?" asked Miss Elvan, offering her hand. "What a pity that I have to go to town! Only just time to catch the train."

"Then I'll walk back to the station with you—may I?"

"I shall be delighted, if you don't mind the trouble. I have an appointment with Miss Cross. She has found rooms which she thinks will suit me, and we're going to look at them together."

"So you have decided for London?"

"I think so. The rooms are at Chelsea, in Oakley Crescent. I know how fond you are of London, and how well you know it. And I know so little; only a street or two here and there. I mean to remedy my ignorance. If ever you have an afternoon to spare, Mr. Warburton, I should be so glad if you would let me go with you to see interesting places."

For an instant, Will was surprised, confused, but Rosamund's entire simplicity and directness of manner rebuked this sensation. He replied in a corresponding tone that nothing would please him more. They were now at the railway station, and the train approached. Rosamund having sprung into a carriage, gave her hand through the window, saying:

"I may be settled in a day or two. You will hear——"

With the sentence unfinished, she drew back, and the train rolled away. For a minute or two, Warburton stood on the platform, his lips mechanically prolonging the smile which had answered Miss Elvan's, and his thoughts echoing her last words. When he turned, he at first walked slowly; then his pace quickened, and he arrived at the Pomfrets' house, as though on urgent business.

In the garden he caught sight of Ralph, recovered from his attack of gout, sitting at his ease, pipe in mouth. Will told of his meeting with Miss Elvan.

"Yes, yes; she's off to London town—wants to live there, like all the rest of the young people. In thirty years' time she'll have had enough of it, and be glad to creep into a quiet corner like this. My wife's in the house, teaching our new maid to make tea-cakes—you shall have some at five o'clock. I wonder whether any girl could be found nowadays who knows how to make tea-cakes? There's Rosamund—she knows no more about that kind of thing than of ship-building. Do you know any young lady who could make a toothsome tea-cake?"

"I'm not quite sure," answered Will reflectively, "but I have one in mind who perhaps does—it wouldn't surprise me."

"That's to your credit. By the bye, you know that Norbert has been here."

"Yes, I heard of it. He wrote to tell me."

"Aye, but he's been twice—did you know that? He was here yesterday."

"Indeed?"

Ralph looked at the other with an odd smile.

"One might have expected a little awkwardness between them," he continued. "Not a bit of it. There again—your girl of to-day; she has a way of her own with all this kind of thing. Why they just shook hands as if they'd never been anything but pleasant friends. All the same, as I tell you, Norbert has been a second time."

"I'm glad to hear it," said Warburton.

Will had purposed getting back to the shop about seven o'clock. He was, indeed, back in London at that hour, but his state of mind tempted him to shirk squalid duty; instead of turning toward Fulham Road, he took his way into the Strand, and there loitered in the evening sunshine, self-reproachful, yet enjoying the unwonted liberty. It was dinner-time ; restaurants exhaled their pungent odours, and Will felt sharpening appetite. For the first time since his catastrophe, he granted himself the dinner of a well-to-do man, and, as would naturally befall in such a case, made his indulgence large.

Several days passed and brought no letter from any one. But at midnight on Saturday, there lay awaiting him a letter addressed in Sherwood's well-known hand. Godfrey began by excusing himself for his delay in replying ; he had had rather a nasty attack of illness, and was only now able to hold his pen. But it was lucky he had not written before ; this very morning there had reached him the very best news. "The father of the man who owes me ten thousand pounds is dying. Off and on he has been ill for a long time, but I hear at length that there can be no doubt whatever that the end is near. I can't pretend to any human feeling in this matter ; the man's death means life for us—so the world goes. Any day now, you may have a telegram from me announcing the event. Of the prompt payment of the debt as soon as my friend inherits, there is no shadow of doubt. I therefore urge you very strongly not to make a disclosure. It will be needless. Wait till we see each other. I am still in Ireland—for a reason which I will explain when we meet."

Will drew a long breath. If ever news came opportunely, it was this. He threw up the window of his stuffy little sitting-room, and looked out into the summer night. The murmur of London once more made music to his ears.

CHAPTER XXIX

ROSAMUND took the Chelsea lodgings proposed to her by Bertha Cross, and in a few days went to live there. The luggage which she brought from Ashtead enabled her to add a personal touch to the characterless rooms: in the place of the landlady's ornaments, which were not things of beauty, she scattered her own *bibelots*, and about the walls she hung a number of her own drawings, framed for the purpose, as well as several which bore the signature, "Norbert Franks." Something less than a year ago, when her father went abroad, their house at Bath had been given up, and the furniture warehoused; for the present, Rosamund and her sister were content to leave things thus. The inheritance of each amounted only to a few hundred pounds.

"It's enough to save one from worry for a year or two," said Rosamund to her friend Bertha. "I'm not extravagant; I can live here very comfortably. And there's a pleasure in the thought that one's work not only *may* succeed but *must*."

"I'm sure I hope so," replied Bertha, "but where's the *must*?"

"What am I to do if it doesn't?" asked Miss Elvan, with her sweet smile, and in a tone of irresistible argument.

"True," conceded her humorous friend. "There's no other way out of the difficulty."

This was on the day of Rosamund's coming to Chelsea. A week later, Bertha found the sitting-room brightened with the hanging water-colours, with curtains of some delicate fabric at the windows, with a new rug before the fire place.

"These things have cost so little," said Rosamund, half apologetically. "And—yes, I was obliged to buy this little tea service; I really couldn't use Mrs. Darby's; it spoilt the taste of the tea. Trifles, but they really have their importance; they help to keep one in the right mind. Oh, I must show you an amusing letter I've had from Winnie. Winifred is prudence itself. She wouldn't spend a sixpence unnecessarily. 'Suppose one fell ill,' she writes, 'what a blessing it would be to feel that one wasn't helpless and dependent. Oh, do be careful with your money, and consider very, very seriously what is the best course to take in your position.' Poor, dear old Winnie! I know she frets and worries about me, and pictures me throwing gold away by the handful. Yet, as you know, that isn't my character at all. If I lay out a few sovereigns to make myself comfortable here, I know what I'm doing; it'll all come back again in work. As you know, Bertha, I'm not afraid of poverty—not a bit! I had very much rather be shockingly poor, living in a garret and half starved, than just keep myself tidily going in lodgings such as these were before I made the little changes. Winnie has a terror of finding herself destitute. She jumped for joy when she was offered that work, and I'm sure she'd be content to live there in the same way for years. She feels safe as long as she needn't touch her money."

Winifred Elvan, since her father's death, had found an engagement as governess in an English family at St. Jean de Luz. This, in the younger sister's eyes, involved a social decline, more disagreeable to her than she chose to confess.

"The one thing," pursued Rosamund, "that I really dread, is the commonplace. If I were utterly, wretchedly, grindingly poor, there'd be at all events a savour of the uncommon about it. I can't imagine myself marrying a prosperous shopkeeper; but if I cared for a clerk who had nothing but a pound a week, I would marry him to-morrow."

"The result," said Bertha, "might be lamentably commonplace."

"Not if it was the right sort of man.—Tell me what you think of that bit." She pointed to a framed drawing. "It's in the valley of Bidassoa."

They talked art for a little, then Rosamund fell into musing, and presently said:

"Don't you think Norbert has behaved very well."

"How well?"

"I mean, it would have been excusable, perhaps, if he had betrayed a little unkind feeling toward me. But nothing of the kind, absolutely nothing. I'm afraid I didn't give him credit for so much manliness. When he came to Ashtead the second time, of course I understood his motive at once. He wished to show me that his behaviour at the first meeting wasn't mere bravado and to assure me that I needn't be afraid of him. There's a great deal of delicacy in that; it really pleased me."

Bertha Cross was gazing at her friend with a puzzled smile.

"You're a queer girl," she remarked.

"Queer? Why?"

"Do you mean that you were really and truly surprised that Mr. Franks behaved like a gentleman?"

"Oh, Bertha!" protested the other. "What a word!"

"Well, like a man, then."

"Perhaps I oughtn't to have felt that," admitted Rosamund thoughtfully. "But I did, and it meant a good deal. It shows how very right I was when I freed myself."

"Are you quite sure of that?" asked Bertha, raising her eyebrows and speaking more seriously than usual.

"I never was more sure of anything."

"Do you know, I can't help thinking it an argument on the other side."

Rosamund looked her friend in the eyes.

"Suppose it means that you were altogether mistaken about Mr. Franks?" went on Bertha, in the same pleasant tone between jest and earnest.

"I wasn't mistaken in my own feeling," said Rosamund in her melodious undertone.

"No; but your feeling, you have always said, was due to a judgment you formed of Mr. Franks' character and motives. And now you confess that it looks very much as if you had judged him wrongly."

Rosamund smiled and shook her head.

"Do you know," asked Bertha, after a pause, "that he has been coming to our house lately?"

"You never mentioned it. But why shouldn't he go to your house?"

"Rather, why should he?" asked Bertha, with a laugh. "Don't trouble to guess. The reason was plain enough. He came to talk about you."

"Oh!" exclaimed the listener with amused deprecation.

"There's no doubt of it; no—shadow—of—doubt. In fact, we've had very pleasant little chats about you. Of course I said all the disagreeable things I could; I knew that was what you would wish."

"Certainly," fell from Rosamund.

"I didn't positively calumniate you, but just the unpleasant little hints that a friend is so well able to throw out; the sort of thing likely to chill any one. I hope you quite approve?"

"Quite."

"Well, the odd thing was that they didn't quite have the effect I aimed at. He talked of you more and more, instead of less and less. Wasn't it provoking, Rosamund?"

Again their eyes encountered.

"I wish," continued Miss Elvan, "I knew how much of this is truth, and how much Bertha's peculiar humour."

"It's substantial truth. That there may be humour in it, I don't deny, but it isn't of my importing."

"When did he last come to see you?" Rosamund inquired.

"Let me see. Just before he went to see you."

"It doesn't occur to you," said Rosamund, slowly meditative, "that he had some other reason—not the apparent one—for coming to your house?"

"It doesn't occur to me, and never will occur to me," was Bertha's amused answer.

When it was time for Bertha to walk homewards, Rosamund put her hat on, and they went out together. Turning to the west, they passed along Cheyne Walk, and paused awhile by old Chelsea Church. The associations of the neighbourhood moved Miss Elvan to a characteristic display of enthusiasm. Delightful to live here! A joy to work amid such memories, of ancient and of latter time!

"I must get Mr. Warburton to come and walk about Chelsea with me," she added.

"Mr. Warburton?"

"He's a great authority on London antiquities. Bertha, if you happen to see Norbert these days, do ask him for Mr. Warburton's address."

"Why not ask your people at Ashtead?" said Bertha.

"I shan't be going there for two or three weeks. Promise to ask Norbert—will you? For me, of course."

Bertha had turned to look at the river. Her face wore a puzzled gravity.

"I'll try to think of it," she replied, walking slowly on.

"He's a great mystery," were Rosamund's next words. "My uncle has no idea what he does, and Norbert, they tell me, is just as ignorant, or at all events, professes to be. Isn't it a queer thing? He came to grief in business two years ago, and since then he has lived out of sight. Uncle Ralph supposes he had to take a clerk's place somewhere, and that he doesn't care to talk about it.

"Is he such a snob?" asked Bertha, disinterestedly.

"No one would think so who knows him. I'm convinced there's some other explanation."

"Perhaps the truth is yet more awful," said Bertha solemnly. "He may have got a place *in a shop*."

"Hush! hush!" exclaimed the other, with a pained look. "Don't say such things! A poor clerk is suggestive—it's possible to see him in a romantic light—but a shopman! If you knew him, you would laugh at the idea. Mystery suits him very well indeed; to tell the truth, he's much more interesting now than when one knew him as a partner in a manufactory of some kind. You see he's unhappy—there are lines in his face——"

"Perhaps," suggested Bertha, "he has married a rich widow and daren't confess it."

CHAPTER XXX

IT was on Saturday night that Godfrey Sherwood came at length to Warburton's lodgings. Reaching home between twelve and one o'clock Will saw a man who paced the pavement near Mrs. Wick's door; the man, at sight of him, hastened forward; there were exclamations of surprise and of pleasure.

"I came first of all at nine o'clock," said Sherwood. "The landlady said you wouldn't be back before midnight, so I came again. Been to the theatre, I suppose?"

"Yes," answered Will, "taking part in a play called 'The Grocer's Saturday Night.'"

"I'd forgotten. Poor old fellow! You won't have much more of *that*, thank Heaven!—Are you too tired to talk to-night?"

"No, no; come in."

The house was silent and dark. Will struck a match to light the candle placed for him at the foot of the stairs, and led the way up to his sitting-room on the first floor. Here he lit a lamp, and the two friends looked at each other. Each saw a change. If Warburton was thin and heavy-eyed, Sherwood's visage showed an even more noticeable falling-off in health.

"What's been the matter with you?" asked Will. "Your letter said you had had an illness, and you look as if you hadn't got over it yet."

"Oh, I'm all right now," cried the other. "Liver

got out of order—or the spleen, or something—I forget. The best medicine was the news I got about old Strangwyn.—There, by Jove! I've let the name out. The wonder is I never did it before, when we were talking. It doesn't matter now. Yes, it's Strangwyn, the whisky man. He'll die worth a million or two, and Ted is his only son. I was a fool to lend that money to Ted, but we saw a great deal of each other at one time, and when he came asking for ten thousand—a mere nothing for a fellow of his expectations—nobody thought his father could live a year, but the old man has held out all this time, and Ted, the rascal, kept swearing he couldn't pay the interest on his debt. Of course I could have made him; but he knew I shouldn't dare to risk the thing coming to his father's ears. I've had altogether about three hundred pounds, instead of the four hundred a year he owed me—it was at four per cent. Now, of course, I shall get all the arrears—but that won't pay for all the mischief that's been done."

"Is it certain," asked Will, "that Strangwyn will pay?"

"Certain? If he doesn't I sue him. The case is plain as daylight."

"There's no doubt that he'll have his father's money?"

"None whatever. For more than a year now, he's been on good terms with the old man. Ted is a very decent fellow, of his sort. I don't say that I care as much for him now as I used to; we've both of us altered; but his worst fault is extravagance. The old man, it must be confessed, isn't very good form; he smells rather of the distillery; but Ted Strangwyn might come of the best family in the land. Oh, you needn't have the least anxiety Strangwyn will pay, principal and interest, as soon as the old man has retired; and that may happen any day, any hour.—How glad I am to see you again, Will! I've known one or two plucky men, but no one like you. I couldn't have gone through it; I should have turned coward after a month of that. Well, it's over, and it'll be something to look back upon. Some day, perhaps, you'll amuse your sister by telling her the story. To tell you the truth, I couldn't bear to come and see you; I should have been too miserably ashamed of myself.—And not a soul has found you out, all this time?"

"No one that I know of."

"You must have suffered horribly from loneliness. —But I have things to tell you, important things." He waved his arm. "Not to-night; it's too late, and you look tired to death."

"Tell on," said Warburton. "If I went to bed I shouldn't sleep—where are you staying?"

"Morley's Hotel. Not at my own expense," Sherwood added hastily. "I'm acting as secretary to a man—a man I got to know in Ireland. A fine fellow! You'll know him very soon. It's about him that I want to tell you. But first of all, that idea of mine about Irish eggs. The trouble was I couldn't get capital enough. My cousin Hackett risked a couple of hundred pounds; it was all lost before the thing could really be set going. I had a bad time after that, Will, a bad time, I tell you. Yet good results came of it. For two or three months I lived on next to nothing—a few pence a day, all told. Of course, if I had let Strangwyn know how badly off I was, he'd have sent a cheque; but I didn't feel I had any right to his money, it was yours, not mine. Besides, I said to myself that, if I suffered, it was only what I deserved; I took it as a sort of expiation of the harm I'd done. All that time I was in Dublin, I tried to get employment but nobody had any use for me—until at last, when I was all but dying of hunger, somebody spoke to me of a certain Milligan, a young and very rich man living in Dublin. I resolved to go and see him, and a lucky day it was. You remember Conolly—Bates's traveller? Well, Milligan is just that man, in appearance; a thorough Irishman, and one of the best hearted fellows that ever lived. Though he's rich I found him living in a very plain way, in a room which looked like a museum, full of fossils, stuffed birds and animals, queer old pictures, no end of such things. Well, I told him plainly who I was, and where I was; and almost without thinking, he cried out—'What could be simpler? Come and be my secretary.'—'You want a secretary?'—'I hadn't thought of it,' said Milligan, 'but now it strikes me it's just what I *do* want. I knew there was something. Yes, yes. come and be my secretary; you're just the man.' He went on to tell me he had a lot of correspondence with sellers of curiosities, and it bored him to write the letters. Would I come for a couple of hours a day? He'd pay me twenty pounds a month. You may suppose I wasn't long in accepting. We began the next day, and in a week's time we were good friends. Milligan told me that he'd always had weak health, and he was convinced his life had been saved by vegetarianism. I myself wasn't feeling at all fit just then; he persuaded me to drop meat, and taught me all about the vegetarian way of living. I hadn't tried it for a month before I found the most wonderful results. Never in my life had I such a clear mind, and such good spirits. It re-made me."

"So you've come to London to hunt for curios?" interposed Will.

"No, no; let me go on. When I got to know Milligan well, I found that he had a large estate somewhere in Connaught. And, as we talked, an idea came to me." Again he sprang up from his chair. "'If I were a landowner on that scale,' I said, 'do you know what I should do—I should make a vegetarian colony; a self-supporting settlement of people who ate no meat, drank no alcohol, smoked no tobacco; a community which, as years went on, might prove to the world that there was the true ideal of civilised life—health of mind and of body, true culture, true humanity!'" The eyes glowed in his fleshless, colourless face; he spoke with arm raised, head thrown back—the attitude of an enthusiastic preacher. "Milligan caught at the idea—caught at it eagerly. 'There's something fine in that!' he said. 'Why shouldn't it be done?' 'You're the man that could do it,' I told him. 'You'd be a benefactor to the human race. Isolated examples are all very well, but what we want is an experiment on a large scale, going on through more than one generation. Let children be born of vegetarian parents, brought up as vegetarians, and this in conditions of life every way simple, natural, healthy. This is the way to convert the world.' So that's what we're working at now, Milligan and I. Of course there are endless difficulties; the thing can't be begun in a hurry; we have to see no end of people, and correspond with the leaders of vegetarianism everywhere. But isn't it a grand idea? Isn't it worth working for?"

Warburton mused, smiling.

"I want you to join us," said Sherwood abruptly.

"Ho, ho! That's another matter."

"I shall bring you books to read."

"I've no time. I'm a grocer."

"Pooh!" exclaimed Sherwood. "In a few days you'll be an independent man.—Yes, yes, I know that you'll have only a small capital, when things are settled; but it's just people with a small capital that we want to enlist; the very poor and the well-to-do will be no use to us. It's too late to-night to go into details. We have time to talk, plenty of time. That you will join us, I feel sure. Wait till you've had time to think about it. For my own part, I've found the work of my life, and I'm the happiest man living!"

He walked round and round the table, waving his arms, and Warburton, after regarding him curiously, mused again, but without a smile.

CHAPTER XXXI

BEHIND his counter next morning, Will thought over Sherwood's story, and laughed to himself wonderingly. Not that any freak of his old partner's—of the man whom he had once regarded as, above all, practical and energetic—could now surprise him; but it seemed astonishing that Godfrey should have persuaded a man of solid means, even a Celt, to pledge himself to such an enterprise. Was the story true? Did Milligan really exist? If any doubt were possible on this point, did it not also throw suspicion on the story of Strangwyn, and the ten thousand pounds? Will grew serious at the reflection. He had never conceived a moment's distrust of Sherwood's honesty, nor did his misgiving now take that form; the question which troubled him throughout to-day was—whether Godfrey Sherwood might be a victim of delusions. Certainly he had a very strange look; that haggard face, those brilliant eyes——

So disquieting was the suspicion that, at closing time, Will could no longer resist an impulse to betake himself to Morley's Hotel. Sherwood had said that Milligan was there only for a few days, until the wealthy Irishman could find a furnished house suitable to his needs whilst he remained in London. Arrived at the hotel, he inquired for his friend; Sherwood had dined and gone out. Will hesitated a moment, then asked whether Mr.

Milligan was to be seen. Mr. Milligan, he learnt, had gone out with Mr. Sherwood. So Milligan did exist. Will's relief at settling this point banished his doubts on all the others. He turned westward again, and through a night of soft, warm rain walked all the way to his lodgings.

On the third day after, late in the evening, Sherwood paid him a second visit. Godfrey was in high spirits. He announced that Milligan had taken a house near the Marble Arch, where he also, as secretary, would have his quarters, and that already a meeting had been convened of the leading London vegetarians. Things were splendidly in train. Then he produced an evening newspaper, with a paragraph, which spoke of the serious illness of Mr. Strangwyn; recovery, it was said, could hardly be hoped for.

"What's more," cried Sherwood. "I've seen Ted Strangwyn himself. Nobody could behave better. The old man, he assured me, couldn't last more than a day or two, and he promised—quite spontaneously, I didn't say a word—to pay his debt in full as soon as ever his father's will was proved, which will be done as quickly as possible.—And now, have you thought over what I said the other night?"

"Thought—yes."

"With not much result, I see. Never mind; you must have time. I want you to meet Milligan. Could you come to lunch next Sunday? He invites you."

Warburton shook his head. He had never cared for the acquaintance of rich men, and was less than ever disposed to sit at their tables. All his anxieties regarding Sherwood's mental condition having been set at rest, he would go on with his grocer's life as long as need be, strengthened with the hope that shone before him.

The end of July had come. After a week of rain, the weather had turned bright, with a coolness at morning and evening very pleasant at this time of year in London streets. Warburton had business in the City which he must needs see to personally; he was on the point of leaving the shop, dressed as became a respectable citizen, silk hat and all, when in the doorway appeared Miss Bertha Cross. A certain surprise marked her smile of recognition; it meant, no doubt, that, never before having seen Mr. Jollyman save bareheaded and aproned, she was struck with the change in his aspect when thus equipped for going abroad. Immediately Mr. Jollyman doffed his hat and stepped behind the counter.

"Please don't let me keep you," said Bertha, with a glance towards Allchin, who was making parcels at the back of the shop. "I only want some—some matches, and one or two trifling things."

Never had she seemed so embarrassed in making a purchase. Her eyes fell, and she half turned away. Mr. Jollyman appeared to hesitate, he also glancing towards Allchin; but the young lady quickly recovered herself, and, taking up a packet of something exhibited on the counter, asked its price. The awkwardness was at an end; Bertha made her purchases, paid for them, and then left the shop as usual.

It was by the last post on the evening after this day that Warburton received a letter of which the exterior puzzled him. Whose could be this graceful, delicate hand? A woman's doubtless; yet he had no female correspondent, save those who wrote from St. Neots. The postmark was London. He opened, "Dear Mr. Warburton"—a glance over the leaf showed him—"Sincerely yours, Rosamund Elvan." H'm!

"Dear Mr. Warburton,—I am settled in my lodgings here, and getting seriously to work. It has occurred to me that you might be able to suggest some quaint corner of old London, unknown to me, which would make a good subject for a water-colour. London has been, I am sure, far too much neglected by artists; if I could mark out a claim here, as the colonists say, I should be lucky. For the present, I am just sketching (to get my hand in) about Chelsea. To-morrow afternoon, about six o'clock, if this exquisite mellow weather continues, I shall be on the Embankment in Battersea Park, near the Albert Bridge, where I want to catch a certain effect of sky and water."

That was all. And what exactly did it mean? Warburton's practical knowledge of women did not carry him very far, but he was wont to theorise at large on the subject, and in this instance it seemed to him that one of his favourite generalities found neat application. Miss Elvan had in a high degree the feminine characteristic of not knowing her own mind. Finding herself without substantial means, she of course meant to marry, and it was natural that she should think of marrying Norbert Franks; yet she could not feel at all sure that she wished to do so; neither was she perfectly certain that Franks would again offer her the choice. In this state of doubt she inclined to cultivate the acquaintance of Franks' intimate friend, knowing that she might thus, very probably, gather hints as to the artist's state of mind, and, if it seemed good to her, could indirectly convey to him a suggestion of her own. Warburton concluded, then, that he was simply being made use of by this typical young lady. That point settled, he willingly lent himself to her device, for he desired nothing better than to see Franks lured back to the old allegiance, and away from the house at Walham Green. So, before going to bed, he posted a reply to Miss Elvan's letter, saying that he should much like a talk with her about the artistic possibilities of obscure London, and that he would walk next day along the Battersea Embankment, with the hope of meeting her.

And thus it came to pass. Through the morning there were showers, but about noon a breeze swept the sky fair, and softly glowing summer reigned over the rest of the day. In his mood of hopefulness, Warburton had no scruple about abandoning the shop at tea-time; he did not even trouble himself to invent a decorous excuse, but told Allchin plainly that he thought he would have a walk. His henchman, who of late had always seemed rather pleased than otherwise when Warburton absented himself, loudly approved the idea.

"Don't you 'urry back, sir. There'll be no business as I can't manage. Don't you think of 'urrying. The air'll do you good."

As he walked away, Will said to himself that no doubt Allchin would only be too glad of a chance of managing the business independently, and that perhaps he hoped for the voluntary retirement of Mr. Jollyman one of these days. Indeed, things were likely to take that course. And Allchin was a good, honest fellow, whom it would be a pleasure to see flourishing.—How much longer would old Strangwyn cumber the world?

With more of elasticity than usual in his rapid stride, Will passed out of Fulham Road into King's Road, and down to the river at Cheyne Walk, whence his eye perceived a sitting figure on the opposite bank. He crossed Albert Bridge ; he stepped down into the Park ; he drew near to the young lady in grey trimmed with black, who was at work upon a drawing. Not until he spoke did she seem aware of his arrival ; then with her brightest smile of welcome, she held out a pretty hand, and in her melodious voice thanked him for so kindly taking the trouble to come.

"Don't look at this," she added. "It's too difficult—I can't get it right——"

What his glance discovered on the block did not strengthen Will's confidence in Rosamund's claim to be a serious artist. He had always taken for granted that her work was amateurish, and that she had little chance of living by it. On the whole, he felt glad to be confirmed in this view ; Rosamund as an incompetent was more interesting to him than if she had given proof of great ability.

"I mustn't be too ambitious," she was saying. "The river suggests dangerous comparisons. I want to find little corners of the town such as no one ever thought of painting——"

"Unless it was Norbert Franks," said Will genially, leaning on his stick with both hands, and looking over her head.

"Yes, I had almost forgotten," she answered with a thoughtful smile. "In those days he did some very good things."

"Some remarkably good things. Of course you know the story of how he and I first met ?"

"Oh, yes. Early morning—a quiet little street —I remember. Where was that ?"

"Over yonder." Will nodded southward. "I hope he'll take that up again some day."

"Oh, but let me do it first," exclaimed Rosamund, laughing. "You mustn't rob me of my chance, Mr. Warburton? Norbert Franks is successful and rich, or going to be ; I am a poor struggler. Of course, in painting London, it's atmosphere one has to try for above all. Our sky gives value, now and then, to forms which in themselves are utterly uninteresting."

"Exactly what Franks used to say to me. There was a thing I wanted him to try—but then came the revolution. It was the long London street, after a hot, fine day, just when the lamps have been lit. Have you noticed how golden the lights are? I remember standing for a long time at the end of Harley Street, enjoying that effect. Franks was going to try it—but then came the revolution."

"For which—you mean, Mr. Warburton—I was to blame."

Rosamund spoke in a very low voice and a very sweet, her head bent.

"Why, yes," replied Will, in the tone of corresponding masculinity, "though I shouldn't myself have used that word. You, no doubt, were the cause of what happened, and so, in a sense, to blame for it. But I know it couldn't be helped."

"Indeed, it couldn't," declared Rosamund, raising her eyes a little, and looking across the river.

She had not in the least the air of a coquette. Impossible to associate any such trivial idea with Rosamund's habitual seriousness of bearing, and with the stamp of her features, which added some subtle charm to regularity and refinement. By temper critical, and especially disposed to mistrustful scrutiny by the present circumstances, Warburton was yet unable to resist the softening influence of this quintessential womanhood. In a certain degree, he had submitted to it during that holiday among the Alps, then, on the whole, he inclined to regard Rosamund impatiently and with slighting tolerance. Now that he desired to mark her good qualities, and so justify himself in the endeavour to renew her conquest of Norbert Franks, he exposed himself to whatever peril might lie in her singular friendliness. True, no sense of danger occurred to him, and for that very reason his state was the more precarious.

"You have seen him lately at Ashtead?" was his next remark.

"More than once. And I can't tell you how glad we were to see each other! I knew in a moment that he had really forgiven me—and I have always wanted to be assured of that. How thoroughly good and straightforward he is! I'm sure we shall be friends all our lives."

"I agree with you," he said, "that there's no better fellow living. Till now, I can't see a sign of his being spoilt by success. And spoilt in the worst sense, I don't think he ever will be, happen what may, there's a simplicity about him which makes his safeguard. But, as for his painting—well, I can't be so sure, I know little or nothing about it, but it's plain that he no longer takes his work very seriously. It pleases people—they pay large prices for it—where's the harm? Still, if he had some one to keep a higher ideal before him——"

He broke off, with a vague gesture. Rosamund looked up at him.

"We must try," she said, with quiet earnestness.

"Oh, I don't know that *I'm* any use," replied Will, with a laugh. "I speak with no authority. But you—yes. *You* might do much. More than any one else possibly could."

"That is exaggerating, Mr. Warburton," said Rosamund. "Even in the old days my influence didn't go for much. You speak of the 'revolution' caused by—by what happened; but the truth is that the revolution had begun before that. Remember I saw 'Sanctuary' while he was painting it, and, but we won't talk of that."

"To tell you the truth," returned Warburton, meeting her eyes steadily, with his pleasantest look, "I saw no harm in 'Sanctuary.' I think he was quite right to do what he could to earn money. He wanted to be married; he had waited quite long enough; if he hadn't done something of the kind, I should have doubted whether he was very much in earnest. No, no; what I call the revolution began when he had lost all hope. At the time he would have given up painting altogether, I believe; if it hadn't been that he owed me money, and knew I wanted it."

Rosamund made a quick movement of interest. "I never heard about that."

"Franks wouldn't talk about it, be sure. He saw me in a hobble—I lost everything, all at once—and he went to work like a brick to get money for me. And that, when he felt more disposed to poison himself than to paint. Do you think I should criticise the work he did under these circumstances?"

"No, indeed! Thank you, Mr. Warburton, for telling me that story."

"How exquisite London is at this time of the year!" Rosamund murmured, as having declared it was time to be walking homewards, they walked slowly towards the bridge. "I'm glad not to be going away. Look at that lovely sky! Look at the tones of those houses.—Oh, I *must* make use of it all! Real use, I mean, as splendid material for art, not only for money-making. Do advise me, Mr. Warburton. Where shall I go to look for bits?"

Walking with bent head, Will reflected.

"Do you know Camberwell?" he asked. "There are good little corners——"

"I don't know it at all. Could you—I'm afraid to ask. You couldn't spare time——?"

"Oh yes, easily. That's to say, during certain hours."

"On Monday say? In the afternoon?"

"Yes."

"How kind of you!" murmured Rosamund. "If I were only an amateur, amusing myself, I couldn't give you the trouble; but it's serious; I *must* earn money before long. You see, there's nothing else I can do. My sister—you know I have a sister?—she has taken to teaching; she's at St. Jean de Luz. But I'm no use for anything of that kind. I must be independent. Why do you smile?"

"Not at you, but at myself. I used to say the same thing. But I had no talent of any kind, and when the smash came——"

They were crossing the bridge. Will looked westward, in the direction of his shop, and it struck him how amusing it would be to startle Rosamund by a disclosure of his social status. Would she still be anxious for his company in search of the picturesque? He could not feel sure—curiosity urged him to try the experiment, but an obscure apprehension closed his lips.

"How very hard for you!" sighed Rosamund. "But don't think," she added quickly, "that I have a weak dread of poverty. Not at all! So long as one can support oneself. Nowadays, when every one strives and battles for money, there's a distinction in doing without it."

Five minutes more, and they were in Oakley Crescent. Rosamund paused before reaching the house in which she dwelt, took the camp-stool from her companion, and offered her hand for good-bye. Only then did Warburton become aware that he had said nothing since that remark of hers about poverty; he had walked in a dream.

CHAPTER XXXII

AUGUST came, and Strangwyn, the great whisky distiller, was yet alive. For very shame, Will kept his thoughts from that direction. The gloomy mood had again crept upon him, in spite of all his reasons for hope; his sleep became mere nightmare, and his day behind the counter a bilious misery.

Since the occasion last recorded, Bertha Cross had not been to the shop. One day, the order was brought by a servant; a week later, Mrs. Cross herself appeared. The querulous lady wore a countenance so nearly cheerful that Warburton regarded her uneasily. She had come to purchase tea, and remarked that it was for use during a seaside holiday; you could never depend on the tea at seaside places. Perhaps, thought Will, the prospect of change sufficed to explain her equanimity. But for the rest of the day he was so glum and curt, that Allchin frequently looked at him with pained remonstrance.

At home, he found a telegram on his table. He clutched at it, rent the envelope. But no; it was not what he expected. Norbert Franks asked him to look in that evening. So, weary and heartsick as he was, he took the train to Notting Hill Gate.

"What is it?" he asked bluntly, on entering the studio.

"Wanted a talk, that was all," replied his friend. "Hope I haven't disturbed you. You told me, you remember, that you preferred coming here."

"All right. I thought you might have news for me."

"Well," said Franks, smiling at the smoke of his cigarette, "there's perhaps something of the sort."

The other regarded him keenly.

"You've done it."

"No—o—o; not exactly. Sit down; you're not in a hurry? I went to Walham Green a few days ago, but Bertha wasn't at home. I saw her mother. They're going away for a fortnight, to Southwold, and I have a sort of idea that I may run down there. I half promised."

Will nodded, and said nothing.

"You disapprove? Speak plainly, old man. What's your real objection? Of course I've noticed before now that you have an objection. Out with it!"

"Have you seen Miss Elvan again?"

"No. Have you?"

"Two or three times."

Franks was surprised.

"Where?"

"Oh, we've had some walks together."

"The deuce you have!" cried Franks, with a laugh.

"Don't you want to know what we talked about," pursued Warburton, looking at him with half-closed eyelids. "Principally about you."

"That's very flattering—but perhaps you abused me?"

"On the whole, no. Discussed you, yes, and

in considerable detail, coming to the conclusion that you were a very decent fellow, and we both of us liked you very much."

Franks laughed gaily, joyously.

"*Que vous êtes aimables, tous-les-deux!* You make me imagine I'm back in Paris. Must I round a compliment in reply?"

"That's as you like. But first I'll tell you the upshot of it all, as it shapes itself to me. Hasn't it even dimly occurred to you that, under the circumstances, it would be—well, say a graceful thing—to give that girl a chance of changing her mind again?"

"What—Rosamund?"

"It never struck you?"

"But, hang it all, Warburton!" exclaimed the artist. "How *should* I have thought of it? You know very well—and then, it's perfectly certain she would laugh at me."

"It isn't certain at all. And, do you know, it almost seems to me a point of honour."

"You're not serious? This is one of your solemn jokes—such as you haven't indulged in lately."

"No, no. Listen," said Will, with a rigid ear nestness on his face as he bent forward in the chair. "She is poor, and doesn't know how she's going to live. You are flourishing, and have all sorts of brilliant things before you; wouldn't it be a generous thing—the kind of thing one might expect of a fellow with his heart in the right place—? You understand me?"

Franks rounded his eyes in amazement.

"But—am I to understand that she *expects* it?"

"Not at all. She hasn't in the remotest way betrayed such a thought—be assured of that.

She isn't the sort of girl to do such a thing. It's entirely my own thought."

The artist changed his seat, and for a moment wore a look of perturbed reflection.

"How the deuce," he exclaimed, "can you come and talk to me like this when you know I've as good as committed myself——?"

"Yes, and in a wobbling, half-hearted way which means you had no right even to think of committing yourself. You care nothing about that other girl——"

"You're mistaken. I care a good deal. In fact——"

"In fact," echoed Warburton with good-natured scorn, "so much that you've all but made up your mind to go down to Southwold whilst she is there! Bosh! You cared for one girl in a way you'll never care for another."

"Well—perhaps—yes that may be true——"

"Of course it's true. If you don't marry *her*, go in for a prize beauty or for an heiress or anything else that's brilliant. Think of the scope before a man like you."

Franks smiled complacently once more.

"Why, that's true," he replied. "I was going to tell you about my social adventures. Who do you think I've been chumming with? Sir Luke Griffin—the great Sir Luke. He's asked me down to his place in Leicestershire, and I think I shall go. He's really a very nice fellow. I always imagined him loud, vulgar, the typical parvenu. Nothing of the kind—no one would guess that he began life in a grocer's shop. Why, he can talk quite decently about pictures, and really likes them."

Warburton listened with a chuckle.

"Has he daughters?"

"Three, and no son. The youngest, about seventeen, an uncommonly pretty girl. Well, as you say, why shouldn't I marry her and a quarter of a million? By Jove! I believe I could. She was here with her father yesterday. I'm going to paint the three girls together.—Do you know, Warburton, speaking without any foolish vanity, what astonishes me is to think of the enormous choice of wives there is for a man of decent appearance and breeding who succeeds in getting himself talked about. Without a joke, I am convinced I know twenty girls, and more or less nice girls, who would have me at once, if I asked them. I'm not a conceited fellow—am I now? I shouldn't say this to any one else. I'm simply convinced of its being a fact."

Warburton declared his emphatic agreement.

"Seeing that," he added, "why are you in such a hurry? Your millionaire grocer is but a stepping-stone; who knows but you may soon chum with dukes? If any man living ought to be cautious about his marriage, it's you."

The artist examined his friend with a puzzled smile.

"I should like to know, Warburton, how much of this is satire, and how much serious advice. Perhaps it's all satire—and rather savage?"

"No, no, I'm speaking quite frankly."

"But, look here, there's the awkward fact that I really have gone rather far with the Crosses."

Will made a movement of all but angry impatience.

"Do you mean," he asked quickly, "that *she* has committed herself in any way?"

"No, that she certainly hasn't," was Franks, deliberate reply, in a voice as honest as the smile which accompanied it.

"My advice then is—break decently off, and either do what I suggested, or go and amuse yourself with millionaire Sir Luke, and extend your opportunities."

Franks mused.

"You are serious about Rosamund?" he asked, after a glance at Warburton's set face.

"Think it over," Will replied, in a rather hard voice. "I saw the thing like that. Of course, it's no business of mine; I don't know why I interfere; every man should settle these matters in his own way. But it was a thought I had, and I've told it you. There's no harm done."

CHAPTER XXXIII

WHEN Warburton reached his lodging the next evening he found a letter on his table. Again the fine feminine hand; it was the second time that Rosamund had written to him. A vague annoyance mingled with his curiosity as he tore the envelope. She began by telling him of a drawing she had made in Camberwell Grove—not bad, it seemed to her, but she wished for his opinion. Then, in a new paragraph:

"I have seen Norbert again. I call him Norbert, because I always think of him by that name, and there's an affectation in writing 'Mr. Franks.' I felt that, when we talked of him, and I really don't know why I didn't simply call him Norbert then. I shall do so in future. You, I am sure, have little respect for silly social conventions, and you will understand me. Yes, I have seen him again, and I feel obliged to tell you about it. It was really very amusing. You know, of course, that all embarrassment was over between us. At Ashtead we met like the best of friends. So, when Norbert wrote that he wanted to see me, I thought nothing could be more natural, and felt quite glad. But, as soon as we met, I saw something strange in him, something seemed to have happened. And—how shall I tell you? It's only a guess of mine—things didn't come to foolish extremities—but I really believe that the poor fellow had somehow persuaded himself that it's his duty to—no, I can't go on, but I'm sure you will understand. I was never so amused at anything.

"Why do I write this to you? I hardly know. But I have just a suspicion that the story may not come to you quite as a surprise. If Norbert thought he had a certain duty—strange idea!—perhaps friends of his might see things in the same way. Even the most sensible people are influenced by curious ideas on one subject. I need not say that, as soon as the suspicion dawned upon me, I did my best to let him understand how far astray he was going. I think he understood. I feel sure he did. At all events he got into natural talk again, and parted in a thoroughly reasonable way.

"I beg that you won't reply to this letter. I shall work on, and hope to be able to see you again before long."

Warburton threw the sheet of paper on to the table, as if dismissing it from his thoughts. He began to walk about the room. Then he stood motionless for ten minutes. "What's the matter with me?" this was the current of his musing. "I used to think myself a fellow of some energy; but the truth is, I know my mind about nothing, and I'm at the mercy of every one who chooses to push me this way or that."

He took up the letter again, and was about to re-read it, but suddenly altered his mind, and thrust the folded paper into his pocket.

Eight days went by. Will had a visit from Sherwood, who brought news that the whisky distiller had seemed a little better, but could not possibly live more than a week or two. As regards the vegetarian colony all went well; practical men were at work on the details of the scheme; Sherwood toiled for ten hours a day at secretarial correspondence. Next day, there came a postcard from Rosamund.

"Work ready to show you. Could you come and have a cup of tea to-morrow afternoon?"

At the conventional hour Will went to Oakley Crescent. Not, however, as he had expected, to find Miss Elvan alone; with her sat Mrs. Pomfret, in London for the afternoon. The simple and kindly lady talked as usual, but Will, nervously observant, felt sure that she was not quite at her ease. On the other hand, nothing could have been more naturally graceful than Rosamund's demeanour; whether pouring out tea, or exhibiting her water-colours, or leading the talk to subjects of common interest, she was charming in her own way, a way which borrowed nothing from the every-day graces of the drawing-room. Her voice, always subdued, had a range of melodious expression which caressed the ear, no matter how trifling the words she uttered, and at moments its slightly tremulous murmur on rich notes suggested depths of sentiment lying beneath this familiar calm. To her aunt she spoke with a touch of playful affection; when her eyes turned to Warburton, their look almost suggested the frankness of simple friendship, and her tone was that of the largest confidence.

Never had Will felt himself so lulled to oblivion of things external; he forgot the progress of time, and only when Mrs. Pomfret spoke of the train she had to catch, made an effort to break the lazy spell and take his leave.

On the morrow, and on the day after that, he shirked business during the afternoon, excusing himself with the plea that the heat of the shop was insufferable. He knew that neglect of work was growing upon him, and again he observed that Allchin seemed rather pleased than vexed by these needless absences. The third day saw him behind the counter until five o'clock, when he was summoned as usual to the back parlour to tea. Laying before him a plate of watercress and slices of brown bread and butter, Mrs. Allchin, a discreetly conversational young woman, remarked on the continued beauty of the weather, and added a hope that Mr. Jollyman would not feel obliged to remain in the shop this evening.

"No, no, it's your husband's turn," Will replied good-naturedly. "He wants a holiday more than I do."

"Allchin want a 'oliday, sir!" exclaimed the woman. "Why he never knows what to do with himself when he's away from business. He enjoys business, does Allchin. Don't you think of him, sir. I never knew a man so altered since he's been kept to regular work all the year round. I used to dread the Sundays, and still more the Bank holidays when we were here first; you never knew who he'd get quarrelling with as soon as he'd nothing to do. But now, sir, why I don't believe you'll find a less quarrelsome man anywhere, and he was saying for a joke only yesterday, that he didn't think he could knock down even a coster, he's so lost the habit."

Will yielded and stole away into the mellowing sunshine. He walked westward, till he found himself on the Embankment by Albert Bridge; here, after hesitating awhile, he took the turn into Oakley Street. He had no thought of calling to see Miss Elvan; upon that he could not venture; but he thought it barely possible that he might meet with her in this neighbourhood, and such a meeting would have been pleasant. Disappointed, he crossed the river, lingered a little in Battersea Park, came back again over the bridge,—and, with a sudden leap of the heart, which all but made his whole body spring forward, saw a slim figure in grey moving by the parapet in front of Cheyne Walk.

They shook hands without speaking, very much as though they had met by appointment.

"Oh, these sunsets!" were Rosamund's first words, when they had moved a few steps together.

"They used to be my delight when I lived there," Will replied, pointing eastward.

"Show me just where it was, will you?"

They turned, and went as far as Chelsea Bridge, where Warburton pointed out the windows of his old flat.

"You were very happy there?" said Rosamund.

"Happy—? Not unhappy, at all events. Yes, in a way I enjoyed my life; chiefly because I didn't think much about it."

"Look at the sky, now."

The sun had gone down in the duskily golden haze that hung above the river's vague horizon. Above, on the violet sky, stood range over range of pleated clouds, their hue the deepest rose, shading to purple in the folds.

"In other countries," continued the soft, murmuring voice, "I have never seen a sky like that. I love this London!"

"As I used to," said Warburton, "and shall again."

They loitered back past Chelsea Hospital, exchanging brief, insignificant sentences. Then for many minutes neither spoke, and in this silence they came to the foot of Oakley Street, where again they stood gazing at the sky. Scarcely changed in form, the western clouds had shed their splendour, and were now so coldly pale that one would have imagined them stricken with moonlight ; but no moon had risen, only in a clear space of yet blue sky glistened the evening star.

"I must go in," said Rosamund abruptly, as though starting from a dream.

CHAPTER XXXIV

SHE was gone, and Warburton stood biting his lips. Had he shaken hands with her? Had he said good-night? He could not be sure. Nothing was present to him but a sense of gawkish confusion, following on a wild impulse which both ashamed and alarmed him, he stood in a bumpkin attitude, biting his lips.

A hansom came crawling by, and the driver called his attention—"Keb, sir?" At once he stepped forward, sprang on to the footboard, and —stood there looking foolish.

"Where to, sir?"

"That's just what I can't tell you," he answered with a laugh. "I want to go to somebody's house, but don't know the address."

"Could you find it in the Directory, sir? They've got one at the corner."

"Good idea."

The cab keeping alongside with him, he walked to the public-house, and there, midway in whisky-and-soda, looked up in the great red volume the name of Strangwyn. There it was,—a house in Kensington Gore. He jumped into the hansom, and, as he was driven down Park Lane, he felt that he had enjoyed nothing so much for a long time; it was the child's delight in "having a ride"; the air blew deliciously on his cheeks, and the trotting clap of the horse's hoofs, the jingle of the bells, aided his exhilaration. And when the driver pulled up, it was with an extraordinary gaiety that Will paid him and shouted good-night.

He approached the door of Mr. Strangwyn's dwelling. Some one was at that moment turning away from it, and, as they glanced at each other, a cry of recognition broke from both.

"Coming to make inquiry?" asked Sherwood. "I've just been doing the same thing."

"Well?"

"No better, no worse. But that means, of course, nearer the end."

"Queer we should meet," said Warburton. "This is the first time I've been here."

"I can quite understand your impatience. It seems an extraordinary case; the poor old man, by every rule, ought to have died weeks ago. Which way are you walking?"

Will answered that he did not care, that he would accompany Sherwood.

"Let us walk as far as Hyde Park Corner, then," said Godfrey. "Delighted to have a talk with you." He slipped a friendly hand under his companion's arm. "Why don't you come, Will, and make friends with Milligan? He's a splendid fellow; you couldn't help taking to him. We are getting on gloriously with our work. For the first time in my life I feel as if I had something to do that's really worth doing. I tell you this scheme of ours has inconceivable importance; it may have results such as one dare not talk about."

"But how long will it be before you really make a start?" asked Warburton, with more interest than he had yet shown in this matter.

"I can't quite say—can't quite say. The details are of course full of difficulty—the thing wouldn't be worth much if they were not. One of Milligan's best points is, that he's a thoroughly practical man—thoroughly practical man. It's no commercial enterprise we're about, but, if it's to succeed, it must be started on sound principles. I'd give anything if I could persuade you to join us, old fellow. You and your mother and sister—you're just the kind of people we want. Think what a grand thing it will be to give a new start to civilisation! Doesn't it touch you?"

Warburton was mute, and, taking this for a sign of the impressionable moment, Sherwood talked on, ardently, lyrically, until Hyde Park Corner was reached.

"Think it over, Will. We shall have you yet; I know we shall. Come and see Milligan."

They parted with a warm hand-grip, and Warburton turned toward Fulham Road.

When Warburton entered the shop the next morning, Allchin was on the lookout for him.

"I want to speak to you, sir," he said, "about this golden syrup we've had from Rowbottom's—"

Will listened, or seemed to listen, smiling at vacancy. To whatever Allchin proposed, he gave his assent, and in the afternoon, without daring to say a word he stole into freedom.

He was once more within sight of Albert Bridge. He walked or prowled—for half an hour close about Oakley Crescent. Then, over the bridge and into the Park. Back again, and more prowling. At last, weary and worn, to the counter and apron, and Allchin's talk about golden syrup.

The next day, just before sunset, he sauntered on the Embankment. He lifted up his eyes, and there, walking towards him, came the slim figure in grey.

"Not like the other evening," said Rosamund, before he could speak, her eyes turning to the dull, featureless west.

He held her hand, until she gently drew it away, and then was frightened to find that he had held it so long. From head to foot, he quivered, deliciously, painfully. His tongue suffered a semi-paralysis, so that, trying to talk, he babbled—something about the sweetness of the air—a scent from the gardens across the river——

"I've had a letter from Bertha Cross," said his companion, as she walked slowly on. "She comes home to-morrow."

"Bertha Cross—? Ah, yes, your friend——"

The name sounded to Warburton as if from a remote past. He repeated it several times to himself.

They stood with face turned toward the lurid south. The air was very still. From away down the river sounded the bells of Lambeth Church, their volleying clang softened by distance to a monotonous refrain, drearily at one with the sadness of the falling night. Warburton heard them, yet heard them not; all external sounds blended with that within him, which was the furious beating of his heart. He moved a hand as if to touch Rosamund's, but let it fall as she spoke.

"I'm afraid I must go. It's really raining——"

Neither had an umbrella. Big drops were beginning to splash on the pavement. Warburton felt one upon his nose.

"To-morrow," he uttered thickly, his tongue hot and dry, his lips quivering.

"Yes, if it's fine," replied Rosamund.

"Early in the afternoon?"

"I can't. I must go and see Bertha."

They were walking at a quick step, and already getting wet.

"At this hour then," panted Will.

"Yes."

Lambeth bells were lost amid a hollow boom of distant thunder.

"I must run," cried Rosamund. "Good-bye."

He followed, keeping her in sight until she entered the house. Then he turned and walked like a madman through the hissing rain—walked he knew not whither—his being a mere erratic chaos, a symbol of Nature's prime impulse whirling amid London's multitudes.

CHAPTER XXXV

TIRED and sullen after the journey home from the seaside, Mrs. Cross kept her room. In the little bay-windowed parlour, Bertha Cross and Rosamund Elvan sat talking confidentially.

"Now, do confess," urged she of the liquid eyes and sentimental accent. "This is a little plot of yours—all in kindness, of course. You thought it best—you somehow brought him to it?"

Half laughing, Bertha shook her head.

"I haven't seen him for quite a long time. And do you really think this kind of plotting is in my way? It would as soon have occurred to me to try and persuade Mr. Franks to join the fire-brigade."

"Bertha! You don't mean anything by that? You don't think I am a danger to him?"

"No, no, no! To tell you the truth, I have tried to think just as little about it as possible, one way or the other. Third persons never do any good in such cases, and more often than not get into horrid scrapes."

"Fortunately," said Rosamund, after musing a moment with her chin on her hand, "I'm sure he isn't serious. It's his good-nature, his sense of honour. I think all the better of him for it. When he understands that I'm in earnest, we shall just be friends again, real friends."

"Then you are in earnest?" asked Bertha, her eyelids winking mirthfully.

Rosamund's reply was a very grave nod, after which she gazed awhile at vacancy.

"But," resumed Bertha, after reading her friend's face, "you have not succeeded in making him understand yet?"

"Perhaps not quite. Yesterday morning I had a letter from him, asking me to meet him in Kensington Gardens. I went, and we had a long talk. Then in the evening, by chance, I saw Mr. Warburton."

"Has that anything to do with the matter?"

"Oh, no!" replied Miss Elvan hastily. "I mention it, because, as I told you once before, Mr. Warburton always likes to talk of Norbert."

"I see. And you talked of him?"

"We only saw each other for a few minutes. The thunder-storm came on.—Bertha, I never knew any one so mysterious as Mr. Warburton. Isn't it extraordinary that Norbert, his intimate friend, doesn't know what he does? I can't help thinking he must write. One can't associate him with anything common, mean."

"Perhaps his glory will burst upon us one of these days," said Bertha.

"It really wouldn't surprise me. He has a remarkable face—the kind of face that suggests depth and force. I am sure he is very proud. He could bear any extreme of poverty rather than condescend to ignoble ways of earning money."

"Is the poor man very threadbare?" asked Bertha. "Has his coat that greenish colour which comes with old age in cheap material?"

"You incorrigible! As far as I have noticed, he is quite properly dressed."

"Oh, oh!" protested Bertha, in a shocked tone.

"Properly dressed! What a blow to my romantic imagination! I thought at least his coat-cuffs would be worn out. And his boots? Oh, surely he is down at heel? Do say that he's down at heel, Rosamund!"

"What a happy girl you are, Bertha," said the other after a laugh. "I sometimes think I would give anything to be like you."

"Ah, but you don't know—you can't see into the gloomy depths, hidden from every eye but my own. For instance, while here we sit, talking as if I hadn't a care in the world I am all the time thinking that I must go to Mr. Jollyman's—the grocer's, that is—as we haven't a lump of sugar in the house."

"Then let me walk with you," said Rosamund. "I oughtn't to have come worrying you to-day, before you had time to settle down. Just let me walk with you to the grocer's, and then I'll leave you at peace."

They presently went forth, and walked for some distance westward along Fulham Road.

"Here's Mr. Jollyman's," said Bertha. "Will you wait for me, or come in?"

Rosamund followed her friend into the shop. Absorbed in thought, she scarcely raised her eyes, until a voice from behind the counter replied to Bertha's "Good-morning"; then, suddenly looking up, she saw that which held her motionless. For a moment she gazed like a startled deer; the next her eyes fell, her face turned away; she fled out into the street.

And there Bertha found her, a few yards from the shop.

"Why did you run away?"

Rosamund had a dazed look.

"Who was that behind the counter?" she asked, under her breath.

"Mr. Jollyman. Why?"

The other walked on. Bertha kept at her side

"What's the matter?"

"Bertha—Mr. Jollyman is Mr. Warburton."

"Nonsense!"

"But he *is*! Here's the explanation—here's the mystery. A grocer—in an apron!"

Bertha was standing still. She, too, looked astonished, perplexed.

"Isn't it a case of extraordinary likeness?" she asked, with a grave smile.

"Oh, dear, no! I met his eye—he showed that he knew me—and then his voice. A grocer—in an apron!"

"This is very shocking," said Bertha, with a recovery of her natural humour. "Let us walk. Let us shake off the nightmare."

The word applied very well to Rosamund's condition; her fixed eyes were like those of a somnambulist.

"But, Bertha!" she suddenly exclaimed, in a voice of almost petulant protest. "He knew you all the time—oh, but perhaps he did not know your name?"

"Indeed he did. He's constantly sending things to the house."

"How extraordinary! Did you ever hear such an astonishing thing in your life?"

"You said more than once," remarked Bertha, "that Mr. Warburton was a man of mystery."

"Oh, but how *could* I have imagined—! a grocer!"

"In an apron!" added the other, with awed voice.

"But, Bertha, does Norbert know? He declared he had never found out what Mr. Warburton did. Was that true, or not?"

"Ah, that's the question. If poor Mr. Franks has had this secret upon his soul! I can hardly believe it. And yet—they are such intimate friends."

"He must have known it," declared Rosamund.

Thereupon she became mute, and only a syllable of dismay escaped her now and then during the rest of the walk to the Crosses' house. Her companion, too, was absorbed in thought. At the door Rosamund offered her hand. No, she would not come in; she had work which must positively be finished this afternoon whilst daylight lasted.

Out of the by-street, Rosamund turned into Fulham Road, and there found a cab to convey her home. On entering the house, she gave instructions that she was at home to nobody this afternoon; then she sat down at the table, as though to work on a drawing, but at the end of an hour her brush had not yet been dipped in colour. She rose, stood in the attitude of one who knows not what to do, and at length moved to the window. Instantly she drew back. On the opposite side of the little square stood a man, looking toward her house; and that man was Warburton.

From safe retirement, she watched him. He walked this way; he walked that; again he stood still, his eyes upon the house. Would he cross over? Would he venture to knock at the door? No, he withdrew; he disappeared.

Presently it was the hour of dusk. Every few minutes Rosamund reconnoitred at the window, and at length, just perceptible to her straining eyes, there again stood Warburton. He came forward. Standing with hand pressed against her side, she waited in nervous anguish for a knock at the front door; but it did not sound. She stood motionless for a long, long time, then drew a deep, deep breath, and trembled as she let herself sink into a chair.

Earlier than usual, she went up to her bedroom. In a corner of the room stood her trunk; this she opened, and from the chest of drawers she took forth articles of apparel, which she began to pack, as though for a journey. When the trunk was half full, she ceased in weariness, rested for a little, and then went to bed.

And in the darkness there came a sound of subdued sobbing. It lasted for some minutes—ceased—for some minutes was again audible. Then silence fell upon the chamber.

Lying awake between seven and eight next morning, Rosamund heard the postman's knock. At once she sprang out of bed, slipped on her dressing-gown, and rang the bell. Two letters were brought up to her; she received them with tremulous hand. Both were addressed in writing, unmistakably masculine; the one was thick, the other was thin; and this she opened first.

"Dear Miss Elvan"—it was Warburton who wrote—"I hoped to see you this evening, as we had appointed. Indeed, I *must* see you, for, as you may imagine, I have much to say. May I come to your house? In any case, let me know place and hour, and let it be as soon as possible. Reply at once, I entreat you. Ever sincerely yours——"

She laid it aside, and broke the other envelope.

"Dear, dearest Rosamund"—thus began Norbert Franks—" our talk this morning has left me in a state of mind which threatens frenzy. You know I haven't too much patience. It is out of the question for me to wait a week for your answer, though I promised. I can't wait even a couple of days. I must see you again to-morrow—must, must, *must*. Come to the same place, there's a good, dear, sweet, beautiful girl! If you don't, I shall be in Oakley Crescent, breaking doors open, behaving insanely. Come early——"

And so on, over two sheets of the very best note-paper, with Norbert's respectable address handsomely stamped in red at the top. (The other missive was on paper less fashionable, with the address, sadly plebeian, in mere handwriting.) Having read to the end, Rosamund finished her dressing and went down to the sitting-room. Breakfast was ready, but, before giving her attention to it, she penned a note. It was to Warburton. Briefly she informed him that she had decided to join her sister in the south of France, and that she was starting on the journey *this morning*. Her address, she added, would be " c/o Mrs. Alfred Coppinger, St. Jean de Luz, Basses Pyrénées." And therewith she remained Mr. Warburton's sincerely.

" Please let this be posted at once," said Rosamund when the landlady came to clear away.

And posted it was.

CHAPTER XXXVI

HIS hands upon the counter, Warburton stared at the door by which first Rosamund, then Bertha Cross, had disappeared. His nerves were a-tremble; his eyes were hot. Of a sudden he felt himself shaken with irresistible mirth; from the diaphragm it mounted to his throat, and only by a great effort did he save himself from exploding in laughter. The orgasm possessed him for several minutes. It was followed by a sense of light-heartedness, which set him walking about, rubbing his hands together, and humming tunes.

At last the burden had fallen from him; the foolish secret was blown abroad; once more he could look the world in the face, bidding it think of him what it would.

They were talking now—the two girls, discussing their strange discovery. When he saw Rosamund this evening—of course he would see her, as she had promised—her surprise would already have lost its poignancy; he had but to tell the story of his disaster, of his struggles, and then to announce the coming moment of rescue. No chance could have been happier than this which betrayed him to these two at the same time; for Bertha Cross's good sense would be the best possible corrective of any shock her more sensitive companion might have received. Bertha Cross's good sense —that was how he thought of her, without touch of emotion; whilst on Rosamund his imagination dwelt with exultant fervour. He saw himself as he would appear in her eyes when she knew all—noble, heroic. What he had done was a fine thing, beyond the reach of ordinary self-regarding mortals, and who more capable than Rosamund of appreciating such courage? After all, fate was kind. In the byways of London it had wrought for him a structure of romance, and amid mean pursuits it exalted him to an ideal of love.

And as he thus dreamt, and smiled and gloried —very much like an aproned Malvolio—the hours went quickly by. He found himself near Albert Bridge, pacing this way and that, expecting at every moment the appearance of the slim figure clad in grey. The sun set; the blind of Rosamund's sitting-room showed that there was lamplight within; and at ten o'clock Warburton still hung about the square, hoping—against his reason —that she might come forth. He went home, and wrote to her.

In a score of ways he explained to himself her holding aloof. It was vexation at his not having confided in her; it was a desire to reflect before seeing him again; it was—and so on, all through the night, which brought him never a wink of sleep. Next morning, he did not go to the shop; it would have been impossible to stand at the counter for ten minutes, he sent a note to Allchin, saying that he was detained by private affairs, then set off for a day-long walk in the country, to kill time until the coming of Rosamund's reply. On his return in the afternoon, he found it awaiting him.

An hour later he was in Oakley Crescent. He stood looking at the house for a moment, then approached, and knocked at the door. He asked if Miss Elvan was at home.

"She's gone away," was the reply of the landlady, who spoke distantly, her face a respectable blank.

"Left for good?"

"Yes, sir," answered the woman, her eyes falling.

"You don't know where she has gone to?"

"It's somewhere abroad, sir—in France, I think. She has a sister there."

This was at five o'clock or so. Of what happened during the next four hours, Will had never a very distinct recollection. Beyond doubt, he called at the shop, and spoke with Allchin; beyond doubt, also, he went to his lodgings and packed a travelling bag. Which of his movements were performed in cabs, which on foot, he could scarce have decided, had he reflected on the matter during the night that followed. That night was passed in the train, on a steamboat, then again on the railway. And before sunrise he was in Paris.

At the railway refreshment-room, he had breakfast, eating with some appetite; then he drove to the terminus of another line. The streets of Paris, dim vistas under a rosy dawn, had no reality for his eyes; the figures flitting here and there, the voices speaking a foreign tongue, made part of a phantasm in which he himself moved no less fantastically. He was in Paris; yet how could that be? He would wake up, and find himself at his lodgings, and get up to go to business in Fulham Road; but the dream bore him on. Now he had taken another ticket. His bag was being registered—for St. Jean de Luz. A long journey lay before him. He yawned violently, half remembering that he had passed two nights without sleep. Then he found himself seated in a corner of the railway carriage, an unknown landscape slipping away before his eyes.

Now for the first time did he seem to be really aware of what he was doing. Rosamund had taken flight to the Pyrenees, and he was in hot pursuit. He grew exhilarated in the thought of his virile energy. If the glimpse of him aproned and behind a counter had been too great a shock for Rosamund's romantic nature, this vigorous action would more than redeem his manhood in her sight. "Yes, I am a grocer; I have lived for a couple of years by selling tea and sugar—not to speak of treacle; but none the less I am the man you drew on to love you. Grocer though I be, I come to claim you!" Thus would he speak, and how could the reply be doubtful? In such a situation, all depends on the man's strength and passionate resolve. Rosamund should be his; he swore it in his heart. She should take him as he was, grocer's shop and all; not until her troth was pledged would he make known to her the prospect of better things. The emotions of the primitive lover had told upon him. She thought to escape him, by flight across Europe? But what if the flight were meant as a test of his worthiness? He seized upon the idea, and rejoiced in it. Rosamund might well have conceived this method of justifying both him and herself. "If he loves me as I would be loved, let him dare to follow!"

To-morrow morning he would stand before her, grocerdom a thousand miles away. They would walk together, as when they were among the Alps. Why, even then, had his heart prompted, had honour permitted, he could have won her. He believed now, what at the time he had refused to admit, that Franks' moment of jealous anger was not without its justification. Again they would meet among the mountains, and the shop in Fulham Road would be seen as at the wrong end of a telescope—its due proportions. They would return together to England, and at once be married. As for the grocery business——

Reason lost itself amid ardours of the natural man.

He paid little heed to the country through which he was passing. He flung himself on to the dark platform, and tottered drunkenly in search of the exit. *Billet*? Why, yes, he had a *billet* somewhere. Hotel? Yes, yes, the hotel,—no matter which. It took some minutes before his brain could grasp the idea that his luggage cheque was wanted; he had forgotten that he had any luggage at all. Ultimately, he was thrust into some sort of a vehicle, which set him down at the hotel door. Food? Good Heavens, no; but something to drink, and a bed to tumble into—quick.

He stood in a bedroom, holding in his hand a glass of he knew not what beverage. Before him was a waiter, to whom—very much to his own surprise—he discoursed fluently in French, or something meant for that tongue. That it was more than sixty hours since he had slept; that he had started from London at a moment's notice; that the Channel had been very rough for the time of the year; that he had never been in this part of France before, and hoped to see a good deal of the Pyrenees, perhaps to have a run into Spain; that first of all he wanted to find the abode of an English lady named Mrs. Cap—Cop—

he couldn't think of the name, but he had written it down in his pocket-book.

The door closed; the waiter was gone; but Warburton still talked French.

"Oui, oui—en effet—très fatigué, horriblement fatigué! Trois nuits sans sommeil—trois nuits—trois!"

His clothes fell in a heap on the floor; his body fell in another direction. He was dead asleep.

CHAPTER XXXVII

AMID struggle and gloom the scene changed. He was in Kew Gardens, rushing hither and thither, in search of some one. The sun still beat upon him, and he streamed at every pore. Not only did he seek in vain, but he could not remember who it was that he sought. This way and that, along the broad and narrow walks, he hurried in torment, until of a sudden, at a great distance, he descried a figure seated on a bench. He bounded forward. In a moment he would see the face, and would know——

When he awoke a sense of strangeness hung about him, and, as he sat up in bed, he remembered. This was the hotel at St. Jean de Luz. What could be the time? He had no matches at hand, and did not know where the bell was. Looking around, he perceived at length a thread of light, of daylight undoubtedly, which must come from the window. He got out of bed, cautiously crossed the floor, found the window, and the means of opening it, then unlatched the shutters which had kept the room in darkness. At once a flood of sunshine poured in. Looking forth, he saw a quiet little street of houses and gardens, and beyond, some miles away, a mountain peak rising against the cloudless blue.

His watch had run down. He rang the bell, and learnt that the hour was nearly eleven.

" I have slept well," he said in his Anglo-French. " I am hungry. Bring me hot water. And find out, if you can, where lives Mrs. Coppinger. I couldn't remember the name last night—Mrs. Coppinger."

In half an hour he was downstairs. The English lady for whom he inquired lived, they told him, outside St. Jean de Luz, but not much more than a mile away. Good, he would go there after lunch. And until that meal was ready, he strolled out to have a look at the sea. Five minutes' walk brought him on to the shore of a rounded bay, sheltered by breakwaters against Atlantic storms: above a sandy beach lay the little town, with grassy slopes falling softly to the tide on either hand.

At noon, he ate and drank heroically, then, having had his way pointed out to him, set forth on the quest. He passed through the length of the town, crossed the little river Nivelle, where he paused for a moment on the bridge, to gaze at the panorama of mountains, all but to the summit clad in soft verdure, and presently turned into an inland road, which led him between pastures and fields of maize, gently upwards. On a height before him stood a house, which he believed to be that he sought; he had written down its unrememberable Basque name, and inquiry of a peasant assured him that he was not mistaken. Having his goal in view, he stood to reflect. Could he march up to the front door, and ask boldly for Miss Elvan? But—the doubt suddenly struck him—what if Rosamund were not living here? At Mrs. Coppinger's her sister was governess; she had bidden him address letters there, but that might be merely for convenience; perhaps she was not Mrs. Coppinger's guest at all, but had an abode somewhere in the town. In that case, he must see her sister—who perhaps, nay, all but certainly, had never heard his name.

He walked on. The road became a hollow lane, with fern and heather and gorse intermingled below the thickets on the bank. Another five minutes would bring him to the top of the hill, to the avenue of trees by which the house was approached. And the nearer he came, the more awkward seemed his enterprise. It might have been better to write a note to Rosamund, announcing his arrival, and asking for an interview. On the other hand that was a timid proceeding; boldly to present himself before her would be much more effective. If he could only be sure of seeing her, and seeing her alone.

For a couple of hours did he loiter irresolutely, ever hoping that chance might help him. Perhaps, as the afternoon grew cooler, people might come forth from the house. His patience at length worn out, he again entered the avenue, half resolved to go up to the door.

All at once he heard voices—the voices of children, and toward him came two little girls, followed by a young lady. They drew near. Standing his ground, with muscles tense, Warburton glanced at the young lady's face, and could not doubt that this was Rosamund's sister; the features were much less notable than Rosamund's, but their gentle prettiness made claim of kindred with her. Forthwith he doffed his hat, and advanced respectfully.

"I think I am speaking to Miss Elvan?"

A nervous smile, a timidly surprised affirmative, put him a little more at his ease.

"My name is Warburton," he pursued, with the

half humorous air of one who takes a liberty which he feels sure will be pardoned. "I have the pleasure of knowing your relatives, the Pomfrets, and——"

"Oh, yes, my sister has often spoken of you," said Winifred quickly. Then, as if afraid that she had committed an indiscretion, she cast down her eyes and looked embarrassed.

"Your sister is here, I think," fell from Warburton, as he threw a glance at the two little girls, who had drawn apart.

"Here? Oh, no. Not long ago she thought of coming, but——"

Will stood confounded. All manner of conjectures flashed through his mind. Rosamund must have broken her journey somewhere. That she had not left England at all seemed impossible.

"I was mistaken," he forced himself to remark carelessly. Then, with a friendly smile, "Forgive me for intruding myself. I came up here for the view.——"

"Yes, isn't it beautiful!" exclaimed Winifred, evidently glad of this diversion from personal topics. And they talked of the landscape, until Warburton felt that he must take his leave. He mentioned where he was staying, said that he hoped to spend a week or so at St. Jean de Luz—and so got away, with an uneasy feeling that his behaviour had not exactly been such as to recommend him to the timid young lady.

Rosamund had broken her journey somewhere, that was evident; perhaps in Paris, where he knew she had friends. If she did not arrive this evening, or to-morrow, her sister would at all events hear that she was coming. But how was he to be informed of her arrival? How could he keep an espial on the house? His situation was wretchedly unlike that he had pictured to himself; instead of the romantic lover, carrying all before him by the energy of passion, he had to play a plotting, almost sneaking part, in constant fear of being taken for a presumptuous interloper. Lucky that Rosamund had spoken of him to her sister. Well, he must wait; though waiting was the worst torture for a man in his mood.

He idled through the day on the seashore. Next morning he bathed, and had a long walk, coming back by way of the Coppingers' house, but passing quickly, and seeing no one. When he returned to the hotel, he was told that a gentleman had called to see him, and had left his card "Mr. Alfred Coppinger." Ho, ho! Winifred Elvan had mentioned their meeting, and the people wished to be friendly. Excellent! This afternoon he would present himself. Splendid. All his difficulties were at an end. He saw himself once more in a gallant attitude.

The weather was very hot—unusually hot, said people at the hotel. As he climbed the hill between three and four o'clock, the sun's ardour reminded him of old times in the tropics. He passed along the shady avenue, and the house door was opened to him by a Basque maid-servant, who led him to the drawing-room. Here, in a dim light which filtered through the interstices of shutters, sat the lady of the house alone.

"Is it Mr. Warburton?" she asked, rising feebly, and speaking in a thin, fatigued, but kindly voice. "So kind of you to come. My husband will be delighted to see you. How did you get up here on such a day? Oh, the terrible heat!"

In a minute or two the door opened to admit Mr. Coppinger, and the visitor, his eyes now accustomed to the gloom, saw a ruddy, vigorous, middle-aged man, dressed in flannels, and wearing the white shoes called *espadrilles*.

"Hoped you would come," he cried, shaking hands cordially. "Why didn't you look in yesterday? Miss Elvan ought to have told you that it does me good to see an Englishman. Here for a holiday? Blazing hot, but it won't last long. South wind. My wife can't stand it. She's here because of the doctors, but it's all humbug; there are lots of places in England would suit her just as well, and perhaps better. Let's have some tea, Alice, there's a good girl. Mr. Warburton looks thirsty, and I can manage a dozen cups or so. Where's Winifred? Let her bring in the kits. They're getting shy; it'll do them good to see a stranger."

Will stayed for a couple of hours, amused with Mr. Coppinger's talk, and pleased with the gentle society of the ladies. The invitation to breakfast being seriously repeated, he rejoiced to accept it. See how Providence favours the daring. When Rosamund arrived, she would find him established as a friend of the Coppingers. He went his way exultingly.

But neither on the morrow, nor the day after, did Winifred receive any news from her sister. Will of course kept to himself the events of his last two days in London; he did not venture to hint at any knowledge of Rosamund's movements. A suspicion was growing in his mind that she might not have left England; in which case, was ever man's plight more ridiculous than his? It would mean that Rosamund had deliberately misled him; but could he think her capable of that? If it were so, and if her feelings toward him had undergone so abruptly violent a change simply because of the discovery she had made—why, then Rosamund was not Rosamund at all, and he might write himself down a most egregious ass.

Had not an inkling of some such thing whispered softly to him before now? Had there not been moments, during the last fortnight, when he stood, as it were, face to face with himself, and felt oddly abashed by a look in his own eyes?

Before leaving his lodgings he had written on a piece of paper: "Poste Restante, St. Jean de Luz, France," and had given it to Mrs. Wick, with the charge to forward immediately any letter or telegram that might arrive for him. But his inquiries at the post-office were vain. To be sure, weeks had often gone by without bringing him a letter; there was nothing strange in this silence; yet it vexed and disquieted him. On the fourth day of his waiting, the weather suddenly broke, rain fell in torrents, and continued for forty-eight hours. Had not the Coppingers' house been open to him he must have spent a wretched time. Returning to the hotel on the second evening of deluge, he looked in at the post-office, and this time a letter was put into his hand. He opened and read it at once.

"Dear old boy, why the deuce have you gone away to the end of the earth without letting me know? I called at your place this evening, and was amazed at the sight of the address which your evil-eyed woman showed me—looking as if she feared I should steal it. I wanted particularly to see you. How long are you going to stay down yonder? Rosamund and I start *for our honeymoon* on Thursday next, and we shall probably be away for a couple of months, in Tyrol. Does this astonish you? It oughtn't to, seeing that you've done your best to bring it about. Yes, Rosamund and I are going to be married, with the least possible delay. I'll tell you all the details some day—though there's very little to tell that you don't know. Congratulate me on having come to my senses. How precious near I was to making a tremendous fool of myself. It's you I have to thank, old man. Of course, as you saw, I should never have cared for any one but Rosamund, and it's pretty sure that she would never have been happy with any one but me. I wanted you to be a witness at our wedding, and now you've bolted, confound you! Write to my London address, and it will be forwarded."

Will thrust the letter into his pocket, went out into the street, and walked to the hotel through heavy rain, without thinking to open his umbrella.

Next morning, the sky was clear again, the sunny air fresh as that of spring. Will rose earlier than usual, and set out on an excursion. He took train to Hendaye, the little frontier town, at the mouth of the Bidassoa, crossed the river in a boat, stepped on to Spanish soil, and climbed the hill on which stands Fuenterabbia.

Later he passed again to the French shore, and lunched at the hotel. Then he took a carriage, and drove up the gorge of Bidassoa, enjoying the wild mountain scenery as much as he had enjoyed anything in his life. The road bridged the river; it brought him into Spain once more, and on as far as to the Spanish village of Vera, where he lingered in the mellowing afternoon. All round him were green slopes of the Pyrenees, green with pasture and with turf, with bracken, with woods of oak. There came by a yoke of white oxen, their heads covered with the wonted sheepskin, and on their foreheads the fringe of red wool tassles; he touched a warm flank with his palm, and looked into the mild, lustrous eyes of the beast that passed near him.

"Vera, Vera," he repeated to himself, with pleasure in the name. He should remember Vera when he was back again behind the counter in Fulham Road. He had never thought to see the Pyrenees, never dreamt of looking at Spain. It was a good holiday.

"Vera, Vera," he again murmured. How came the place to be so called? The word seemed to mean *true*. He mused upon it.

He dined at the village inn, then drove at dusk back to Hendaye, down the great gorge; crags and precipices, wooded ravines and barren heights glooming magnificently under a sky warm with afterglow; beside him the torrent leapt and roared, and foamed into whiteness.

And from Hendaye the train brought him back to St. Jean de Luz. Before going to bed, he penned a note to Mr. Coppinger, saying that he was unexpectedly obliged to leave for England, at an early hour next day, and regretted that he could not come to say good-bye. He added a postscript. "Miss Elvan will, of course, know of her sister's marriage to Norbert Franks. I hear it takes place to-morrow. Very good news."

This written, he smoked a meditative pipe, and went upstairs humming a tune.

CHAPTER XXXVIII

TOUCHING the shore of England, Will stamped like a man who returns from exile. It was a blustering afternoon, more like November than August; livid clouds pelted him with rain, and the wind chilled his face; but this suited very well with the mood which possessed him. He had been away on a holiday—a more expensive holiday than he ought to have allowed himself, and was back full of vigour. Instead of making him qualmish, the green roarers of the Channel had braced his nerves, and put him in good heart; the boat could not roll and pitch half enough for his spirits. A holiday—a run to the Pyrenees and back; who durst say that it had been anything else? The only person who could see the matter in another light was little likely to disclose her thoughts.

At Dover he telegraphed to Godfrey Sherwood: "Come and see me to-night." True, he had been absent only a week, but the time seemed to him so long that he felt it must have teemed with events. In the railway carriage he glowed with good fellowship toward the other passengers; the rain-beaten hop-lands rejoiced his eyes, and the first houses of London were so many friendly faces greeting his return. From the station he drove to his shop. Allchin, engaged in serving a lady, forgot himself at the sight of Mr. Jollyman, and gave a shout of welcome. All was right, nothing troublesome had happened; trade better than usual at this time of year.

"He'll have to put up the shutters," said Allchin confidentially, with a nod in the direction of the rival grocer. "His wife's been making a row in the shop again—disgraceful scene—talk of the 'ole neighbourhood. She began throwing things at customers, and somebody as was badly hit on the jaw with a tin of sardines complained to the police. We shall be rid of him very soon, you'll see, sir."

This gave Warburton small satisfaction, but he kept his human thoughts to himself, and presently went home. Here his landlady met him with the announcement that only a few hours ago she had forwarded a letter delivered by the post this morning. This was vexatious; several days must elapse before he could have the letter back again from St. Jean de Luz. Sure that Mrs. Wick must have closely scrutinised the envelope, he questioned her as to handwriting and postmark, but the woman declared that she had given not a glance to these things, which were not her business. Couldn't she even remember whether the writing looked masculine or feminine? No; she had not the slightest idea; it was not her business to "pry"; and Mrs. Wick closed her bloodless lips with virtuous severity.

He had tea and walked back again to the shop, where as he girt himself with his apron, he chuckled contentedly.

"Has Mrs. Cross looked in?" he inquired.

"Yes, sir," answered his henchman, "she was here day before yes'day, and asked where you was. I said you was travelling for your health in foreign parts."

"And what did she say to that?"

"She said 'Oh'—that's all, sir. It was a very small order she gave. I can't make out how she manages to use so little sugar in her 'ouse. It's certain the servant doesn't have her tea too sweet—what do *you* think, sir?"

Warburton spoke of something else.

At nine o'clock he sat at home awaiting his visitor. The expected knock soon sounded and Sherwood was shown into the room. Will grasped his hand, calling out: "What news?"

"News?" echoed Godfrey, in a voice of no good omen. "Haven't you heard?"

"Heard what?"

"But your telegram—? Wasn't that what it meant?"

"What do *you* mean?" cried Will. "Speak, man! I've been abroad for a week. I know nothing; I telegraphed because I wanted to see you, that was all."

"Confound it! I hoped you knew the worst. Strangwyn is dead."

"He's dead?" Well, isn't that what we've been waiting for?"

"Not the old man," groaned Sherwood, "not the old man. It's Ted Strangwyn that's dead. Never was such an extraordinary case of bad luck. And his death—the most astounding you ever heard of. He was down in Yorkshire for the grouse. The dogcart came round in the morning, and as he stood beside it, stowing away a gun or something, the horse made a movement forward, and the wheel went over his toe. He thought nothing of it. The next day he was ill; it turned to tetanus; and in a few hours he died. Did you ever in your life hear anything like that?"

Warburton had listened gravely. Towards the

end, his features began to twitch, and, a moment after Godfrey had ceased, a spasm of laughter overcame him.

"I can't help it, Sherwood," he gasped. "It's brutal, I know, but I can't help it."

"My dear boy," exclaimed the other, with a countenance of relief, "I'm delighted you can laugh. Talk about the irony of fate—eh? I couldn't believe my eyes when I saw the paragraph in the paper yesterday. But, you know," he added earnestly, "I don't absolutely give up hope. According to the latest news, it almost looks as if old Strangwyn might recover; and, if he does, I shall certainly try to get this money out of him. If he has any sense of honour——"

Will again laughed, but not so spontaneously.

"My boy," he said, "it's all up, and you know it. You'll never see a penny of your ten thousand pounds."

"Oh, but I can't help hoping——"

"Hope as much as you like. How goes the other affair?"

"Why, there, too, odd things have been happening. Milligan has just got engaged, and, to tell you the truth, to a girl I shouldn't have thought he'd ever have looked twice at. It's a Miss Parker, the daughter of a City man. Pretty enough if you like, but as far as I can see, no more brains than a teapot, and I can't for the life of me understand how a man like Milligan—. But of course, it makes no difference; our work goes on. We have an enormous correspondence."

"Does Miss Parker interest herself in it?" asked Will.

"Oh, yes, in a way, you know; as far as she can. She has turned vegetarian, of course. To tell you the truth, Warburton, it vexes me a good deal. I didn't think Milligan could do such a silly thing. I hope he'll get married quickly. Just at present, the fact is, he isn't quite himself."

Again Warburton was subdued by laughter.

"Well, I thought things might have been happening whilst I was away," he said, "and I wasn't mistaken. Luckily, I have come back with a renewed gusto for the shop. By the bye, I'm going to keep that secret no longer. I'm a grocer, and probably shall be a grocer all my life, and the sooner people know it the better. I'm sick of hiding away. Tell Milligan the story; it will amuse Miss Parker. And, talking of Miss Parker, do you know that Norbert Franks is married? His old love—Miss Elvan. Of course it was the sensible thing to do. They're off to Tyrol. As soon as I have their address, I shall write and tell him all about Jollyman's."

"Of course, if you really feel you must," said Godfrey, with reluctance. "But remember that I still hope to recover the money. Old Strangwyn has the reputation of being an honourable man——"

"Like Brutus," broke in Warburton, cheerfully. "Let us hope. Of course we will hope. Hope springs eternal——"

Days went by, and at length the desired letter came back from St. Jean de Luz. Seeing at a glance that it was from his sister, Will reproached himself for having let more than a month elapse without writing to St. Neots. Of his recent "holiday" he had no intention of saying a word. Jane wrote a longer letter than usual, and its tenor was disquieting. Their mother had not been at all well lately; Jane noticed that she was becoming very weak. "You know how she dreads to give trouble, and cannot bear to have any one worry about her. She has seen Dr. Edge twice in the last few days, but not in my presence, and I feel sure that she has forbidden him to tell me the truth about her. I dare not let her guess how anxious I am, and have to go on in my usual way, just doing what I can for her comfort. If you would come over for a day, I should feel very glad. Not having seen mother for some time, you would be better able than I to judge how she looks." After reading this Will's self-reproaches were doubled. At once he set off for St. Neots.

On arriving at The Haws, he found Jane gardening, and spoke with her before he went in to see his mother.

He had been away from home, he said, and her letter had strayed in pursuit of him.

"I wondered," said Jane, her honest eyes searching his countenance. "And it's so long since you sent a word; I should have written again this afternoon."

"I've been abominably neglectful," he replied, "and time goes so quickly."

"There's something strange in your look," said the girl. "What is it, I wonder? You've altered in some way I don't know how."

"Think so? but never mind me; tell me about mother."

They stood among the garden scents, amid the flowers, which told of parting summer, and conversed with voices softened by tender solicitude. Jane was above all anxious that her brother's visit should seem spontaneous, and Will promised not to hint at the news she had sent him. They entered the house together. Mrs. Warburton, after her usual morning occupations, had lain down on the couch in the parlour, and fallen asleep; as soon as he beheld her face, Will understood his sister's fears. White, motionless, beautiful in its absolute calm, the visage might have been that of the dead; after gazing for a moment, both, on the same impulse, put forth a hand to touch the unconscious form. The eyelids rose; a look of confused trouble darkened the features; then the lips relaxed in a happy smile.

"Will—and you find me asleep?—I appeal to Jane; she will tell you it's only an accident. Did you ever before see me asleep like this, Jane?"

At once she rose, and moved about, and strove to be herself; but the effort it cost her was too obvious; presently she had to sit down, with tremulous limbs, and Will noticed that her forehead was moist.

Not till evening did he find it possible to lead the conversation to the subject of her health. Jane had purposely left them alone. Her son having said that he feared she was not so well as usual, Mrs. Warburton quietly admitted that she had recently consulted her doctor.

"I am not young, Will, you know. Sixty-five next birthday."

"But you don't call that old!" exclaimed her son.

"Yes, it's old for one of my family, dear. None of us, that I know of, lived to be much more than sixty, and most died long before. Don't let us wear melancholy faces," she added, with that winning smile which had ever been the blessing of all about her. "You and I, dear, are too sensible, I hope, to complain or be frightened because life must have an end. When my time comes,

I trust to my children not to make me unhappy by forgetting what I have always tried to teach them. I should like to think—and I know—that you would be sorry to lose me; but to see you miserable on my account, or to think you miserable after I have gone—I couldn't bear that."

Will was silent, deeply impressed by the calm voice, the noble thought. He had always felt no less respect than love for his mother, especially during the latter years, when experience of life better enabled him to understand her rare qualities; but a deeper reverence took possession of him whilst she was speaking. Her words not only extended his knowledge of her character; they helped him to an understanding of himself, to a clearer view of life, and its possibilities.

"I want to speak to you of Jane," continued Mrs. Warburton, with a look of pleasant reflection. "You know she went to see her friend, Miss Winter, a few weeks ago. Has she told you anything about it?"

"Nothing at all."

"Well, do you know that Miss Winter has taken up flower-growing as a business, and it looks as if she would be very successful. She is renting more land, to make gardens of, and has two girls with her, as apprentices. I think that's what Jane will turn to some day. Of course she won't be really obliged to work for her living, but, when she is alone, I'm certain she won't be content to live just as she does now—she is far too active; but for me, I daresay she would go and join Miss Winter at once."

"I don't much care for that idea of girls going out to work when they could live quietly at home," said Will.

"I used to have the same feeling," answered his mother, "but Jane and I have often talked about it, and I see there is something to be said for the other view. At all events, I wanted to prevent you from wondering what was to become of her when she was left alone. To be sure," she added, with a bright smile, "Jane may marry. I hope she will. But I know she won't easily be persuaded to give up her independence. Jane is a very independent little person."

"If she has that in mind," said Will, "why shouldn't you both go and live over there, in Suffolk? You could find a house, no doubt——"

Mrs. Warburton gently shook her head.

"I don't think I could leave The Haws. And—for the short time——"

"Short time? but you are not seriously ill, mother."

"If I get stronger," said Mrs. Warburton, without raising her eyes, "we must manage to send Jane into Suffolk. I could get along very well alone. But there—we have talked enough for this evening, Will. Can you stay over to-morrow? Do, if you could manage it. I am glad to have you near me."

When they parted for the night, Will asked his sister to meet him in the garden before breakfast, and Jane nodded assent.

CHAPTER XXXIX

THE garden was drenched in dew, and when about seven o'clock, the first sunbeam pierced the grey mantle of the east, every leaf flashed back the yellow light. Will was walking there alone, his eyes turned now and then to the white window of his mother's room.

Jane came forth with her rosy morning face, her expression graver than of wont.

"You are uneasy about mother," were her first words. "So am I, very. I feel convinced Dr. Edge has given her some serious warning; I saw the change in her after his last visit."

"I shall go and see him," said Will.

They talked of their anxiety, then Warburton proposed that they should walk a little way along the road, for the air was cool.

"I've something I want to tell you," he began, when they had set forth. "It's a little startling —rather ludicrous, too. What should you say if some one came and told you he had seen me serving behind a grocer's counter in London?"

"What do you mean, Will?"

"Well, I want to know how it would strike you. Should you be horrified?"

"No; but astonished."

"Very well. The fact of the matter is then," said Warburton, with an uneasy smile, "that for a couple of years I *have* been doing that. It came about in this way——"

He related Godfrey Sherwood's reckless proceedings, and the circumstances which had decided him to take a shop. No exclamation escaped the listener; she walked with eyes downcast, and, when her brother ceased, looked at him very gently, affectionately.

"It was brave of you, Will," she said.

"Well, I saw no other way of making good the loss; but now I am sick of living a double life—*that* has really been the worst part of it, all along. What I want to ask you, is—would it be wise or not to tell mother? Would it worry and distress her? As for the money, you see there's nothing to worry about; the shop will yield a sufficient income, though not as much as we hoped from Applegarth's; but of course I shall have to go on behind the counter."

He broke off, laughing, and Jane smiled, though with a line of trouble on her brow.

"That won't do," she said, with quiet decision.

"Oh, I'm getting used to it."

"No, no, Will, it won't do. We must find a better way. I see no harm in shopkeeping, if one has been brought up to it; but you haven't, and it isn't suitable for you. About mother—yes, I think we'd better tell her. She won't worry on account of the money; that isn't her nature, and it's very much better that there should be confidence between us all."

"I haven't enjoyed telling lies," said Will, "I assure you."

"That I'm sure you haven't, poor boy!—but Mr. Sherwood? Hasn't he made any effort to help you. Surely he——"

"Poor old Godfrey!" broke in her brother, laughing. "It's a joke to remember that I used to think him a splendid man of business, far more practical than I. Why, there's no dreamier muddlehead living."

He told the stories of Strangwyn and of Milligan with such exuberance of humour that Jane could not but join in his merriment.

"No, no; it's no good looking in that direction. The money has gone, there's no help for it. But you can depend on Jollyman's. Of course the affair would have been much more difficult without Allchin. Oh, you must see Allchin some day!"

"And absolutely no one has discovered the secret?" asked Jane.

Will hesitated, then.

"Yes, one person. You remember the name of Miss Elvan? A fortnight ago—imagine the scene—she walked into the shop with a friend of hers, a Miss Cross, who has been one of my customers from the first. As soon as she caught sight of me she turned and ran; yes, ran out into the street in indignation and horror. Of course she must have told her friend, and whether Miss Cross will ever come to the shop again, I don't know. I never mentioned that name to you, did I? The Crosses were friends of Norbert Franks. And, by the bye, I hear that Franks was married to Miss Elvan a few days ago—just after her awful discovery. No doubt she told him, and perhaps he'll drop my acquaintance."

"You don't mean that?"

"Well, not quite; but it wouldn't surprise me if his wife told him that really one mustn't be too intimate with grocers. In future, I'm going to tell everybody; there shall be no more hiding and sneaking. That's what debases a man; not the selling of sugar and tea. A short time ago, I had got into a vile state of mind; I felt like poisoning myself. And I'm convinced it was merely the burden of lies weighing upon me. Yes, yes, you're quite right; of course, mother must be told. Shall I leave it to you, Jane? I think you could break it better."

After breakfast, Will walked into St. Neots, to have a private conversation with Dr. Edge, and whilst he was away Jane told her mother the story of the lost money. At the end of an hour's talk, she went out into the garden, where presently she was found by her brother, who had walked back at his utmost pace, and wore a perturbed countenance.

"You haven't told yet?" were his first words, uttered in a breathless undertone.

"Why?" asked Jane startled.

"I'm afraid of the result. Edge says that every sort of agitation must be avoided."

"I have told her," said Jane, with quiet voice, but anxious look. "She was grieved on your account, but it gave her no shock. Again and again she said how glad she was you had let us know the truth."

"So far then, good."

"But Dr. Edge—what did he tell you?"

"He said he had wanted to see me, and thought of writing. Yes, he speaks seriously."

They talked for a little, then Will went into the house alone, and found his mother as she sat in her wonted place, the usual needlework on her lap. As he crossed the room, she kept her eyes upon him in a gaze of the gentlest reproach, mingled with a smile, which told the origin of Will's wholesome humour.

"And you couldn't trust me to take my share of the trouble?"

"I knew only too well," replied her son, "that your own share wouldn't content you."

"Greedy mother!—Perhaps you were right, Will. I suppose I should have interfered, and made everything worse for you; but you needn't have waited quite so long before telling me. The one thing that I can't understand is Mr. Sherwood's behaviour. You had always given me such a different idea of him. Really, I don't think he ought to have been let off so easily."

"Oh, poor old Godfrey! What could he do? He was sorry as man could be, and he gave me all the cash he could scrape together——"

"I'm glad he wasn't a friend of mine," said Mrs. Warburton. "In all my life, I have never quarrelled with a friend, but I'm afraid I must have fallen out with Mr. Sherwood. Think of the women who entrust their all to men of that kind, and have no strong son to save them from the consequences."

After the mid-day meal all sat together for an hour or two in the garden. By an evening train, Will returned to London. Jane had promised to let him have frequent news, and during the ensuing week she wrote twice with very favourable accounts of their mother's condition. A month went by without any disquieting report, then came a letter in Mrs. Warburton's own hand.

"My dear Will," she wrote, "I can't keep secrets as long as you. This is to inform you that a week ago I let The Haws, on annual tenancy, to a friend of Mr. Turnbull's, who was looking for such a house. The day after to-morrow we begin our removal to a home which Jane has taken near to Miss Winter's in Suffolk. That she was able to find just what we wanted at a moment's notice encourages me in thinking that Providence is on our side, or, as your dear father used to say, that the oracle has spoken. In a week's time I hope to send news that we are settled. You are forbidden to come here before our departure, but will be invited to the new home as soon as possible. The address is——" etc.

The same post brought a letter from Jane.

"Don't be alarmed by the news," she wrote. "Mother has been so firm in this resolve since the day of your leaving us, that I could only obey her. Wonderful and delightful to tell, she seems better in health. I dare not make too much of this, after what Dr. Edge said, but for the present she is certainly stronger. As you suppose, I am going to work with Miss Winter. Come and see us when we are settled, and you shall hear all our plans. Everything has been done so quickly, that I live in a sort of a dream. Don't worry, and of course don't on any account come."

These letters arrived in the evening, and, after reading them, Warburton was so moved that he had to go out and walk under the starry sky, in quiet streets. Of course the motive on which his mother had acted was a desire to free him as soon as possible from the slavery of the shop; but that slavery had now grown so supportable, that he grieved over the sacrifice made for his sake. After all, would he not have done better to live on with his secret? And yet—and yet——

CHAPTER XL

WITH curiosity which had in it a touch of amusement, Will was waiting to hear from Norbert Franks. He waited for nearly a month, and was beginning to feel rather hurt at his friend's neglect, perhaps a little uneasy on another score, when there arrived an Italian postcard, stamped Venice. "We have been tempted as far as this," ran the hurried scrawl. "Must be home in ten days. Shall be delighted to see you again." Warburton puckered his brows and wondered whether a previous letter or card had failed to reach him. But probably not.

At the end of September, Franks wrote from his London address, briefly but cordially, with an invitation to luncheon on the next day, which was Sunday. And Warburton went.

He was nervous as he knocked at the door; he was rather more nervous as he walked into the studio. Norbert advanced to him with a shout of welcome, and from a chair in the background rose Mrs. Franks. Perceptibly changed, both of them. The artist's look was not quite so ingenuous as formerly; his speech, resolute in friendliness, had not quite the familiar note. Rosamund, already more mature of aspect, smiled somewhat too persistently, seemed rather too bent on showing herself unembarrassed. They plunged into talk of Tyrol, of the Dolomites, of Venice, and, so talking, passed into the dining-room.

"Queer little house this, isn't it?" said Mrs. Franks as she sat down to table. "Everything is sacrificed to the studio; there's no room to turn anywhere else. We must look at once for more comfortable quarters."

"It's only meant for a man living alone," said the artist, with a laugh. Franks laughed frequently, whether what he said was amusing or not. "Yes, we must find something roomier."

"A score of sitters waiting for you, I suppose?" said Warburton.

"Oh, several. One of them such an awful phiz that I'm afraid of her. If I make her presentable, it'll be my greatest feat yet. But the labourer is worthy of his hire, you know, and this bit of beauty-making will have its price."

"You know how to interpret *that*, Mr. Warburton," said Rosamund, with a discreetly confidential smile. "Norbert asks very much less than any other portrait painter of his reputation would."

"He'll grow out of that bad habit," Will replied. His note was one of joviality, almost of bluffness.

"I'm not sure that I wish him to," said the painter's wife, her eyes straying as if in a sudden dreaminess. "It's a distinction nowadays not to care for money. Norbert jokes about making an ugly woman beautiful," she went on earnestly, "but what he will really do is to discover the very best aspect of the face, and so make something much more than an ordinary likeness."

Franks fidgeted, his head bent over his plate.

"That's the work of the great artist," exclaimed Warburton, boldly flattering.

"Humbug!" growled Franks, but at once he laughed and glanced nervously at his wife.

Though this was Rosamund's only direct utterance on the subject, Warburton discovered from the course of the conversation, that she wished to be known as her husband's fervent admirer, that she took him with the utmost seriousness, and was resolved that everybody else should do so. The "great artist" phrase gave her genuine pleasure; she rewarded Will with the kindest look of her beautiful eyes, and from that moment appeared to experience a relief, so that her talk flowed more naturally. Luncheon over, they returned to the studio, where the men lit their pipes, while Rosamund, at her husband's entreaty, exhibited the sketches she had brought home.

"Why didn't you let me hear from you?" asked Warburton. "I got nothing but that flimsy postcard from Venice."

"Why, I was always meaning to write," answered the artist. "I know it was too bad. But time goes so quickly——"

"With you, no doubt. But if you stood behind a counter all day——"

Will saw the listeners exchange a startled glance, followed by an artificial smile. There was an instant's dead silence.

"Behind a counter—?" fell from Norbert, as if he failed to understand.

"The counter; *my* counter!" shouted Will blusterously. "You know very well what I mean. Your wife has told you all about it."

Rosamund flushed, and could not raise her eyes.

"We didn't know," said Franks, with his nervous little laugh, "whether you cared—to talk about it——"

"I'll talk about it with any one you like. So you *do* know? That's all right. I still owe my apology to Mrs. Franks for having given her such a shock. The disclosure was really too sudden."

"It is I who should beg you to forgive me, Mr. Warburton," replied Rosamund, in her sweetest accents. "I behaved in a very silly way. But my friend Bertha Cross treated me as I deserved. She declared that she was ashamed of me. But do not, pray do not, think me worse than I was. I ran away really because I felt I had surprised a secret. I was embarrassed,—I lost my head. I'm sure you don't think me capable of really mean feelings?"

"But, old man," put in the artist, in a half pained voice, "what the deuce does it all mean? Tell us the whole story, do."

Will told it, jestingly, effectively.

"I was *quite* sure," sounded, at the close, in Rosamund's voice of tender sympathy, "that you had some noble motive. I said so at once to Bertha."

"I suppose," said Will, "Miss Cross will never dare to enter the shop again?"

"She doesn't come!"

"Never since," he answered laughingly. "Her mother has been once or twice, and seems to regard me with a very suspicious eye. Mrs. Cross was told no doubt?"

"That I really can't say," replied Rosamund, averting her eyes. "But doesn't it do one good to hear such a story, Norbert?" she added impulsively.

"Yes, that's pluck," replied her husband, with the old spontaneity, in his eyes the old honest look which hitherto had somehow been a little obscured.

"I know very well that *I* couldn't have done it."

Warburton had not looked at Rosamund since her explanation and apology. He was afraid of meeting her eyes; afraid as a generous man who shrinks from inflicting humiliation. For was it conceivable that Rosamund could support his gaze without feeling humiliated? Remembering what had preceded that discovery at the shop; bearing in mind what had followed upon it; he reflected with astonishment on the terms of her self-reproach. It sounded so genuine; to the ears of her husband it must have been purest, womanliest sincerity. As though she could read his thoughts, Rosamund addressed him again in the most naturally playful tone.

"And you have been in the Basque country since we saw you. I'm so glad you really took your holiday there at last; you often used to speak of doing so. And you met my sister—Winifred wrote to me all about it. The Coppingers were delighted to see you. Don't you think them nice people? Did poor Mrs. Coppinger seem any better?"

In spite of himself, Will encountered her look, met the beautiful eyes, felt their smile envelop him. Never till now had he known the passive strength of woman, that characteristic which at times makes her a force of Nature rather than an individual being. Amazed, abashed, he let his head fall—and mumbled something about Mrs. Coppinger's state of health.

He did not stay much longer. When he took his leave, it would have seemed natural if Franks had come out to walk a little way with him, but his friend bore him company only to the door.

"Let us see you as often as possible, old man. I hope you'll often come and lunch on Sunday; nothing could please us better."

Franks' handgrip was very cordial, the look and tone were affectionate, but Will said to himself that the old intimacy was at an end; it must now give place to mere acquaintanceship. He suspected that Franks was afraid to come out and walk with him, afraid that it might not please his wife. That Rosamund was to rule—very sweetly of course, but unmistakably—no one could doubt who saw the two together for five minutes. It would be, in all likelihood, a happy subjugation, for Norbert was of anything but a rebellious temper; his bonds would be of silk; the rewards of his docility would be such as many a self-assertive man might envy. But when Warburton tried to imagine himself in such a position, a choked laugh of humorous disdain heaved his chest.

He wandered homewards in a dream. He relived those moments on the Embankment at Chelsea, when his common sense, his reason, his true emotions, were defeated by an impulse now scarcely intelligible; he saw himself shot across Europe, like a parcel despatched by express; and all that fury and rush meaningless as buffoonery at a pantomime! Yet this was how the vast majority of men "fell in love"—if ever they did so at all. This was the prelude to marriages innumerable, marriages destined to be dull as ditchwater or sour as verjuice. In love, forsooth! Rosamund at all events knew the value of that, and had saved him from his own infatuation. He owed her a lifelong gratitude.

That evening he re-read a long letter from Jane which had reached him yesterday. His sister gave him a full description of the new home in

Suffolk, and told of the arrangement she had made with Miss Winter, whereby, in a twelvemonth, she would be able to begin earning a little money, and, if all went well, before long would become self-supporting. Could he not run down to see them? Their mother had borne the removal remarkably well, and seemed, indeed, to have a new vigour; possibly the air might suit her better than at The Haws. Will mused over this, but had no mind to make the journey just yet. It would be a pain to him to see his mother in that new place; it would shame him to see his sister at work, and to think that all this change was on his account. So he wrote to mother and sister, with more of expressed tenderness than usual, begging them to let him put off his visit yet a few weeks. Presently they would be more settled. But of one thing let them be sure; his daily work was no burden whatever to him, and he hardly knew whether he would care to change it for what was called the greater respectability of labour in an office. His health was good; his spirits could only be disturbed by ill news from those he loved. He promised that at all events he would spend Christmas with them.

September went by. One of the Sundays was made memorable by a visit to Ashtead. Will had requested Franks to relate in that quarter the story of Mr. Jollyman, and immediately after hearing it, Ralph Pomfret wrote a warm-hearted letter which made the recipient in Fulham chuckle with contentment. At Ashtead he enjoyed himself in the old way, gladdened by the pleasure with which his friends talked of Rosamund's marriage. Mrs. Pomfret took an opportunity of speaking to him apart, a bright smile on her good face.

"Of course we know who did much, if not

everything, to bring it about. Rosamund came and told me how beautifully you had pleaded Norbert's cause, and Norbert confided to my husband that, but for you, he would most likely have married a girl he really didn't care about at all. I doubt whether a *mere man* ever did such a thing so discreetly and successfully before!"

In October, Will began to waver in his resolve not to go down into Suffolk before Christmas. There came a letter from his mother which deeply moved him; she spoke of old things as well as new, and declared that in her husband and in her children no woman had ever known truer happiness. This was at the middle of the week; Will all but made up his mind to take an early train on the following Sunday. On Friday he wrote to Jane, telling her to expect him, and, as he walked home from the shop that evening he felt glad that he had overcome the feelings which threatened to make this first visit something of a trial to his self-respect.

"There's a telegram a-waiting for you, sir," said Mrs. Wick, as he entered.

The telegram contained four words:

"Mother ill. Please come."

CHAPTER XLI

HAPPEN what might in the world beyond her doors, Mrs. Cross led the wonted life of domestic discomfort and querulousness. An interval there had been this summer, a brief, uncertain interval, when something like good-temper seemed to struggle with her familiar mood; it was the month or two during which Norbert Franks resumed his friendly visitings. Fallen out of Mrs. Cross's good graces since his failure to become her tenant a couple of years ago, the artist had but to present himself again to be forgiven, and when it grew evident that he came to the house on Bertha's account, he rose into higher favour than ever. But this promising state of things abruptly ended. One morning, Bertha, with a twinkle in her eyes, announced the fact of Franks' marriage. Her mother was stricken with indignant amaze.

"And you laugh about it?"

"It's so amusing," answered Bertha.

Mrs. Cross examined her daughter.

"I don't understand you," she exclaimed, in a tone of irritation. "I do *not* understand you, Bertha! All I can say is, behaviour more disgraceful I *never*——"

The poor lady's feelings were too much for her. She retreated to her bedroom, and there passed the greater part of the day. But in the evening curiosity overcame her sullenness. Having obtained as much information about the artist's marriage as Bertha could give her, she relieved herself in an acrimonious criticism of him and Miss Elvan.

"I never liked to say what I really thought of that girl," were her concluding words. "Now your eyes are opened. Of course you'll never see her again?"

"Why, mother?" asked Bertha. "I'm very glad she has married Mr. Franks. I always hoped she would, and felt pretty sure of it."

"And you mean to be friends with them both?"

"Why not?—But don't let us talk about that," Bertha added good-humouredly. "I should only vex you. There's something else I want to tell you, something you'll really be amused to hear."

"Your ideas of amusement, Bertha——"

"Yes, yes, but listen. It's about Mr. Jollyman. Who do you think Mr. Jollyman really is?"

Mrs. Cross heard the story with bent brows and lips severely set.

"And why didn't you tell me this before, pray?"

"I hardly know," answered the girl, thoughtfully, smiling. "Perhaps because I waited to hear more to make the revelation more complete. But——"

"And this," exclaimed Mrs. Cross, "is why you wouldn't go to the shop yesterday?"

"Yes," was the frank reply. "I don't think I shall go again."

"And, pray, why not?"

Bertha was silent.

"There's one very disagreeable thing in your character, Bertha," remarked her mother severely, "and that is your habit of hiding and concealing. To think that you found this out more than a week ago! You're very, very unlike your father. *He* never kept a thing from me, never for an hour. But you are always *full* of secrets. It isn't nice—it isn't at all nice."

Since her husband's death Mrs. Cross had never ceased discovering his virtues. When he lived, one of the reproaches with which she constantly soured his existence was that of secretiveness. And Bertha, who knew something and suspected more of the truth in this matter, never felt it so hard to bear with her mother as when Mrs. Cross bestowed such retrospective praise.

"I have thought it over," she said quietly, disregarding the reproof, "and on the whole I had rather not go again to the shop."

Thereupon Mrs. Cross grew angry, and for half an hour clamoured as to the disadvantage of leaving Jollyman's for another grocer's. In the end she did not leave him, but either went to the shop herself or sent the servant. Great was her curiosity regarding the disguised Mr. Warburton, with whom, after a significant coldness, she gradually resumed her old chatty relations. At length, one day in autumn, Bertha announced to her that she could throw more light on the Jollyman mystery; she had learnt the full explanation of Mr. Warburton's singular proceedings.

"From those people, I suppose?" said Mrs. Cross, who by this phrase signified Mr. and Mrs. Franks. "Then I don't wish to hear one word of it."

But as though she had not heard this remark, Bertha began her narrative. She seemed to repeat what had been told her with a quiet pleasure.

"Well, then," was her mother's comment, "after all, there's nothing disgraceful."

"I never thought there was."

"Then why have you refused to enter his shop?"

"It was awkward," replied Bertha.

"No more awkward for you than for me," said Mrs. Cross. "But I've noticed, Bertha, that you are getting rather selfish in some things—I don't of course say in *everything*—and I think it isn't difficult to guess where that comes from."

Soon after Christmas they were left, by a familiar accident, without a servant; the girl who had been with them for the last six months somehow contrived to get her box secretly out of the house, and disappeared (having just been paid her wages) without warning. Long and loudly did Mrs. Cross rail against this infamous behaviour.

The next morning, a young woman came to the house and inquired for Mrs. Cross; Bertha, who had opened the door, led her into the dining room, and retired. Half an hour later, Mrs. Cross came into the parlour, beaming.

"There now! If that wasn't a good idea! Who do you think sent that girl, Bertha?—Mr. Jollyman."

Bertha kept silence.

"I had to go into the shop yesterday, and I happened to speak to Mr. Jollyman of the trouble I had in finding a good servant. It occurred to me that he *might* just possibly know of some one. He promised to make inquiries, and here at once comes the nicest girl I've seen for a long time. She had to leave her last place because it was too hard; just fancy, a shop where she had to cook for sixteen people, and see to five bedrooms; no wonder she broke down, poor thing. She's been resting for a month or two: and she lives in the same house as a person named Mrs.

Hopper, who is the sister of the wife of Mr. Jollyman's assistant. And she's quite content with fifteen pounds—quite."

As she listened, Bertha wrinkled her forehead, and grew rather absent. She made no remark, until, after a long account of the virtues she had already descried in Martha—this was the girl's name—Mrs. Cross added that of course she must go at once and thank Mr. Jollyman.

"I suppose you still address him by that name?" fell from Bertha.

"That name? Why, I'd really almost forgotten that it wasn't his real name. In any case, I couldn't use the other in the shop, could I?"

"Of course not; no."

"Now you speak of it, Bertha," pursued Mrs. Cross, "I wonder whether he knows that I know who he is?"

"Certainly he does."

"When one thinks of it, wouldn't it be better, Bertha, for you to go to the shop again now and then? I'm afraid the poor man may feel hurt. He *must* have noticed that you never went again after that discovery, and one really wouldn't like him to think that you were offended."

"Offended?" echoed the girl with a laugh. "Offended at what?"

"Oh, some people, you know, might think his behaviour strange—using a name that's not his own, and—and so on."

"Some people might, no doubt. But the poor man, as you call him, is probably quite indifferent as to what we think of him."

"Don't you think it would be well if you went in and just thanked him for sending the servant?"

"Perhaps," replied Bertha, carelessly.

But she did not go to Mr. Jollyman's, and Mrs. Cross soon forgot the suggestion.

Martha entered upon her duties, and discharged them with such zeal, such docility, that her mistress never tired of lauding her. She was a young woman of rather odd appearance; slim and meagre and red-headed, with a never failing simper on her loose lips, and blue eyes that frequently watered; she had somehow an air of lurking gentility in faded youth. Undeniable as were the good qualities she put forth on this scene of innumerable domestic failures, Bertha could not altogether like her. Submissive to the point of slavishness, she had at times a look which did not harmonize at all with this demeanour, a something in her eyes disagreeably suggestive of mocking insolence. Bertha particularly noticed this on the day after Martha had received her first wages. Leave having been given her to go out in the afternoon to make some purchases, she was rather late in returning, and Bertha, meeting her as she entered, asked her to be as quick as possible in getting tea; whereupon the domestic threw up her head and regarded the speaker from under her eyelids with an extraordinary smile; then with a "Yes, miss, this minute, miss" scampered upstairs to take her things off. All that evening her behaviour was strange. As she waited at the supper table she seemed to be subduing laughter, and in clearing away she for the first time broke a plate; whereupon she burst into tears, and begged forgiveness so long and so wearisomely that she had at last to be ordered out of the room.

On the morrow all was well again; but Bertha could not help watching that singular countenance, and the more she observed, the less she liked it.

The more "willing" a servant the more toil did Mrs. Cross exact from her. When occasions of rebuke or of dispute were lacking, the day would have been long and wearisome for her had she not ceaselessly plied the domestic drudge with tasks, and narrowly watched their execution. The spectacle of this slave-driving was a constant trial to Bertha's nerves; now and then she ventured a mild protest, but only with the result of exciting her mother's indignation. In her mood of growing moral discontent, Bertha began to ask herself whether acquiescence in this sordid tryanny was not a culpable weakness, and one day early in the year—a wretched day of east-wind—when she saw Martha perched on an outer window-sill cleaning panes, she found the courage to utter resolute disapproval.

"I don't understand you, Bertha," replied Mrs. Cross, the muscles of her face quivering as they did when she felt her dignity outraged. "What do we engage a servant for? Are the windows to get so dirty we can't see through them?"

"They were cleaned not many days ago," said her daughter, "and I think we could manage to see till the weather's less terrible."

"My dear, if we *managed* so as to give the servant no trouble at all, the house would soon be in a pretty state. Be so good as not to interfere. It's really an extraordinary thing that as soon as I find a girl who almost suits me, you begin to try to spoil her. One would think you took a pleasure in making my life miserable——"

Overwhelmed with floods of reproach, Bertha had either to combat or to retreat. Again her nerves failed her, and she left the room.

At dinner that day there was a roast leg of mutton, and, as her habit was, Mrs. Cross carved the portion which Martha was to take away for herself. One very small and very thin slice, together with one unwholesome little potato, represented the servant's meal. As soon as the door had closed, Bertha spoke in an ominously quiet voice.

"Mother, this won't do. I am very sorry to annoy you, but if you call that a dinner for a girl who works hard ten or twelve hours a day, I don't. How she supports life, I can't understand. You have only to look into her face to see she's starving. I can bear the sight of it no longer."

This time she held firm. The conflict lasted for half an hour, during which Mrs. Cross twice threatened to faint. Neither of them ate anything, and in the end Bertha saw herself, if not defeated, at all events no better off than at the beginning, for her mother clung fiercely to authority, and would obviously live in perpetual strife rather than yield an inch. For the next two days domestic life was very unpleasant indeed; mother and daughter exchanged few words; meanwhile Martha was tasked, if possible, more vigorously than ever, and fed mysteriously, meals no longer doled out to her under Bertha's eyes. The third morning brought another crisis.

"I have a letter from Emily," said Bertha at breakfast, naming a friend of hers who lived in the far north of London. "I'm going to see her to-day."

"Very well," answered Mrs. Cross, between rigid lips.

"She says that in the house where she lives, there's a bed-sitting-room to let. I think, mother, it might be better for me to take it."

"You will do just as you please, Bertha."

"I shall have dinner to-day with Emily, and be back about tea-time."

"I have no doubt," replied Mrs. Cross, "that Martha will be so obliging as to have tea ready for you. If she doesn't feel *strong* enough, of course I will see to it myself."

CHAPTER XLII

ON the evening before, Martha had received her month's wages, and had been promised the usual afternoon of liberty to-day; but, as soon as Bertha had left the house, Mrs. Cross summoned the domestic, and informed her bluntly that the holiday must be postponed.

"I'm very sorry, mum," replied Martha, with an odd, half-frightened look in her watery eyes. "I'd promised to go and see my brother as has just lost his wife; but of course, if it isn't convenient, mum——"

"It really is not, Martha. Miss Bertha will be out all day, and I don't like being left alone You shall go to-morrow instead."

Half an hour later, Mrs. Cross went out shopping, and was away till noon. On returning, she found the house full of the odour of something burnt.

"What's this smell, Martha?" she asked at the kitchen door, "what is burning?"

"Oh, it's only a dishcloth as was drying and caught fire, mum," answered the servant.

"Only! What do you mean?" cried the mistress, angrily. "Do you wish to burn the house down?"

Martha stood with her arms akimbo, on her thin, dough-pale face the most insolent of grins, her teeth gleaming, and her eyes wide.

"What do you mean?" cried Mrs. Cross. "Show me the burnt cloth at once."

"There you are, mum!"

And Martha, with a kick, pointed to something on the floor. Amazed and wrathful, Mrs. Cross saw a long roller-towel, half a yard of it burnt to tinder; nor could any satisfactory explanation of the accident be drawn from Martha, who laughed, sobbed, and sniggered by turns as if she were demented.

"Of course you will pay for it," exclaimed Mrs. Cross for the twentieth time. "Go on with your work at once, and don't let me have any more of this extraordinary behaviour. I can't think what has come to you."

But Martha seemed incapable of resuming her ordinary calm. Whilst serving the one o'clock dinner—which was very badly cooked—she wept and sighed, and when her mistress had risen from the table, she stood for a long time staring vacantly before she could bestir herself to clear away. About three o'clock, having several times vainly rung the sitting-room bell, Mrs. Cross went to the kitchen. The door was shut, and, on trying to open it, she found it locked. She called "Martha," again and again, and had no reply, until, all of a sudden, a shrill voice cried from within—"Go away! Go away!" Beside herself with wrath and amazement, the mistress demanded admission; for answer, there came a violent thumping on the door at the other side, and again the voice screamed—"Go away! Go away!"

"What's the matter with you, Martha?" asked Mrs. Cross, beginning to feel alarmed.

"Go away!" replied the voice fiercely.

"Either you open the door this moment, or I call a policeman."

This threat had an immediate effect, though

not quite of the kind that Mrs. Cross hoped. The key turned with a snap, the door was flung open, and there stood Martha, in a Corybantic attitude, brandishing a dinner-plate in one hand, a poker in the other; her hair was dishevelled, her face red, and fury blazed in her eyes.

"You *won't* go away?" she screamed "There, then—there goes one of your plates!"

She dashed it to the floor.

"You *won't* go away?—There goes one of your dishes!—and there goes a basin!—And there goes a tea-cup!"

One after another, the things she named perished upon the floor. Mrs. Cross stood paralysed, horror-stricken.

"You think you'll make me pay for them?" cried Martha frantically. "Not me—not me! It's you as owes me money—money for all the work I've done as wasn't in my wages, and for the food as I haven't had, when I'd ought to. What do you call *that*?" She pointed to a plate of something on the kitchen table. "Is that a dinner for a human being, or is it a dinner for a beetle? D'you think I'd eat it, and me with money in my pocket to buy better? You want to make a walkin' skeleton of me, do you?—but I'll have it out of you, I will—There goes another dish! And there goes a sugar-basin! And *here* goes your teapot!"

With a shriek of dismay, Mrs. Cross sprang forward. She was too late to save the cherished object, and her aggressive movement excited Martha to yet more alarming behaviour.

"You'd hit me, would you? Two can play at that game—you old skinflint, you! Come another step nearer, and I'll bring this poker on your head! You thought you'd get somebody you could do as you liked with, didn't you? You thought because I was willing, and tried to do my best, as I could be put upon to any extent, did you? It's about time you learnt your mistake, you old cheese-parer! You and me has an account to settle. Let me get at you—let me get at you——"

She brandished the poker so menacingly that Mrs. Cross turned and fled. Martha pursued, yelling abuse and threats. The mistress vainly tried to shut the sitting-room door against her; in broke the furious maid, and for a moment so handled her weapon that Mrs. Cross with difficulty escaped a dangerous blow. Round and round the table they went, until, the cloth having been dragged off, Martha's feet caught in it, and she fell heavily to the floor. To escape from the room, the terrified lady must have stepped over her. For a moment there was silence. Then Martha made an attempt to rise, fell again, again struggled to her knees, and finally collapsed, lying quite still and mute.

Trembling, panting, Mrs. Cross moved cautiously nearer, until she could see the girl's face. Martha was asleep, unmistakably asleep; she had even begun to snore. Avoiding her contact with as much disgust as fear, Mrs. Cross got out of the room, and opened the front door of the house. This way and that she looked along the streets, searching for a policeman, but none was in sight. At this moment, approached a familiar figure, Mr. Jollyman's errand boy, basket on arm; he had parcels to deliver here.

"Are you going back to the shop at once?" asked Mrs. Cross, after hurriedly setting down her groceries in the passage.

"Straight back, mum."

"Then run as quickly as ever you can, and tell Mr. Jollyman that I wish to see him immediately—immediately. Run! Don't lose a moment!"

Afraid to shut herself in with the sleeping fury, Mrs. Cross remained standing near the front door, which every now and then she opened to look for a policeman. The day was cold; she shivered, she felt weak, wretched, ready to sob in her squalid distress. Some twenty minutes passed, then, just as she opened the door to look about again, a rapid step sounded on the pavement, and there appeared her grocer.

"Oh, Mr. Jollyman!" she exclaimed. "What I have just gone through! That girl has gone raving mad—she has broken almost everything in the house, and tried to kill me with the poker. Oh, I am so glad you've come! Of course there's never a policeman when they're wanted. Do please come in."

Warburton did not at once understand who was meant by "that girl," but when Mrs. Cross threw open the sitting-room door, and exhibited her domestic prostrate in disgraceful slumber, the facts of the situation broke upon him. This was the girl so strongly recommended by Mrs. Hopper.

"But I thought she had been doing very well——"

"So she had, so she had, Mr. Jollyman—except for a few little things—though there was always something rather strange about her. It's only to-day that she broke out. She is mad, I assure you, raving mad!"

Another explanation suggested itself to Warburton.

"Don't you notice a suspicious odour?" he asked significantly.

"You think it's *that*!" said Mrs. Cross, in a horrified whisper. "Oh, I daresay you're right. I'm too agitated to notice anything. Oh, Mr. Jollyman! Do, do help me to get the creature out of the house. How shameful that people gave her a good character. But everybody deceives me—everybody treats me cruelly, heartlessly. Don't leave me alone with that creature, Mr. Jollyman. Oh, if you knew what I have been through with servants! But never anything so bad as this—never! Oh, I feel quite ill—I must sit down——"

Fearful that his situation might become more embarrassing than it was, Warburton supported Mrs. Cross into the dining-room, and by dint of loudly cheerful talk in part composed her. She consented to sit with the door locked, whilst her rescuer hurried in search of a policeman. Before long, a constable's tread sounded in the hall; Mrs. Cross told her story, exhibited the ruins of her crockery on the kitchen floor, and demanded instant expulsion of the dangerous rebel. Between them, Warburton and the man in authority shook Martha into consciousness, made her pack her box, put her into a cab, and sent her off to the house where she had lived when out of service; she all the time weeping copiously, and protesting that there was no one in the world so dear to her as her outraged mistress. About an hour was thus consumed. When at length the policeman had withdrawn, and sudden quiet reigned in the house, Mrs. Cross seemed again on the point of fainting.

"How can I ever thank you, Mr. Jollyman!" she exclaimed, half hysterically, as she let herself sink into the armchair. "Without you, what would have become of me! Oh, I feel so weak, if I had strength to get myself a cup of tea——"

"Let me get it for you," cried Warburton. "Nothing easier. I noticed the kettle by the kitchen fire."

"Oh, I cannot allow, you, Mr. Jollyman—you are too kind—I feel so ashamed——"

But Will was already in the kitchen, where he bestirred himself so effectually that in a few minutes the kettle had begun to sing. Just as he went back to the parlour, to ask where tea could be found, the front door opened, and in walked Bertha.

"Your daughter is here, Mrs. Cross," said Will, in an undertone, stepping toward the limp and pallid lady.

"Bertha," she cried. "Bertha, are you there? Oh, come and thank Mr. Jollyman! If you knew what has happened whilst you were away!"

At the room door appeared the girl's astonished face. Warburton's eyes fell upon her.

"It's a wonder you find me alive, dear," pursued the mother. "If one of those blows had fallen on my head——!"

"Let me explain," interposed Warburton quietly. And in a few words he related the events of the afternoon.

"And Mr. Jollyman was just getting me a cup of tea, Bertha," added Mrs. Cross. "I do feel ashamed that he should have had such trouble."

"Mr. Jollyman has been very kind indeed," said Bertha, with look and tone of grave sincerity. "I'm sure we cannot thank him enough."

Warburton smiled as he met her glance.

"I feel rather guilty in the matter," he said, "for it was I who suggested the servant. If you will let me, I will do my best to atone by trying to find another and a better."

"Run and make the tea, my dear," said Mrs.

Cross. "Perhaps Mr. Jollyman will have a cup with us——"

This invitation was declined. Warburton sought for his hat, and took leave of the ladies, Mrs. Cross overwhelming him with gratitude, and Bertha murmuring a few embarrassed words. As soon as he was gone, mother and daughter took hands affectionately, then embraced with more tenderness than for a long, long time.

"I shall never dare to live alone with a servant," sobbed Mrs. Cross. "If you leave me, I must go into lodgings, dear."

"Hush, hush, mother," replied the girl, in her gentlest voice. "Of course I shall not leave you."

"Oh, the dreadful things I have been through! It was drink, Bertha; that creature was a drunkard of the most dangerous kind. She did her best to murder me. I wonder I am not at this moment lying dead.—Oh, but the kindness of Mr. Jollyman! What a good thing I sent for him! And he speaks of finding us another servant; but, Bertha, I shall never try to manage a servant again—never. I shall always be afraid of them; I shall dread to give the simplest order. You, my dear, must be the mistress of the house; indeed you must. I give over everything into your hands. I will never interfere; I won't say a word, whatever fault I may have to find; not a word. Oh, that creature; that horrible woman will haunt my dreams. Bertha, you don't think she'll hang about the house, and lie in wait for me, to be revenged? We must tell the policeman to look out for her. I'm sure I shall never venture to go out alone, and if you leave me in the house with a new servant, even for an hour, I must be in a room with the door locked. My nerves will never recover from this shock. Oh, if you knew how ill I feel! I'll have a cup of tea, and then go straight to bed."

Whilst she was refreshing herself, she spoke again of Mr. Jollyman.

"Do you think I ought to have pressed him to stay, dear? I didn't feel sure."

"No, no, you were quite right not to do so," replied Bertha. "He of course understood that it was better for us to be alone."

"I thought he would. Really, for a grocer, he is so very gentlemanly."

"That's not surprising, mother."

"No, no; I'm always forgetting that he isn't a grocer by birth. I think, Bertha, it will only be right to ask him to come to tea some day before long."

Bertha reflected, a half-smile about her lips.

"Certainly," she said, "if you would like to."

"I really should. He was so very kind to me. And perhaps—what do you think?—ought we to invite him in his proper name?"

"No, I think not," answered Bertha, after a moment's reflection. "We are not supposed to know anything about that."

"To be sure not.—Oh, that dreadful creature. I see her eyes, glaring at me, like a tiger's. Fifty times at least did she chase me round this table. I thought I should have dropped with exhaustion; and if I had, one blow of that poker would have finished me. Never speak to me of servants, Bertha. Engage any one you like, but do, do be careful to make inquiries about her. I shall never wish even to know her name; I shall never look at her face; I shall never speak a word to her. I leave all the responsibility to you, dear. And now, help me upstairs. I'm sure I could never get up alone. I tremble in every limb——"

CHAPTER XLIII

WARBURTON'S mother was dead. The first effect upon him of the certainty that she could not recover from the unconsciousness in which he found her when summoned by Jane's telegram, was that of an acute remorse; it pierced him to the heart that she should have abandoned the home of her life-time, for the strangeness and discomfort of the new abode, and here have fallen, stricken by death—the cause of it, he himself, he so unworthy of the least sacrifice. He had loved her; but what assurance had he been wont to give her of his love? Through many and many a year it was much if he wrote at long intervals a hurried letter. How seldom had he cared to go down to St. Neots, and, when there, how soon had he felt impatient of the little restraints imposed upon him by his mother's ways and prejudices. Yet not a moment had she hesitated, ill and aged, when, at so great a cost to herself, it seemed possible to make life a little easier for him. This reproach was the keenest pain with which nature had yet visited him.

Something of the same was felt by his sister, partly on her own, partly on his account, but as soon as Jane became aware of his self torment, her affection and her good sense soon brought succour to them both. She spoke of the life their mother had led since coming into Suffolk, related a hundred instances to prove how full of interest and contentment it had been, bore witness to the seeming improvement of health, and the even cheerfulness of spirits which had accompanied it. Moreover, there was the medical assurance that life could not in any case have been prolonged; that change of place and habits counted for nothing in the sudden end which some months ago had been foretold. Jane confessed herself surprised at the ease with which so great and sudden a change was borne; the best proof that could have been given of their mother's nobleness of mind. Once only had Mrs. Warburton seemed to think regretfully of the old home; it was on coming out of church one morning, when, having stood for a moment to look at the graveyard, she murmured to her daughter that she would wish to be buried at St. Neots. This, of course, was done; it would have been done even had she not spoken. And when, on the day after the funeral, brother and sister parted to go their several ways, the sadness they bore with them had no embitterment of brooding regret. A little graver than usual, Will took his place behind the counter, with no word to Allchin concerning the cause of his absence. He wrote frequently to Jane, and from her received long letters, which did him good, so redolent were they of the garden life, even in mid-winter, and so expressive of a frank, sweet, strong womanhood, like that of her who was no more.

Meanwhile his business flourished. Not that he much exerted himself, or greatly rejoiced to see his till more heavily laden night after night, by natural accretion custom flowed to the shop in fuller stream; Jollyman's had established a reputation for quality and cheapness, and began seriously to affect the trade of small rivals in the district. As Allchin had foretold, the hapless grocer with the drunken wife sank defeated before the end of the year; one morning his shop did not open, and in a few days the furniture of the house was carried off by some brisk creditor. It made Warburton miserable to think of the man's doom; when Allchin, frank barbarian as he was, loudly exulted. Will turned away in shame and anger. Had the thing been practicable he would have given money out of his own pocket to the ruined struggler. He saw himself as a merciless victor; he seemed to have his heel on the other man's head, and to crush, crush——

At Christmas he was obliged to engage a second assistant. Allchin did not conceal his dislike of this step, but he ended by admitting it to be necessary. At first, the new state of things did not work quite smoothly; Allchin was inclined to an imperious manner, which the newcomer, by name Goff, now and then plainly resented. But in a day or two they were on fair terms, and ere long they became cordial.

Then befell the incident of Mrs. Cross' Martha.

Not without uneasiness had Warburton suggested a servant on the recommendation of Mrs. Hopper, but credentials seemed to be fairly good, and when, after a week or two, Mrs. Cross declared herself more than satisfied, he blessed his good luck. Long ago he had ceased to look for the reappearance at the shop of Bertha Cross; he thought of the girl now and then, generally reverting in memory to that day when he had followed her and her mother into Kew Gardens—a recollection which had lost all painfulness, and shone idyllically in summer sunlight, but it mattered nothing to him that Bertha showed herself no more. Of course she knew his story from Rosamund, and in all likelihood she felt her self-respect concerned in holding aloof from an acquaintance of his ambiguous standing. It mattered not a jot.

Yet when the tragi-comedy of Martha's outbreak unexpectedly introduced him to the house at Walham Green, he experienced a sudden revival of the emotions of a year ago. After his brief meeting with Bertha, he did not go straight back to the shop, but wandered a little in quiet by-ways, thinking hard and smiling. Nothing more grotesque than the picture of Mrs. Cross amid her shattered crockery, Mrs. Cross pointing to the prostrate Martha, Mrs. Cross panting forth the chronicle of her woes; but Mrs. Cross' daughter was not involved in this scene of pantomime; she walked across the stage, but independently, with a simple dignity, proof against paltry or ludicrous circumstance. If any one could see the laughable side of such domestic squalor, assuredly it was Bertha herself; of that Will felt assured. Did he not remember her smile when she had to discuss prices and qualities in the shop? Not many girls smile with so much implication of humorous comment.

He had promised to look out for another servant, but hardly knew how to go to work. First of all, Mrs. Hopper was summoned to an interview in the parlour behind the shop, and Martha's case was fully discussed. With much protesting and circumlocution, Mrs. Hopper brought herself at length to own that Martha had been known to "take too much," but that was so long ago, and the girl had solemnly declared, etc., etc. However, as luck would have it, she did know of another girl, a really good general servant, who had only just been thrown out of a place by the death of her mistress, and who was living at home in Kentish Town. Thither sped Warburton; he saw the girl and her mother, and, on returning, sent a note to Mrs. Cross, in which he detailed all he had learnt concerning the new applicant. At the close he wrote: "You are aware, I think, that the name under which I do business is not my own. Permit me, in writing to you on a private matter, to use my own signature"—which accordingly followed. Moreover, he dated the letter from his lodgings, not from the shop.

The next day brought him a reply; he found it on his breakfast table, and broke the envelope with amused curiosity Mrs. Cross wrote that "Sarah Walker" had been to see her, and if inquiries proved satisfactory, would be engaged. "We are very greatly obliged for the trouble you have taken. Many thanks for your kind inquiries as to my health. I am glad to say that the worst of the shock has passed away, though I fear that I shall long continue to feel its effects." A few remarks followed on the terrible difficulties of the servant question; then "Should you be disengaged on Sunday next, we shall be glad if you will take a cup of tea with us."

Over his coffee and egg, Will pondered this invitation. It pleased him, undeniably, but caused him no undue excitement. He would have liked to know in what degree Mrs. Cross' daughter was a consenting party to the step. Perhaps she felt that, after the services he had rendered, the least one could do was to invite him to tea. Why should he refuse? Before going to business, he wrote a brief acceptance. During the day, a doubt now and then troubled him as to whether he had behaved discreetly, but on the whole he looked forward to Sunday with pleasant expectation.

How should he equip himself? Should he go dressed as he would have gone to the Pomfrets', in his easy walking attire, jacket and soft-felt? Or did the circumstances dictate chimney-pot and frock-coat? He scoffed at himself for fidgeting over the point; yet perhaps it had a certain importance. After deciding for the informal costume, at the last moment he altered his mind, and went arrayed as society demands; with the result that, on entering the little parlour—that name suited it much better than drawing-room—he felt over-dressed, pompous, generally absurd. His cylinder seemed to be about three feet high; his gloves stared their newness; the tails of his coat felt as though they wrapped several times round his legs, and still left enough to trail upon the floor as he sat on a chair too low for him. Never since the most awkward stage of boyhood had he felt so little at ease "in company." And he had a conviction that Bertha Cross was laughing at him. Her smile was too persistent; it could only be explained as a compromise with threatening merriment.

A gap in the conversation prompted Warburton to speak of a little matter which was just now interesting him. It related to Mr. Potts, the shop-keeper in Kennington Lane, whom he used to meet, but of whom for a couple of years and more, he had quite lost sight. Stirred by reproach of conscience, he had at length gone to make inquiries; but the name of Potts was no longer over the shop.

"I went in and asked whether the old man was dead; no, he had retired from business and was lodging not far away. I found the house—a rather grimy place, and the door was opened by a decidedly grimy woman. I saw at once that she didn't care to let me in. What was my business? and so on; but I held firm, and got at last into a room on the second floor, an uncomfortable sitting-room, where poor old Potts welcomed me. If only he had known my address, he said, he should have written to tell me the news. His son in America, the one I knew, was doing well, and sent money every month, enough for him to live upon. 'But was he comfortable in those lodgings?' I asked. Of course I saw that he wasn't, and I saw too that my question made him nervous. He looked at the door, and spoke in a whisper. The upshot of it was that he had fallen into the hands of a landlady who victimised him; just because she was an old acquaintance, he didn't feel able to leave her. 'Shall I help you to get away?' I asked him, and his face shone with hope. Of course the woman was listening at the keyhole; we both knew that. When I went away she had run half down the stairs, and I caught her angry look before she hid it with a grin. I must find decent lodgings for the old fellow, as soon as possible. He is being bled mercilessly."

"How very disgraceful!" exclaimed Mrs. Cross. "Really, the meanness of some women of that class!"

Her daughter had her eyes cast down, on her lips the faintest suggestion of a smile.

"I wonder whether we could hear of anything suitable," pursued her mother, "by inquiring of people we know out at Holloway. I'm thinking of the Boltons, Bertha."

Mr. Potts' requirements were discussed, Bertha interesting herself in the matter, and making various suggestions. The talk grew more animated. Warburton was led to tell of his own experience in lodgings. Catching Bertha's eye, he gave his humour full scope on the subject of Mrs. Wick, and there was merriment in which even Mrs. Cross made a show of joining.

"Why," she exclaimed, "do you stay in such very uncomfortable rooms?"

"It doesn't matter," Will replied, "it's only for a time."

"Ah, you have other views?"

"Yes," he answered, smiling cheerfully, "I have other views."

CHAPTER XLIV

TOWARD the end of the following week, Mrs. Cross came to the shop. She had a busy air, and spoke to Warburton in a confidential undertone,

"We have been making inquiries, and at last I think we have heard of something that might suit your poor friend. This is the address. My daughter went there this morning, and had a long talk with the woman, and she thinks it really might do; but perhaps you have already found something?"

"Nothing at all," answered Will. "I am much obliged to you. I will go as soon as possible."

"We shall be so glad to hear if it suits," said Mrs. Cross. "Do look in on Sunday, will you? We are always at home at five o'clock.—Oh, I have written out a little list of things," she added, laying her grocery order on the counter. "Please tell me what they come to."

Warburton gravely took the cash, and Mrs. Cross, with her thinly gracious smile, bade him good-day.

He did not fail to "look in" on Sunday, and this time he wore his ordinary comfortable clothing. The rooms recommended for Mr. Potts had seemed to him just what were needed, and on his own responsibility he had taken them. Moreover, he had been to Kennington, and had made known to the nervous old man the arrangements that were proposed for him.

"But will he be allowed to leave?" asked Bertha, in her eyes the twinkle for which Will watched.

"He won't dare, he tells me, to give notice; but he'll only have to pay a week's rent in lieu of it. I have promised to be with him at ten to-morrow morning, to help him to get away. I shall take my heaviest walking-stick; one must be prepared for every emergency. Glance over the police news on Tuesday, Mrs. Cross, just to see whether I have come to harm."

"We shall be very anxious indeed," replied the literal lady, with pained brow. "Couldn't you let us hear to-morrow evening? I know only too well what dreadful creatures the women of that class can be. I very strongly advise you, Mr. Warburton, to be accompanied by a policeman. I beg you will."

Late on the Monday afternoon, Jollyman's errand boy left a note for Mrs. Cross. It informed her that all had gone well, though "not without uproar. The woman shrieked insults from her doorstep after our departing cab. Poor Mr. Potts was all but paralytic with alarm, but came round famously at sight of the new lodgings. He wants to thank you both."

It was on this same evening that Warburton had a visit from Godfrey Sherwood. A fortnight ago, just after Easter, had taken place the marriage of Mr. Milligan and Miss Parker; and Sherwood, whilst his chief was absent on the honeymoon, had run down to the seaside for a change of air. To-night, he presented himself unexpectedly, and his face was the prologue to a moving tale.

"Read that, Warburton——" he held out a

letter. " Read that, and tell me what you think of human nature."

It was a letter from Milligan, who, with many explanations and apologies, wrote to inform his secretary that the Great Work could not be pursued, that the vegetarian colony in Ireland, which was to civilise the world, must—so far as he was concerned—remain a glorious dream. The fact of the matter was, Mrs. Milligan did not like it. She had tried vegetarianism ; it did not suit her health ; moreover, she objected to living in Ireland, on account of the dampness of the climate. Sadly, reluctantly, Mrs. Milligan's husband had to forgo his noble project. In consequence, he would have no need henceforth of a secretary, and Sherwood must consider their business relations at an end.

" He encloses a very liberal cheque," said Godfrey. " But what a downfall ! I foresaw it. I hinted my fears to you as soon as Miss Parker appeared on the scene. Poor old Milligan ! A lost man—sunk in the commonplace—hopelessly whelmed in vulgar matrimony. Poor old fellow ! "

Warburton chuckled.

" But that isn't all," went on the other, " Old Strangwyn is dead, really dead at last. I wrote several times to him ; no acknowledgment of my letters. Now it's all over. The ten thousand pounds——"

He made a despairing gesture. Then :

" Take that cheque, Warburton. It's all I have ; take it, old fellow, and try to forgive me. You won't ? Well, well, if I live, I'll pay you yet ; but I'm a good deal run down, and these disappointments have almost floored me. To tell you the truth, the vegetarian diet won't do. I feel as weak as a cat. If you knew the heroism it has cost me, down at the seaside, to refrain from chops and steaks. Now I give it up. Another month of cabbage and lentils and I should be sunk beyond recovery. I give it up. This very night I shall go and have a supper, a real supper, in town. Will you come with me, old man? What's before me, I don't know. I have half a mind to go to Canada as farm labourer; it would be just the thing for my health; but let us go and have one more supper together, as in the old days. Where shall it be?"

So they went into town, and supped royally, with the result that Warburton had to see his friend home. Over the second bottle, Godfrey decided for an agricultural life in the Far West, and Will promised to speak for him to a friend of his, a lady who had brothers farming in British Columbia; but, before he went, he must be assured that Warburton really forgave him the loss of that money. Will protested that he had forgotten all about it; if any pardon were needed, he granted it with all his heart. And so with affectionate cordiality they bade each other good-night.

To his surprise, he received a letter from Sherwood, a day or two after, seriously returning to the British Columbia project, and reminding him of his promise. So, on Sunday, Will called for the first time without invitation at Mrs. Cross', and, being received with no less friendliness than hitherto, began asking news of Bertha's brothers; whereupon followed talk upon Canadian farming life, and the mention of Godfrey Sherwood. Bertha undertook to write on the subject by the next mail; she thought it likely enough that her brothers might be able to put Mr. Sherwood into the way of earning a living.

"What do you think we did yesterday?" said Mrs. Cross. "We took the liberty of calling upon Mr. Potts. We had to go and see Mrs. Bolton, at Holloway, and, as it was so near, we thought we might venture—using your name as our introduction. And the poor old gentleman was delighted to see us—wasn't he, Bertha? Oh, and he is so grateful for our suggestion of the lodgings."

Bertha's smile betrayed a little disquiet. Perceiving this, Warburton spoke with emphasis.

"It was kind of you. The old man feels a little lonely in that foreign region; he's hardly been out of Kennington for forty years. A very kind thought, indeed."

"I am relieved," said Bertha; "it seemed to me just possible that we had been guilty of a serious indiscretion. Good intentions are very dangerous things."

When next Warburton found time to go to Holloway, he heard all about the ladies' visit. He learnt, moreover, that Mr. Potts had told them the story of his kindness to the sick lad at St. Kitts, and of his first visit to Kennington Lane.

CHAPTER XLV

WHEN Bertha, at her mother's request, undertook the control of the house, she knew very well what was before her.

During a whole fortnight, Mrs. Cross faithfully adhered to the compact. For the first time in her life, she declared, she was enjoying peace. Feeling much shaken in her nervous system, she rose late, retired early, and, when downstairs, reclined a good deal on the sofa. She professed herself unable to remember the new servant's name, and assumed an air of profound abstraction whenever " what do you call her " came into the room. Not a question did she permit herself as to the details of household management. Bertha happening (incautiously) to complain of a certain joint supplied by the butcher, Mrs. Cross turned a dreamy eye upon it, and said, in the tone of one who speaks of long ago, " In my time he could always be depended upon for a small shoulder " ; then dismissed the matter as in no way concerning her.

But repose had a restorative effect, and, in the third week, Mrs. Cross felt the revival of her energies. She was but fifty-three years old, and in spite of languishing habits, in reality had very fair health. Caring little for books, and not much for society, how was she to pass her time if denied the resource of household affairs ? Bertha observed the signs of coming trouble. One morning, her mother came downstairs earlier than usual, and after fidgeting about the room, where her daughter was busy at her drawing-board, suddenly exclaimed:

"I wish you would tell that girl to make my bed properly. I haven't closed my eyes for three nights, and I ache from head to foot. The way she neglects my room is really shameful——"

There followed intimate details, to which Bertha listened gravely.

"That shall be seen to at once, mother," she replied, and left the room.

The complaint, as she suspected, had very little foundation. It was only the beginning; day after day did Mrs. Cross grumble about this, that and the other thing, until Bertha saw that the anticipated moment was at hand. The great struggle arose out of that old point of debate, the servant's meals. Mrs. Cross, stealing into the kitchen, had caught a glimpse of Sarah's dinner, and so amazed was she, so stirred with indignation to the depth of her soul, that she cast off all show of respect for the new order, and overwhelmed Bertha with rebukes. Her daughter listened quietly until the torrent had spent its force, then said with a smile:

"Is this how you keep your promise, mother?"

"Promise? Did I promise to look on at wicked waste? Do you want to bring us to the workhouse, child?"

"Don't let us waste time in talking about what we settled a month ago," replied Bertha decisively. "Sarah is doing very well, and there must be no change. I am quite content to pay her wages myself. Keep your promise, mother, and let us live quietly and decently."

"If you call it living decently to pamper a servant until she bursts with insolence——"

"When was Sarah insolent to you? She has never been disrespectful to me. Quite the contrary, I think her a very good servant indeed. You know that I have a good deal of work to do just now, and—to speak quite plainly—I can't let you upset the orderly life of the house. Be quiet, there's a dear. I insist upon it."

Speaking thus, Bertha laid her hands on her mother's shoulders, and looked into the foolish, angry face so steadily, so imperturbably, with such a light of true kindness in her gentle eyes, yet at the same time such resolution about the well-drawn lips that Mrs. Cross had no choice but to submit. Grumbling she turned; sullenly she held her tongue for the rest of the day; but Bertha, at all events for a time, had conquered.

The Crosses knew little and saw less of their kith and kin. With her husband's family, Mrs. Cross had naturally been on cold terms from an early period of her married life; she held no communication with any of the name, and always gave Bertha to understand that, in one way or another, the paternal uncles and aunts had "behaved very badly." Of her own blood, she had only a brother ten years younger than herself, who was an estate agent at Worcester. Some seven years had elasped since their last meeting, on which occasion Mrs. Cross had a little difference of opinion with her sister-in-law. James Rawlings was now a widower, with three children, and during the past year or two not unfriendly letters had been exchanged between Worcester and Walham Green. Utterly at a loss for a means of passing her time, Mrs. Cross, in these days of domestic suppression, renewed the correspondence, and was surprised by an invitation to pass a few days at her brother's house. This she made known to Bertha about a week after the decisive struggle.

"Of course, you are invited, too, but—I'm afraid you are too busy?"

Amused by her mother's obvious wish to go to Worcester unaccompanied, Bertha answered that she really didn't see how she was to spare the time just now.

"But I don't like to leave you alone here——"

Her daughter laughed at this scruple. She was just as glad of the prospect of a week's solitude as her mother in the thought of temporary escape from the proximity of pampered Sarah. The matter was soon arranged, and Mrs. Cross left home.

This was a Friday. The next day, sunshine and freedom putting her in holiday mood, Bertha escaped into the country, and had a long ramble like that, a year ago, on which she had encountered Norbert Franks. Sunday morning she spent quietly at home. For the afternoon she had invited a girl friend. About five o'clock, as they were having tea, Bertha heard a knock at the front door. She heard the servant go to open, and, a moment after, Sarah announced, "Mr. Warburton."

It was the first time that Warburton had found a stranger in the room, and Bertha had no difficulty in reading the unwonted look with which he advanced to shake hands.

"No bad news, I hope?" she asked gravely, after presenting him to the other visitor.

"Bad news?—"

"I thought you looked rather troubled——"

Her carefully composed features resisted Will's scrutiny.

"Do I? I didn't know it—but, yes," he added,

abruptly, "you are right. Something has vexed me—a trifle."

"Look at these drawings of Miss Medwin's. They will make you forget all vexatious trifles."

Miss Medwin was, like Bertha, a book illustrator, and had brought work to show her friend. Warburton glanced at the drawings with a decent show of interest. Presently he inquired after Mrs. Cross, and learnt that she was out of town for a week or so; at once his countenance brightened, and so shamelessly that Bertha had to look aside, lest her disposition to laugh should be observed. Conversation of a rather artificial kind went on for half an hour, then Miss Medwin jumped up and said she must go. Bertha protested, but her friend alleged the necessity of making another call, and took leave.

Warburton stood with a hand upon his chair. Bertha, turning back from the door, passed by him, and resumed her seat.

"A very clever girl," she said, with a glance at the window.

"Very, no doubt," said Will, glancing the same way.

"Won't you sit down?"

"Gladly, if you don't think I am staying too long. I had something I wanted to talk about. That was why I felt glum when I came in and found a stranger here. It's such a long time since I had any part in ordinary society, that I'm forgetting how to behave myself."

"I must apologise for you to Miss Medwin, when I see her next," said Bertha, with drollery in her eyes.

"She will understand if you tell her I'm only a grocer," remarked Will, looking at a point above her head.

"That might complicate things."

"Do you know," resumed Warburton. "I feel sure that the Franks will never again invite me to lunch or dine there. Franks is very careful when he asks me to go and see them; he always adds that they'll be alone—quite alone."

"But that's a privilege."

"So it may be taken; but would it surprise you if they really preferred to see as little of me as possible?"

Bertha hesitated, smiling, and said at length with a certain good-humoured irony:

"I think I should understand."

"So do I, quite," exclaimed Will, laughing. "I wanted to tell you that I've been looking about me, trying to find some way of getting out of the shop. It isn't so easy. I might get a clerkship at a couple of pounds a week, but that doesn't strike me as preferable to my present position. I've been corresponding with Applegarth, the jam manufacturer, and he very strongly advises me to stick to trade. I'm not sure that he isn't right."

There was silence. Each sat with drooping eyes.

"Do you know," Warburton then asked, "why I turned grocer?"

"Yes."

"It was a fortunate idea. I don't see how else I should have made enough money, these three years, to pay the income I owed to my mother and sister, and to support myself. Since my mother's death——"

Her look arrested him.

"I am forgetting that you could not have known of that. She died last autumn; by my father's will, our old house, at St. Neots then became mine; it's let; the rent goes to my sister, and out of the shop profits I easily make up what her own part of the lost capital used to yield. Jane is going in for horticulture, making a business of what was always her chief pleasure, and before long she may be independent ; but it would be shabby to get rid of my responsibilities at her expense—don't you think so ? "

" Worse than shabby."

" Good. I like to hear you speak so decidedly. Now, if you please "—his own voice was not quite steady—" tell me in the same tone whether you agree with Applegarth—whether you think I should do better to stick to the shop and not worry with looking for a more respectable employment."

Bertha seemed to reflect for a moment, smiling soberly.

" It depends entirely on how you feel about it."

" Not entirely," said Warburton, his features nervously rigid ; " but first let me tell you how I do feel about it. You know I began shopkeeping as if I were ashamed of myself. I kept it a dead secret ; hid away from everybody ; told elaborate lies to my people ; and the result was what might have been expected—before long I sank into a vile hypochrondria, saw everything black or dirty grey, thought life intolerable. When common sense found out what was the matter with me, I resolved to have done with snobbery and lying ; but a sanguine friend of mine, the only one in my confidence, made me believe that something was going to happen—in fact, the recovery of the lost thousands ; and I foolishly held on for a time. Since the awful truth has been divulged, I have felt a different man. I can't say that I glory in grocerdom, but the plain fact is that I see nothing degrading in it, and I do my day's work as a matter of course. Is it any worse to stand behind a counter than to sit in a counting-house? Why should retail trade be vulgar, and wholesale quite re-pectable? This is what I've come to, as far as my own thought and feeling go."

"Then," said Bertha, after a moment's pause, "why trouble yourself any more?"

"Because——"

His throat turned so dry that he had to stop with a gasp. His fingers were doing their best to destroy the tassels on the arm of his easy chair. With an effort, he jerked out the next words.

"One may be content to be a grocer; but what about one's wife?"

With head bent, so that her smile was half concealed, Bertha answered softly—

"Ah, that's a question."

CHAPTER XLVI

AFTER he had put the question, the reply to which meant so much to him, Will's eyes, avoiding Bertha, turned to the window. Though there wanted still a couple of hours to sunset, a sky overcast was already dusking the little parlour. Distant bells made summons to evening service, and footfalls sounded in the otherwise silent street.

"It's a question," he resumed, "which has troubled me for a long time. Do you remember—when was it? A year ago?—going one Sunday with Mrs. Cross to Kew?"

"I remember it very well."

"I happened to be at Kew that day," Will continued, still nervously. "You passed me as I stood on the bridge. I saw you go into the Gardens, and I said to myself how pleasant it would be if I could have ventured to join you in your walk. You knew me—as your grocer. For me to have approached and spoken, would have been an outrage. That day I had villainous thoughts."

Bertha raised her eyes; just raised them till they met his, then bent her head again.

"We thought your name was really Jollyman," she said, in a half-apologetic tone.

"Of course you did. A good invention, by the bye, that name, wasn't it?"

"Very good indeed," she answered, smiling.

"And you used to come to the shop." pursued Will. "And I looked forward to it. There was something human in your way of talking to me."

"I hope so."

"Yes, but—it made me ask myself that question. I comforted myself by saying that of course the shop was only a temporary expedient; I should get out of it; I should find another way of making money; but, you see, I'm as far from that as ever; and if I decide to go on shopkeeping—don't I condemn myself to solitude?"

"It *is* a difficulty," said Bertha, in the tone of one who lightly ponders an abstract question.

"Now and then, some time ago, I half persuaded myself that, even though a difficulty, it needn't be a fatal one." He was speaking now with his eyes steadily fixed upon her; "but that was when you still came to the shop. Suddenly you ceased——"

His voice dropped. In the silence, Bertha uttered a little "Yes."

"I have been wondering what that meant——"

His speech was a mere parched gasp. Bertha looked at him, and her eyebrows contracted, as if in sympathetic trouble. Gently she asked: "No explanation occurred to you?"

With a convulsive movement, Will changed his position, and by so doing seemed to have released his tongue.

"Several," he said, with a strange smile. "The one which most plagued me, I should very likely do better to keep to myself; but I won't; you shall know it. Perhaps you are prepared for it. Do you know that I went abroad last summer?"

"I heard of it."

"From Miss Elvan?"

"From Mrs. Franks."

"Mrs. Franks—yes. She told you, then, that I had been to St. Jean de Luz? She told you that I had seen her sister?"

"Yes," replied Bertha, and added quickly. "You had long wished to see that part of France."

"That wasn't my reason for going. I went in a fit of lunacy. I went because I thought Miss Elvan was there. They told me at her Chelsea lodgings that she had gone to St. Jean de Luz. This was on the day after she came into the shop with you. I had been seeing her. We met here and there, when she was sketching. I went crazy. Don't for a moment think the fault was hers—don't dream of anything of the kind. I, I alone, ass, idiot, was to blame. She must have seen what had happened, and, in leaving her lodgings, she purposely gave a false address, never imagining that I was capable of pursuing her across Europe. At St. Jean de Luz I heard of her marriage——"

He stopped, breathless. The short sentences had been flung out explosively. He was hot and red.

"Did you suspect anything of all that?" followed in a more restrained tone. "If so, of course I understand——"

Bertha seemed to be deep in meditation. A faint smile was on her lips. She made no answer.

"Are you saying to yourself," Will went on vehemently, "that, instead of being merely a foolish man, I have shown myself to be shameless? It was foolish, no doubt, to dream that an educated girl might marry a grocer; but when he begins his suit by telling such a story as this—! Perhaps I needn't have told it at all. Perhaps you had never had a suspicion of such things? All the same, it's better so. I've had enough of lies to last me for all my life; but now that I've told you, try to believe something else; and that is—that I never loved Rosamund Elvan —never—never!"

Bertha seemed on the point of laughing; but she drew in her breath, composed her features, let her eyes wander to a picture on the wall.

"Can you believe that?" Will asked, his voice quivering with earnestness, as he bent forward to her.

"I should have to think about it," was the answer, calm, friendly.

"The fit of madness from which I suffered is very common in men. Often it has serious results. No end of marriages come about in that way. Happily I was in no danger of that. I simply made a most colossal fool of myself. And all the time—all the time, I tell you, believe it or not, as you will or can—I was in love with *you*."

Again Bertha drew in her breath, more softly than before.

"I went one day from St. Jean de Luz over the border into Spain, and came to a village among the mountains, called Vera. And there my madness left me. And I thought of you—thought of you all the way back to St. Jean de Luz, thought of you as I had been accustomed to do in England, as if nothing had happened. Do you think it pained me then that Rosamund was Mrs. Franks? No more than if I had never seen her; by that time, fresh air and exercise were doing their work, and at Vera I stood a sane man once more. I find it hard to believe now that I really behaved in that frantic way. Do you remember coming once to the shop to ask for a box to send to America? As you talked to me that morning, I knew what I know better still now, that there was no girl that I *liked* as I liked you, no girl whose face had so much meaning for me, whose voice and way of speaking so satisfied me. But you don't understand—I can't express it—it sounds stupid——"

"I understand very well," said Bertha, once more on the impartial note.

"But the other thing, my insanity?"

"I should have to think about that," she answered, with a twinkle in her eyes.

Will paused a moment, then asked in a shamefaced way:

"Did you suspect anything of the sort?"

Bertha moved her head as if to reply, but after all, kept silence. Thereupon Warburton stood up and clutched his hat.

"Will you let me see you again—soon? May I come some afternoon in this week, and take my chance of finding you at home?—Don't answer. I shall come, and you have only to refuse me at the door. It's only—an importunate tradesman."

Without shaking hands, he turned and left the room.

Dreamily he walked homewards; dreamily, often with a smile upon his face, he sat through the evening, now and then he pretended to read, but always in a few minutes forgetting the page before him. He slept well; he arose in a cheerful but still dreamy, mood; and without a thought of reluctance he went to his day's work.

Allchin met him with a long-drawn face, saying: "She's dead, sir." He spoke of his consumptive sister-in-law, whom Warburton had befriended, but whom nothing had availed to save.

"Poor girl," said Will kindly. "It's the end of much suffering."

"That's what I say, sir," assented Allchin. "And poor Mrs. Hopper, she's fair worn out with nursing her. Nobody can feel sorry."

Warburton turned to his correspondence.

The next day, at about four o'clock, he again called at the Crosses. Without hesitation the servant admitted him, and he found Bertha seated at her drawing. A little gravely perhaps, but not at all inhospitably, she rose and offered her hand.

"Forgive me," he began, "for coming again so soon."

"Tell me what you think of this idea of a book-cover," said Bertha, before he had ceased speaking.

He inspected the drawing, found it pretty, yet ventured one or two objections; and Bertha, after smiling to herself for a little, declared that he had found the weak points.

"You are really fond of this work?" asked Will. "You would be sorry to give it up?"

"Think of the world's loss," Bertha answered with raised eyebrows.

He sat down and kept a short silence, whilst the girl resumed her pencil.

"There were things I ought to have told you on Sunday." Will's voice threatened huskiness. "Things I forgot. That's why I have come again so soon. I ought to have told you much more about myself. How can you know my character —my peculiarities—faults? I've been going over all that. I don't think I'm ill-tempered, or unjust or violent, but there are things that irritate me. Unpunctuality for instance. Dinner ten minutes late makes me fume; failure to keep an appointment makes me hate a person, I'm rather a grumbler about food; can't stand a potato ill-boiled or an under-done chop. Then —ah yes! restraint is intolerable to me. I must come and go at my own will. I must do and refrain just as I think fit. One enormous advantage of my shopkeeping is that I'm my own master. I can't subordinate myself, won't be ruled. Fault-finding would exasperate me; dictation would madden me. Then yes, the money matter. I'm not extravagant, but I hate parsimony. If it pleases me to give away a sovereign I must be free to do it. Then—yes, I'm not very tidy in my habits; I have no respect for furniture; I like, when it's comfortable, to sit with my boots on the fender; and—I loathe antimacassars."

In the room were two or three of these articles, dear to Mrs. Cross. Bertha glanced at them, then bent her head and bit the end of her pencil.

"You can't think of anything else?" she asked, when Will had been silent for a few seconds.

"Those are my most serious points." He rose. "I only came to tell you of them, that you might add them to the objection of the shop."

Bertha also rose. He moved toward her to take leave.

"You will think?"

Turning half way, Bertha covered her face with her hands, like a child who is bidden "not to look." So she stood for a moment; then, facing Will again, said:

"I have thought."

"And——?"

"There is only one thing I am sorry for—that you are nothing worse than a grocer. A grocer's is such a clean, dainty, aromatic trade. Now if you kept an oil shop—there would be some credit in overlooking it. And you are so little even of a grocer, that I should constantly forget it. I should think of you simply as a very honest man—the most honest man I ever knew."

Warburton's face glowed.

"Should—should?" he murmured. "Can't it be *shall*?"

And Bertha, smiling now without a touch of roguishness, smiling in the mere joy of her heart, laid a hand in his.

CHAPTER XLVII

WHEN Mrs. Cross came home she brought with her a changed countenance. The lines graven by habitual fretfulness and sourness of temper, by long-indulged vices of the feminine will, could not of course be obliterated, but her complexion had a healthier tone, her eyes were brighter, and the smile with which she answered Bertha's welcome expressed a more spontaneous kindliness than had appeared on her face for many a year. She had recovered, indeed, during her visit to the home of her childhood, something of the grace and virtue in which she was not lacking before her marriage to a man who spoilt her by excess of good nature. Subject to a husband firm of will and occasionally rough of tongue, she might have led a fairly happy and useful life. It was the perception of this truth which had strengthened Bertha in her ultimate revolt. Perhaps, too, it had not been without influence on her own feeling and behaviour during the past week.

Mrs. Cross had much to relate. At the tea-table she told all about her brother's household, described the children, lauded the cook and housemaid—"Ah, Bertha, if one could get such servants here! But London ruins them."

James Rawlings was well-to-do; he lived in a nice, comfortable way, in a pretty house just outside the town. "Oh, and the air, Bertha. I hadn't been there a day before I felt a different creature." James had been kindness itself. Not a word about old differences. He regretted that his niece had not come, but she must come very soon. And the children—Alice, Tom, and little Hilda, so well-behaved, so intelligent. She had brought photographs of them all. She had brought presents—all sorts of things."

After tea, gossip continued. Speaking of the ages of the children, the eldest eight, the youngest four, Mrs. Cross regretted their motherless state. A lady-nurse had care of them, but with this person their father was not quite satisfied. He spoke of making a change. And here Mrs. Cross paused, with a little laugh.

"Perhaps uncle thinks of marrying again?" said Bertha.

"Not a bit of it, my dear," replied her mother eagerly. "He expressly told me that he should *never* do that. I shouldn't wonder if—but let bygones be bygones. No, he spoke of something quite different. Last night we were talking, when the children had gone to bed, and all at once he startled me by saying—'If only you could come and keep house for me.' The idea!"

"A wonderfully good idea it seems to me," said Bertha, reflectively.

"But how is it possible, Bertha? Are you serious?"

"Quite. I think it might be the very best thing for you. You need something to do, mother. If Uncle James really wishes it, you ought certainly to accept."

Fluttered, not knowing whether to look pleased or offended, surprised at her daughter's decisiveness, Mrs. Cross began urging objections. She doubted whether James was quite in earnest; he had admitted that Bertha could not be left alone, yet she could hardly go and live in his house as well.

"Oh, don't trouble about me, mother," said the listener. "Nothing is simpler."

"But what would you do?"

"Oh, there are all sorts of possibilities. At the worst"—Bertha paused a moment, face averted, and lips roguish—"I could get married."

And so the disclosure came about. Mrs. Cross seemed so startled as to be almost pained; one would have thought that no remotest possibility of such a thing had ever occurred to her.

"Then Mr. Warburton *has* found a position?" she asked at length.

"No, he keeps to the shop."

"But—my dear—you don't mean to tell me—?"

The question ended in a mere gasp. Mrs. Cross' eyes were darkened with incredulous horror.

"Yes," said Bertha, calmly, pleasantly, "we have decided that there's no choice. The business is a very good one; it improves from day to day; now that there are two assistants, Mr. Warburton need not work so hard as he used to."

"But, my dearest Bertha, you mean to say that you are going to be the wife of a *grocer*?"

"Yes, mother, I really have made up my mind to it. After all, is it so *very* disgraceful?"

"What will your friends say? What will——"

"Mrs. Grundy?" interposed Bertha.

"I was going to say Mrs. Franks——"

Bertha nodded, and answered laughingly:

"That's very much the same thing, I'm afraid."

CHAPTER XLVIII

NORBERT FRANKS was putting the last touches to a portrait of his wife; a serious portrait, full length, likely to be regarded as one of his most important works. Now and then he glanced at the original, who sat reading; his eye was dull, his hand moved mechanically, he hummed a monotonous air.

Rosamund having come to the end of her book, closed it, and looked up.

"Will that do?" she asked, after suppressing a little yawn.

The painter merely nodded. She came to his side, and contemplated the picture, inclining her head this way and that with an air of satisfaction.

"Better than the old canvas I put my foot through, don't you think?" asked Franks.

"Of course there's no comparison. You've developed wonderfully. In those days——"

Franks waited for the rest of the remark, but his wife lost herself in contemplation of the portrait. Assuredly he had done nothing more remarkable in the way of bold flattery. Any one who had seen Mrs. Franks only once or twice, and at her best, might accept the painting as a fair "interpretation" of her undeniable beauty; those who knew her well would stand bewildered before such a counterfeit presentment.

"Old Warburton must come and see it," said the artist presently.

Rosamund uttered a careless assent. Long since she had ceased to wonder whether Norbert harboured any suspicions concerning his friend's brief holiday in the south of France. Obviously, he knew nothing of the dramatic moment which had preceded, and brought about, his marriage; nor would he ever know.

"I really ought to go and look him up." Franks added. "I keep on saying I'll go to-morrow and to-morrow. Any one else would think me an ungrateful snob; but old Warburton is too good a fellow. To tell the truth, I feel a little ashamed when I think of how he's living. He ought to have a percentage on my income. What would have become of me if he hadn't put his hand into his pocket when he was well off and I was a beggar?"

"But don't you think his business must be profitable?" asked Rosamund, her thoughts only half attentive to the subject.

"The old chap isn't much of a business man, I fancy," Franks answered with a smile. "And he has his mother and sister to support. And no doubt he's always giving away money. His lodgings are miserable. It makes me uncomfortable to go there. Suppose we ask him to lunch on Sunday?"

Rosamund reflected for a moment.

"If you like—I had thought of asking the Fitz-james girls."

"You don't think we might have him at the same time?"

Rosamund pursed her lips a little, averting her eyes as she answered:

"Would he care for it? And he said—didn't he?—that he meant to tell everybody, everywhere, how he earned his living. Wouldn't it be just a little——?

Franks laughed uneasily.

"Yes, it might be just a little—. Well, he must come and see the picture quietly. And I'll go and look up the poor old fellow to-night, I really will."

This time, the purpose was carried out. Franks returned a little after midnight, and was surprised to find Rosamund sitting in the studio. A friend had looked in late in the evening, she said, and had stayed talking.

"All about her husband's pictures, so tiresome! She thinks them monuments of genius!"

"His last thing isn't half bad," said Franks, good-naturedly.

"Perhaps not. Of course I pretended to think him the greatest painter of modern times. Nothing else will satisfy the silly little woman. You found Mr. Warburton?"

Franks nodded, smiling mysteriously

"I have news for you."

Knitting her brows a little his wife looked interrogation.

"He's going to be married. Guess to whom."

"Not to——?"

"Well——?"

"Bertha Cross——?"

Again Franks nodded and laughed. An odd smile rose to his wife's lips; she mused for a moment, then asked:

"And what position has he got?"

"Position? His position behind the counter, that's all. Say's he shan't budge. By the bye, his mother died last autumn; he's in easier circumstances; the shop does well, it seems. He thought of trying for something else, but talked it over with Bertha Cross, and they decided to stick to groceries. They'll live in the house at Walham Green. Mrs. Cross is going away—to keep house for a brother of hers."

Rosamund heaved a sigh, murmuring:

"Poor Bertha!"

"A grocer's wife," said Franks, his eyes wandering. "Oh, confound it! Really you know—" He took an impatient turn across the floor. Again his wife sighed and murmured:

"Poor Bertha!"

"Of course," said Franks, coming to a pause, "there's a good deal to be said for sticking to a business which yields a decent income, and promises much more."

"Money!" exclaimed Rosamund scornfully. "What is money?"

"We find it useful," quietly remarked the other.

"Certainly we do; but you are an artist, Norbert, and money is only an accident of your career. Do we ever talk about it, or think about it? Poor Bertha! With her talent!"

The artist paced about, his hands in his jacket pockets. He was smiling uneasily.

"Did you know anything of this kind was going on?" he asked, without looking at his wife.

"I had heard nothing whatever. It's ages since Bertha was here."

"Yet you don't seem very much surprised."

"And you?" asked Rosamund, meeting his eyes. "Were you profoundly astonished?"

"Why, yes. It came very unexpectedly. I

had no idea they saw each other—except in the shop."

"And it vexes you?" said Rosamund, her eyes upon his face.

"Vexes? Oh, I can't say that." He fidgeted, turned about, laughed. "Why should it vex me? After all, Warburton is such a thoroughly good fellow, and if he makes money——"

"Money!"

"We *do* find it useful, you know," insisted Franks, with a certain obstinacy,

Rosamund was standing before the picture, and gazing at it.

"That she should have no higher ambition! Poor Bertha!"

"We can't all achieve ambitions," cried Franks from the other end of the room. "Not every girl can marry a popular portrait-painter."

"A great artist!" exclaimed his wife, with emphasis.

As she moved slowly away, she kept her look still turned upon the face which smiled from the easel. Watching her tremulous eyebrows, her uncertain lips, one might have fancied that Rosamund sought the solution of some troublesome doubt, and hoped, only hoped, to find it in that image of herself so daringly glorified.

THE END

THE HOGARTH PRESS

A New Life For A Great Name

This is a paperback list for today's readers – but it holds to a tradition of adventurous and original publishing set by Leonard and Virginia Woolf when they founded The Hogarth Press in 1917 and started their first paperback series in 1924.

Now, after many years of partnership, Chatto & Windus · The Hogarth Press are proud to launch this new series. Our choice of books does not echo that of the Woolfs in every way – times have changed – but our aims are the same. Some sections of the list are light-hearted, some serious: all are rigorously chosen, excellently produced and energetically published, in the best Hogarth Press tradition. We hope that the new Hogarth Press paperback list will be as prized – and as avidly collected – as its illustrious forebear.

A list of our books already published, together with some of our forthcoming titles, follows. If you would like more information about Hogarth Press books, write to us for a catalogue:

40 William IV Street, London WC2N 4DF

Please send a large stamped addressed envelope

HOGARTH FICTION

Behind A Mask: The Unknown Thrillers of Louisa May Alcott
Edited and Introduced by Madeleine Stern

Death of a Hero by Richard Aldington
New Introduction by Christopher Ridgway

The Amazing Test Match Crime by Adrian Alington
New Introduction by Brian Johnston

Epitaph of a Small Winner by Machado de Assis
Translated and Introduced by William L. Grossman

Mrs Ames by E.F. Benson
Paying Guests by E.F. Benson
Secret Lives by E.F. Benson
New Introductions by Stephen Pile

Ballantyne's Folly by Claud Cockburn
New Introduction by Andrew Cockburn
Beat the Devil by Claud Cockburn
New Introduction by Alexander Cockburn

Chance by Joseph Conrad
New Introduction by Jane Miller

Lady Into Fox & A Man in the Zoo by David Garnett
New Introduction by Neil Jordan

The Whirlpool by George Gissing
New Introduction by Gillian Tindall

Morte D'Urban by J.F. Powers
Prince of Darkness and other stories by J.F. Powers
New Introductions by Mary Gordon

Mr Weston's Good Wine by T.F. Powys
New Introduction by Ronald Blythe

The Revolution in Tanner's Lane by Mark Rutherford
New Introduction by Claire Tomalin
Catharine Furze by Mark Rutherford
Clara Hopgood by Mark Rutherford
New Afterwords by Claire Tomalin

The Last Man by Mary Shelley
New Introduction by Brian Aldiss

The Island of Desire by Edith Templeton
Summer in the Country by Edith Templeton
New Introductions by Anita Brookner

Christina Alberta's Father by H.G. Wells
Mr Britling Sees It Through by H.G. Wells
New Introductions by Christopher Priest

Frank Burnet by Dorothy Vernon White
New Afterword by Irvin Stock

George Gissing

The Whirlpool

New Introduction by Gillian Tindall

'Marriage rarely means happiness, either for man or woman . . .'

In *The Whirlpool* George Gissing explores sympathetically, but without illusions, his vision of married life: an existence often leading to 'envy, hatred, fear'. This magnificent novel, a masterpiece of English social realism, is a powerful diagnosis of human institutions and the suffering of those caught up in them.

George Gissing

Born in Exile

New Introduction by Gillian Tindall

Godwin Peak is a man fated to a life in exile. At university in the Midlands, at work in London, or studying for the church in Exeter, he always feels an outsider. For Peak, a natural intellectual, has been born into the working class at a time when social mobility seems virtually impossible.

Written four years before Hardy's *Jude the Obscure* and poignantly autobiographical, *Born in Exile* is one of the most powerful of Victorian novels, revealing the ambition, the rage and resignation of an individual trying to come to terms with his age.

George Gissing

The Emancipated

New Introduction by John Halperin

Miriam Baske, a young widow, leaves behind the grey stone chapels and flinty hearts of Lancashire for the sun and artistic splendour of Italy – where she meets a host of her countrymen doing the Grand Tour. To Miriam's surprise, the English abroad are a different breed from those back home: in the Bay of Naples, passion rules over reason. But will life change when they return to their own hearthsides?

A proclamation of hope, of freedom in the midst of Victorian darkness, *The Emancipated* is reminiscent of George Eliot's *Middlemarch*; for it tells us as much about Victorian society – with all its prejudices and rigid conventions – as it does about one woman's growth to human understanding.